THE WHISPERING WIND

Two lives, one heartbreaking story

Lexa Dudley

Matador
9 Priory Business Park,
Wistow Road, Kibworth Beauchamp,
Leicestershire. LE8 0RX
Tel: (+44) 116 279 2299
Fax: (+44) 116 279 2277
Email: books@troubador.co.uk
Web: www.troubador.co.uk/matador

ISBN 978 1780885 025

British Library Cataloguing in Publication Data.
A catalogue record for this book is available from the British Library.

Printed and bound in the UK by TJ International, Padstow, Cornwall
Typeset by Troubador Publishing Ltd, Leicester, UK

Matador is an imprint of Troubador Publishing Ltd

For Kit

To all who love the island of Sardinia
And those who will fall under her spell in time.

ACKNOWLEDGEMENTS

I would like to thank everyone who encouraged me to finish this book.

To Charlie Wilson for her excellent editing and understanding.

To Mel for her friendship and all her help when everything crashed.

To my friends in Sardinia for all their patience with my unending questions about their island over the years.

And finally to my husband, Kit, who has lived the book and taken me back to 'my island' every year for research.

Thank you.

Lexa

Dedication
Su Fischidu de su Bentu
To the Spirit of Sardegna:
In some other place and in some other time
people have lived and loved. Their lives touched
by those who have a profound effect, the one
upon another, where souls and kindred spirits entwine
for eternity.

Season's Love

Softly on a heavy blossom laden morn
when fragrant breezes did gently blow,
warmed by a sun's silent fiery glow
their love, on a whispering wind, was born.
Spring wooed their tender love to flower,
a bloom with divine enchanted power.
Summer gave her early sun at dawn
kindling the flame of passion to ignite;
nurturing it under her dazzling light,
turning fields of green to golden corn.
Amber autumn brought warm languid days
spent together in winsome, carefree ways.
But winter sent only icy winds to mourn
for cherished dreams once more to bring
the sweet return of their awaking spring.

INTRODUCTION

People who have grown up with mobile phones and the Internet have no concept of what communication was like in the late 1960s. Phone calls had to be booked through the exchange, taking hours if not days. The Italian post, never known for its reliability, was only marginally better than in Sardinia. The fact that one local postman was imprisoned on the island for hiding some letters for seven years because, he didn't know where to deliver them, gives some idea of the problem.

Sardinia has always been known as 'the forgotten island', and perhaps that is still true today. Certainly, in 1969 it was well off the tourist route. It can become an itch that can't be scratched, as it gets under your skin. The Sards call it *Mal di Sardegna*; an illness which is helped by regular visits to the island, which has a wild magical beauty all of its own.

The Sards themselves are a fiercely independent people who have survived continual occupation of their homeland with a tremendous dignity and pride. If I can convey to the reader a small amount of the charm and magic of this island and its people, then I will be more than happy. In the words of my late and dear friend:

'I have one ambition or rather hope: to communicate to others my faith in Sardinia, my loving solicitude for this land to which many people have applied the much abused but still accurate title of the unknown island, this land which so few people really try to know and to understand. But anyone who looks beyond certain off-putting or banal aspects of this island will finish up loving it.' Marcello Serra

Barumini is a large Bronze Age monument known as a Nuraghe for which there is no parallel anywhere in the world, and is described as I first saw it, but since then the authorities have adopted a scorched earth policy to stop the grass from growing between the stones, creating a rather grey and bleak monument. It was inscribed on the UNESCO list of World Heritage Sites in 1997 as Su Nuraxi di Barumini.

Many of the roads travelled on by Elise and Beppe are now motorways, thanks to EU funding. But if the traveller moves off these roads, he will still discover the 'old Sardinia', with its small villages and friendly people.

All places are as I describe them, except for Santa Cella, and the villa at Pula which are imaginary along with all the characters. Any likeness to anyone living or dead is purely coincidental.

I first visited Sardinia in 1972. It was love at first sight, and I still feel the same way about the island and its people after all these years. To me, it will always be the 'enchanted island', and long may it remain that way.

Lexa Dudley, 2012

PROLOGUE

A gentle breeze fluttered through the peach grove, but gave no respite from the midday sun. The rows of peach and lemon trees offered no shade, and the branches of the tall cypress trees surrounding the orchard seemed to trap and intensify the relentless rays, creating an overwhelming heat that pervaded everything. Only the strident call of the cicadas broke the unnerving quiet that descended over the parched land.

One exception to the dryness was a small area at the end of the garden where an old standpipe dripped, making the ground damp. This area was bordered by giant prickly pears, and growing through their great spines were masses of pink and white wild roses, together with honeysuckle; their strong sweet scents mingling languorously in the oppressive air.

The rows of peach and lemon trees, planted with military precision, gave way to a mantle of green vineyards, which in turn blended into fields of golden barley, before finally fading into the hazy, distant mountains that rose from all sides of the Campidano.

This hard-baked Sardinian soil, that has drained the strength of all who have worked it since pre-Carthaginian times, produces men as tough and durable as the ancient land itself, and the two brothers working in this grove were no exception. The elder of them leaned heavily on his shovel and surveyed the work that the two of them had done. He watched his younger brother as he put the finishing touches to the hoses and turned on the water from the huge standpipe in the centre of the grove, allowing the water to gush into the newly dug trenches before being swallowed up by the thirsty earth.

He had promised to help in the peach grove today, but now he was tired, having lain awake most of the night listening to music, drinking whisky and trying to fight the demon depression that lurked in his mind. He had kept his promise to his brother, but now he needed to sleep.

'Are you alright? You look awful.' asked his younger brother looking concerned.

He didn't reply. He was busy undoing the rough bandaging on his normally well manicured hands. His mind went back to the time when, as a child, he had worked beside his father in this same grove; when he returned home at night his mother had bathed his hands in salt water to harden them and ease the pain. He shoved the bandaging into his pocket and sighed as he put his hands up to his brow to try to stop the relentless pounding in his head.

'I don't know how the hell you stand this heat all the time.'

'Probably because I don't drink like you do and, I am used to it.'

The elder brother shrugged and walked to the bottom of the grove to collect his shirt. Nearing the hedge of prickly pears, he became aware of the suffocating, heavy scent coming from the roses and rampant honeysuckle. The sun dazzled between the leaves of the overhanging lemon trees and the ever-changing light was mesmerising. The summer heat closed in on him and he felt weak. His feet turned to clay as he became rooted to the spot and beads of sweat stood out on his forehead as an icy chill ran down his spine. He felt unable to breathe and a dull, sick feeling welled up in the pit of his stomach.

Coming toward him through the now blurred lines of trees, and moving slowly, as if in a dream, was a young woman, her arms outstretched to greet him. Her long, golden hair flowed over her shoulders, glinting in the sun, and her white cotton dress seemed to intensify the bright light. He put his hands up to shield his eyes from the glare as the girl came nearer. He turned to see if his brother was there, but seeing no one he looked back and was surprised to see that the young girl now appeared to be beside him. He knew her. He knew her so well that all his senses cried out as he stared at her once familiar face.

Stirred memories and lost dreams rushed in on him from days long gone, and a deep yearning filled his soul. He found it difficult to catch his breath with his heart pounding as if it would burst. The world about him began to spin and tears sprang to his eyes.

'I've come back, darling,' she whispered, laying a soft, cooling hand on his fevered skin.

Everything fell out of focus as he reached forward, in desperation, to embrace his long-lost love, crying out as he fell to the ground.

'I always knew you would!'

PART ONE

PART ONE

CHAPTER ONE

Sardinia April 1969

The plane touched down on the hot concrete runway and taxied to the hanger. The strong smell of aviation fuel hung in the heat of a Mediterranean afternoon, and the air was thick with fumes. The deafening whirring of engines hit Elise as she stepped onto the aircraft steps. She stood out from her fellow passengers with her long blond hair and pale complexion, and her short blue cotton dress showed off her neatly shaped legs. She followed the crowd of excited locals into the hanger, where they hurried to meet their relatives or friends. Elise collected her case and found a young porter to carry it out of the building, and then she stood looking around for someone to help her.

At that moment, a small man stepped forward to shake her hand.

'Signora Raynesford?' he asked with a polite bow.

'*Si* ,' she replied, nervously.

'Me Efisio Fozzi,' he said, stabbing his barrel chest with a short, stubby finger. 'I take you to villa. Do you have a pleasant journey? I hope you enjoy your stay. To follow me, please.'

The words were run together with such well-rehearsed charm and speed that Elise didn't have time to answer him, but followed, meekly, as he took her suitcase from the porter and set off to find the car. Efisio bundled the case into the boot of the Fiat and then rushed round to hold the door open, to allow her to climb into the passenger seat. Once inside the car, she put her shoulder bag down by her feet and took a quick survey of the airport.

Efisio was talking to the man in the next car and although Elise was unable to understand the Sard language, she realised they were talking about her as they kept looking at her.

Elmas was such a small airport, its main building a large Nissen hut with a tin roof and huge open doors. It was teeming with waves of people as some left and others arrived, all in the one building. Families, some of them carrying insulated food boxes in order to constantly feed their broods during their journeys, came and went, welcoming arrivals or bidding vociferous farewells to those departing. Above all the chatter and bustle could be heard the constant whirring propellers and whining engines of the aircraft parked on the runway, waiting to take off.

Efisio climbed in the car beside her. He was a short, tubby little man with a paunch overhanging the wide leather belt which miraculously held up a faded pair of brown cotton trousers; he looked like a Toby jug, Elise thought. His shirt was immaculately white and straining at the buttons. His head was a shiny, weathered, bald pate with a fringe of dark hair, and his face round and swarthy, from which shone a pair of eyes like two brown beads.

'Your husband Signora. He no come?'

'No he has had to go to America. How far is it to the villa?' she replied in her near-perfect Italian, before he could bombard her again with another stream of words.

'About thirty minutes, signora,' he replied. 'You speak Italian, which is very good. There are few visitors, who speak the language,' he replied, obviously pleased that he was not going to have to battle on in his broken English.

Efisio started the car and with a sudden lurch they shot forwards on the start of a most nerve wracking drive through the outskirts of Cagliari. He pointed out the sights of interest with great enthusiasm, but still managed to sound like a tape recording; having driven this route so many times before, usually speaking over a babble of disinterested visitors, it had become automatic.

'This is Via San Paulo. Up on your left is Colle Tuvumannu, one of the oldest sites in the area. On your right are the salt flats.'

At this point, he negotiated a sharp left-hand bend and before Elise could recover he had made another turn to the right. She bit her lip, as she held tightly onto her seat. They came to a road junction and took a right-hand fork which doubled back on itself, narrowly missing an approaching lorry. The blaring of horns drowned out the insults exchanged by the two drivers.

Crossing a narrow iron bridge, barely wide enough to take two vehicles, Elise saw that the buildings fell away on either side, and below, in the narrow, river-like opening, fishermen were busy preparing their boats. She glimpsed the great ribs of an old boat lying in a sleepy yard and the round tower of a small dwelling. A little further on, the bridge continued over a wide estuary where men and boys stood close to the railing, fishing the brackish water below, while men in boats helped others who were wading in the shallows, collecting mussels in large hoop-shaped nets. The smell of the fresh sea air filled the car and Elise smiled to herself.

The car sped along the coast road, with the sea rolling in on the left and a huge expanse of salt water flats with great flocks of pink flamingos on the right. The sun was dipping fast, daubing the land and seascape with its fiery rays and turning the pools of water blood-red.

Elise thought that the little man appeared to be afraid of the approaching dark, for he was driving like the devil possessed, gripping the steering wheel so hard that his knuckles stood out white against his sallow skin. They raced on through Pula, with its neat homesteads, vineyards, and orange and lemon groves.

A small crossroad lay ahead, and Efisio signalled that he was turning left. The tarmac road ceased and they bumped down a dusty track, full of potholes and boulders. A farmhouse seemed to jump by on the right. Elise noticed as they bumped past that the family was busy unloading a donkey and they waved at Efisio as the car shot by. There were small vineyards and even smaller olive groves.

They passed a small church that rested under the shade of an old olive tree and, suddenly there was a high, plastered wall. The car swung perilously through the old gateway, swerved around another huge, gnarled olive tree and came to a shuddering halt.

'We have arrived, signora,' announced Efisio proudly, and in a somewhat surprised tone added, 'you were very silent, signora. I frightened you, *non?*'

'*Non*,' lied Elise, greatly relieved that the journey was over. '*Non*, not at all. Thank you.'

Efisio heaved himself out of the car and came round to hold the door open for Elise. As she stepped out, a woman appeared in the doorway of the villa. She was round and happy looking, with a dark complexion. Her glossy, black hair was wound into a neat bun at the nape of her neck. She was dressed in a white blouse and a long, dark maroon skirt, which was covered by a freshly laundered white apron. She beamed as she came forward offering her hand to Elise in greeting.

'Signora Raynesford. I am Maria Fozzi. Welcome to Sardinia. I hope you will be very happy here. We were expecting you and your husband.'

'He has been called away to America, so I decided to come on my own.'

Elise was ushered into the villa where the smell of cooking, polish and wood smoke greeted her.

'Welcome Signora.' repeated the woman smiling.

'Thank you, Signora Fozzi. I am sure I will be very happy here.'

'Ah, you speak excellent Italian. How wonderful. You must be hungry, signora? If you are ready I will show you your room. Efisio will take up your luggage, and when you have freshened up, I will serve you supper.'

Elise smiled and nodded.

They were standing in a large room, running the full length of the villa, which served as hall, sitting room and dining room. Despite its size, it had a cosy atmosphere. She took in the cheerful rugs that adorned the terracotta tiled floors and the hand-woven tapestries that softened the starkness of the white-washed walls. On either side of the large fireplace the walls were covered with shelves of books and ornaments. She sighed contentedly; reading wouldn't be a problem here, she thought with pleasure.

Maria led the way across the room to the stone staircase that turned on itself as it climbed to the second floor. Ornate iron railings ran up the side of the stairs and on around the stairwell, forming a gallery that overlooked part of the room below. Through the railings rambled the largest cheese plant Elise had ever seen, its dark shiny leaves contrasting with the dull white of the plaster.

At the top of the stairs, Maria stopped at a door leading off the gallery. She opened the door into a corridor area which had a large built-in wardrobe on the left and a door into the en suite bathroom on the right. Walking through the short corridor, Maria turned on the light and stood aside to let Elise into the bedroom.

'This is your room, signora. Tomorrow you will see it has beautiful views of the sea from the French windows.'

'Grazia, Maria. It's lovely.'

'We could eat in about an hour; would that be alright with you, signora? I thought perhaps anti-pasta, followed by spaghetti, with a little meat and salad to follow?'

'No, please, just spaghetti for tonight. I am tired, and won't eat a lot. Please, signora.'

Maria nodded and left. Efisio, who had followed directly behind them, brought in her suitcase and placed it on a large wooden chest.

'If you need anything, signora, please let us know.' And bowing politely, he too left.

On her own again at last, Elise took stock of the new surroundings that were to be home for the next eight weeks. She plumped down on the bed and looked around her. There were two windows, both shuttered.

On the right-hand side of the room was a pair of French doors, also shuttered. The walls were painted white, with tapestries hanging on them and a cluster of paintings of coastal scenes. On either side of the grand, hand-carved double bed were chests of drawers. Maria had placed fresh flowers in a small vase on one, and a basket of fruit on the other. A large fan turned slowly above the bed, giving a gentle movement of air. The whole room gave an air of freshness and felt inviting.

It didn't take Elise long to unpack her case, wash and shower. She sat on the edge of the bed to dry herself, and caught her reflection in the mirror. The bruises on her upper arms and back were turning a blue-yellow colour, and red welts stood out on the remainder of her pale skin.

The night before last came back in vivid detail.

William, her husband, who was a representative for a large oil company, had always travelled a lot, and to begin with she had gone with him. But she had grown to hate the endless cocktail parties, with the inane gossip, and had finally stayed at home. This time it had been different, two months on the Mediterranean island of Sardinia in early spring sounded wonderful, and she had begged William to allow her to rent a villa near the oil refinery at Sarroch so she could join him there. He had been reluctant, but she had gone ahead and arranged it all, and was looking forward to a holiday.

But the night before, William, returning late after a night at a private gaming party, had woken her and demanded that she let him have money to pay off his huge gambling debts. She had refused. The money her father had left her was dwindling fast, as her husband lost it on the roulette tables or betting on the horses. She had stood firm, but it had cost her dearly. He had hit her repeatedly with his fists and beaten her with a leather belt until she had managed to escape into the bathroom and lock the door.

He had continued banging on the door until his drunken shouting woke the housekeeper, who came to see what was happening. William had sworn at the woman, and told Elise he was going to America as his plans had changed, then left the house cursing at the top of his voice. Elise had been appalled and frightened by his reaction. He was moody and petulant, but he had never been violent before and she had been shocked by his outburst.

The following morning, Elise had told the housekeeper she was no longer needed and paid her two months in lieu. She had rung her dear friend and solicitor, James Bennet, to arrange to stay with him that night, and it had been he who suggested that she go to the villa alone and enjoy some peace away from everything. But it wasn't until now, in Sardinia, that she felt really safe.

Elise sighed heavily, and having finished drying and dressing, she went rather timidly down the stone staircase to the dining room area. There was a large homemade table at which the single place setting on the far end looked rather lost. Maria bustled in and told Elise to be seated; she obeyed. Efisio arrived with a carafe of red wine and a basket of freshly baked bread, while Maria set a huge plate of spaghetti in front of her.

'Buon appetito,' they chorused, and stood watching to see if everything was to her liking.

Elise sipped the dark-red wine and then started her meal, conscious of the two pairs of dark eyes taking in her every move.

'The spaghetti is delicious, as is the wine,' she told them, at which they departed, beaming, leaving her alone to enjoy her meal.

Suddenly feeling hungry, Elise still couldn't do justice to all the pasta that Maria had piled on her plate. On her return Elise explained, as politely as she could, that she wasn't used to eating quite as much, adding that what she had eaten was superb. The Sardinian woman seemed happy with that and added that she had enjoyed cooking it.

The fire in the sitting room looked inviting, but the journey from Heathrow to Milan, then on to Alghero and finally Cagliari, had been tiring. Elise knew that if she sat in front of the warm embers, she would be asleep in no time; so she said goodnight to Maria and made her way up to bed. Tonight, she hoped she would sleep peacefully away from London, William and her unfulfilled marriage. But tiredness rapidly overcame her, and she soon dropped into a deep sleep.

CHAPTER TWO

Elise woke to the sound of someone whistling outside her window. It was a momentary shock to find she wasn't in her bed in London, with the rumble of traffic as a constant background noise. The realisation that she was on her own, at peace, from William and away from his anger, made her smile and she sighed contentedly.

Slipping out of the sheets, she crossed the room and opened one of the shutters opposite her bed. The light was bright and the sun was showing the promise of a long, hot day. It highlighted the huge bourganvilia that clambered over the plastered wall, making a vivid show in the incandescent light. The whistling continued, but Elise couldn't see who was finding the morning so exhilarating.

Crossing to the other window, by her bed, she carefully opened the shutters. Below was the courtyard, surrounded by old buildings with uneven, ochre-coloured tiles and white-washed walls, all shaded by the huge olive tree that Efisio had so narrowly missed on their arrival the previous night.

Behind the low building was a vineyard, and it was the young man working there who was responsible for the whistling. Elise watched him for a moment. He was tall and dark, and seemed totally absorbed in his work. Afraid that she might be seen, Elise moved away from the window. She suddenly felt weak and realised she must still be tired and a bit hungry.

She went to the French doors and threw them back against the wall. They opened onto a small, narrow balcony with its own wooden staircase leading to the garden below. A little river ran down to the beach and a bridge crossed it to a cottage on the other side, which was half hidden by the tall reeds. In the distance she could see a spit of land running out to the sea, topped by an ancient tower.

Elise looked down to see that this side of the villa was completely covered by the prolific ramblings of another huge bourgenvillia that entwined its way up the walls and onto the roof. Eager to explore, Elise showered and pulled on cotton jeans and a shirt, making sure that none of her bruises could be seen. She was about to descend the stairs when the sound of raised voices made her stop.

'Maria, I haven't time to take a lonely English woman on boat trips, or any trips at all come to that.'

'Hush!' said Maria. 'She will hear you, and she speaks excellent Italian.'

The conversation then continued *in Sardu*, so Elise was unable to understand what was said. She waited until there was a break in the conversation and went down the stairs. Her heart sank a little because, once again, her single place setting looked so lonely, there at the end of the huge table.

'*Buon giorno, signora.* I hope you slept well?' said Maria, suddenly appearing from nowhere, making Elise jump.

'Yes, thank you, Maria.'

'Would the signora like an English breakfast, with tea or coffee?'

'Thank you, a continental breakfast would be lovely. Please.'

Coffee came, hot and strong, with fresh crusty bread, brioche and peach preserve. Elise took her coffee and sat by the French window. All the shutters were thrown open, giving a view over the terrace to the sea beyond. She finished her breakfast and crossed the room to inspect the books in the large bookcase by the fireplace. There was a generous selection of books in different languages.

Maria entered to clear the table.

'There are lots of books on Sardinia that you might find interesting, signora.'

When Maria left, Elise searched the bookcase and found a large copy of *Sardegna Encantevoile*. She spread it out on the table and became so absorbed in the photographs of the Sard people and their various customs, together with the intriguing places of the island, that she didn't hear Maria's return, and the sound of her voice made Elise jump again.

'S'Cusa, signora, but you would be better outside in the sun. You look pale and thin. Take the book with you and Efisio will bring you a drink. After the first of May, you can go for a swim, and that will build up your appetite,' commanded Maria in a soft, motherly fashion.

'Why after the first of May?' asked Elise, obviously curious.

'We have a large festa then. It's the island's saint's day, the *Sagra di Sant' Efisio,* and on that day we have the official opening of the lido at Poetto in Cagliari, so you can swim,' she said.

'Do I have to go there to swim?' ventured Elise.

'Oh no, but no one swims before the season opens. At least, none of the local people, not unless they are completely mad. The sea is far too cold. Now, you go out in the sun before it gets any hotter,' Maria added, smiling.

Elise went to her room and changed into a brightly coloured bikini, tying a striped cotton kikoi around her waist. Ever since she had been to Kenya with her father, when she was in her teens, she had always carried these with her. The oblong piece of material was worn by all the Kenyans, and she found them better than a dressing gown. Finally, she pulled on a long silk top over it all making sure that none of her bruises could be seen; she picked up a towel and returned downstairs to collect her book. But Maria had beaten her to it; the book was already outside on a long, low table on the terrace. Elise smiled Maria obviously intended to mother her during her stay and tears sprang to her eyes at the kindness. It was all so different from her life at home, and the thought of William made her momentarily catch her breath.

Stepping out from the cool of the shaded balcony into the comparative heat of the morning, Elise plumped down on a padded reclining chair and once more began to read about the island and its people. The sun shone brightly from a cloudless sky, but it never seemed too hot because a pleasant breeze sprang constantly from the sea.

She found it hard to concentrate and she thought of James, her long-term friend, who had always been there for her. Since the death of her father, he had become the only man she could trust, but she knew that he wasn't interested in her, or any woman for that matter. She was glad she had taken his advice and come down here on her own.

Efisio broke into her thoughts when he arrived with freshly squeezed and lightly sweetened lemon juice in an ice-frosted glass, crammed to the top with tinkling ice. The sound alone was cooling, and the semi-sharp taste made Elise feel refreshed.

'Would it be possible to have my lunch outside on the terrace?' she asked.

'Of course, signora,' replied Efisio.

In no time, Maria was outside laying the table and presently the meal was brought out, together with a carafe of rosé wine.

'Thank you, Maria, that is wonderful, and very kind.'

Whatever it is about Mediterranean countries that produce the need for a siesta after a good meal and wine, it certainly caught up with Elise that afternoon; so with little difficulty, she once more climbed the stone stairs and entered the coolness of her room. She lay on the newly made bed and was soon fast asleep.

It was past four when she awoke. Sitting up drowsily, she decided to wash her hair as it was lank and sticky from the heat. The coolness of the shower's final rinse as the water splashed over her head and body was refreshing, and she gasped as the cold water flowed through her long hair. She dressed, grabbed her comb and headed out through the French doors to the balcony, and then down the outside staircase to sit by the river.

The sun shone on the white sand, making it hot under her bare feet as she hurried to the water's edge. She searched for a spot to sit where the reeds were thin and she could see the still, dark water slip slowly by on its reluctant way to the sea. The cooling breeze coming from the sea blew through her hair as she combed it into place.

She watched the swallows as they dipped and rose about her, collecting mud for their nests, or feeding on the midges that hovered above the smooth, gliding water. The movement of the river was so slow that the only ripples on its surface came from the swallows as they dipped their wings or beaks into the water; or shivered as the breeze hurried over the surface. The reeds were reflected in the river, together with the overhanging trees, giving it the appearance of a huge, dark mirror. The trees and the reeds trembled in the breeze, while the cicadas chirped their grating song, accompanied by the gentle wash of the sea on the nearby beach and the relentless chatter of the ever-present sparrows.

Elise's hair was soon dry, so she decided to walk along the beach towards the point with the tower, the one she could see from her bedroom window. The sand was still hot, so she walked along the water's edge, allowing the small waves to wash over her feet, enjoying the feeling of the sand and water on her bare skin.

Her mind went back to holidays in Wales as a child, and she suddenly realised why Sardinia seemed so familiar to her. It was just like the beaches of Wales, with the long stretches of sand, rocky headlands, small bays and sunlit coves. She remembered how her father would take her along the water's edge, searching for things that had been washed up with the last tide. The walks together on the cliffs, picking wild flowers she would later press and label. He would always photograph the flowers and tell her both their Latin and common names. She smiled as she remembered how her mother had chided her father for allowing her to collect so many little treasures.

Elise reached the end of the beach where the sand gave way to stones and rocks. The little bay fell back, only to open up into a much larger one which was impossible to see from the villa. The bay stretched in a broad sweep for miles and at the far end of the point, which ran out to sea, was the round tower she could see from her room. She would ask Efisio or Maria what they were when she returned to the villa.

She turned to retrace her steps, and was surprised to find that she couldn't see the villa at all from where she was; it was well hidden behind the heavily wooded area that grew so close to the beach. She sauntered back slowly, stopping every now and then to pick up a shell or pretty stone that caught her eye. She loved the fact that she could do as she pleased without the fear of ridicule or criticism from William. She sighed and wondered, not for the first time, why she had married him.

As she ambled on slowly, savouring the peace of the place, Elise let her mind wander back over her life. After her father's death, James had been moved to Scotland with his firm. She had found it difficult in London on her own. She hadn't wanted to go back to the country and her mother. She met William, with all his obvious charms. He was tall, spoke a number of languages including German, French and Italian. In fact they often spoke Italian together when they didn't want others to know what they were saying. He had treated her like a woman and although ten years older than her they seemed to have a lot in common. They had got engaged in a whirlwind of romance. James had travelled down from Scotland to try to persuade her against it, but she had gone ahead; much to the delight of her mother, who believed William to be everything a woman, could want in a man. Elise had insisted that James give her away, much to the disapproval of both William and her mother, but she had won the day. William had chosen Kenya for the honeymoon and it all seemed so wonderful. How had she got everything so very wrong?

She reached the villa just as the sun was beginning to sink behind the great mountain range that lay in the distance. The whole scene seemed to take on a technicoloured appearance, with muted shades of purple and green and a blazing crimson sunset. The cicadas were still chirping in the reeds and trees, and somehow they sounded as if they had recruited outside help for the evening and night chorus, for they seemed twice as loud when accompanied by the local frogs. However, the sparrows were now, at last, silent in the trees. A breeze sprang up to rustle through the reeds and trees once more. With the setting sun, the air took on a slight chill, and Elise shivered. She quickened her pace, pausing for a moment at the doors that opened onto the terrace, where she left the shells and pebbles she had collected in a neat pile.

It was warm inside the villa where Efisio was busy lighting the evening fire.

'That walk has certainly bought some roses into your cheeks,' he said.

'What is that tower on the point further up the beach, the one I can see from the bedroom window?' asked Elise.

'That's Nora. The tower was built as protection against Mohammedans raiders. It is known as Coltellazzo, or sometimes San Efisio. Below is the very ancient town of Nora, with its Phoenician and Roman remains.'

Again, Efisio sounded like the tape recording. He was obviously well practised in answering visitor's questions.

'It's all in the books,' he said, looking at Elise, and grinned. 'Well, you know what I mean,'

At that moment, Maria came into the room and began to lay the table. Efisio nodded at Elise and left with the empty log basket.

'You have some colour in your cheeks,' she remarked.

'Yes, so Efisio said.' Elise paused, and then went on hesitantly, 'Maria, where do you and Efisio eat your meals?'

'In the kitchen; why do you ask?'

'Would it be possible for me to join you? Would it be an imposition to ask if I could eat with you? Would it be a problem?'

Maria stared at Elise with some surprise.

'But you're a visitor, signora. It is not right for you to eat in the kitchen with us! That is not what you pay for.'

'If you don't want me to, I quite understand,' said Elise slowly, suddenly feeling awkward. 'It's just that… well… if I'm to stay here for weeks, I shall be very lonely on my own; and besides, I shall never have a chance to see what the Sard people are really like, and I need to practise my Italian. If at all possible I would much rather be with you and not regarded as a visitor. However, it's up to you… or perhaps you could eat in here?'

'Signora. We would very much like you to join us. However, I have to warn you: if you eat with the family, it can be very noisy,' Maria said, 'Would you like to start tonight?'

'Yes, please, Maria,' replied Elise, and then added: 'If you have any mealtimes when you don't want me, all you have to do is say so. Thank you very much.'

Elise ran up the stairs two at a time. Mealtimes would be something to look forward to from now on.

After showering and dressing in a white blouse and a long cotton skirt, Elise collected the book on Sardinia from the sitting room and went to join Maria in the kitchen. It was a pleasant and homely place, with a long, pine table in the middle around which a number of ill-matched pine chairs were arranged. It reminded her of her grandfather's farmhouse kitchen and all the warmth there. A stove stood in one corner, with two pots simmering away on it.

Elise put her book on the table and crossed over to the stove.

'*Posso?*' she asked Maria with her hand on the lid.

Maria nodded and Elise lifted the lid. A cloud from the fragrant aroma of tomatoes and herbs came up to meet her. She peered into the other pan. This one contained a similar mixture, though not quite as thick.

'That one is for tomorrow's sauce,' said Maria, pointing to the second pan. 'I'm cooking it today and then will leave it overnight to cool, as it always tastes better. I cooked the other yesterday. See how concentrated it is?'

'It looks and smells out of this world,' affirmed Elise. 'What time do you usually eat?'

'Not until half-past eight or nine, but if you are hungry, we can have it now.'

'Thank you, but I'll eat whenever you do,' replied Elise, and she settled down at the table to look at her book.

'There are a lot of questions about the island I want to ask Efisio.' her finger poised over a photo of one of the coastal towers.

'He's not the one to ask. You need to ask Beppe,' replied Maria.

'Who is he?'

'He is a friend who works at the villa. He lives in the flat at the end of the vinery. You can see it from your room. He looks after the vines and generally helps here.'

'I think I saw him this morning. He was whistling very cheerfully. But I am sure he is far too busy to answer any of my questions.'

'Yes, that was him,' said Maria, giving Elise a sideways glance.

'He has gone to his village at Santa Cella, to celebrate his brother's birthday. They have all gone.'

'All?' echoed Elise. 'Who is all?'

'Well. We have two sons and a daughter. We all live in the cottage across the river.'

'I saw it this morning. It looks rather sweet.'

'Sweet it may be.' Maria moved her plump shoulders expressively. 'It's a little cramped too, but we manage. We all eat over here in the kitchen, unless the guests disapprove. They are good children, and we are truly blessed. They all help when they are not working. And work is hard to find on the island.'

'What are their names?' enquired Elise.

'The eldest, who is like his father to look at, is called Ignazio. He's eighteen and works part-time at the cantina in Pula, and is training in viticulture. Then there is my daughter, Margherita; she is sixteen and they say she looks like me,' said Maria, with a note of pride. 'She helps me here when I am really busy. Then there is

Predu. He works on the neighbouring farm whenever he can.'

'And who does he look like?' asked Elise.

'He is like my brother and nearly as tall as him already, though he is only fourteen.'

'Will I be in the way if I come to eat with you when they all come here?' ventured Elise.

'Oh, signora. You will be very welcome, as long as you don't mind the terrible noise. As I said, it will be a bit rowdy, but it will make it easier for me.'

Efisio shuffled into the room. He looked surprised to see Elise sitting at the table.

'I asked Maria if I could eat with you,' she said uncomfortably. 'I hope you don't mind?'

'Maria told me, signora. I'm very pleased,' he replied, his manner rather belying his words.

Elise, determined to break down his resistance, said, 'Maria and Efisio, will you please call me, Elise? That is my first name, and if I am going to be with your family, you can't keep calling me "signora" all the time.'

The two Sards looked at one another.

'What is the matter?' asked Elise.

'We're not used to such openness from strangers,' said Efisio. 'Foreigners always like to give the orders. After all, an English couple staying last year told me, in no uncertain terms, when they couldn't understand our attempts at English, that they couldn't speak Italian and why should they? They had won the war, and it was time the Italians stepped into line.'

'Efisio replied *in Sardu*,' cut in Maria, 'that he was not an Italian, and he has been rather cool towards all English after such an outburst. But you are a completely different character, and you speak Italian; perhaps that is the difference,' she added.

'Thank you, Maria, but do you mind?' asked Elise turning to Efisio.

'No, signora. I don't mind. I would be delighted,' said Efisio, his brown eyes lighting up with his warm smile. 'And now, would the signora – would Elise – like something to drink?'

Elise smiled at him.

'Yes, please. Is it your local wine?'

Efisio smiled and nodded.

Maria busied herself with the cooking, while Elise settled down with her book and enjoyed the wine given to her. Efisio sat himself at the table and hid himself behind the local newspaper: *l'Unione Sarda*. The silence was broken only occasionally as Maria chattered to her husband or he read something from the paper. Although Elise found little difficulty in understanding their Italian, the *Sardu* they spoke together was something quite different. Even so, she sensed they were talking about her by the smiling glances that they both gave her from time to time.

'Dinner in twelve minutes,' Maria announced at last.

Elise looked up from her book; she had been lost in it for nearly an hour.

Efisio rose to lay the table, excusing himself as he spread a freshly laundered cloth in front of her. Earthenware plates were set at each place, together with the cutlery and glassware. Efisio collected a large jug from the side and went out to the vinery, returning with it brimming with the dark local wine.

'It's homemade in our cantina,' he said proudly. 'We grow the grapes and press them here ourselves.'

'Is it the same as the wine we drank earlier?'

'No, and not the same as the visitors have either. This is younger and better. Beppe and I make all the wine drunk here in the villa, but some is for the visitors, and this is for the family; and as you are to be with the family… well… try it,' he said, smiling awkwardly.

Elise was touched by his genuine gesture of friendship, and returned his smile. Efisio said grace and they tucked into proccutto and melon then Maria's spaghetti with the rich tomato sauce, topped with a liberal helping of pecorino – a hard Sardinian sheep's cheese and a green salad with beautiful home-baked Sardinian bread, washed down by their wine.

'It's funny how a country's wines always go so well with the local food,' said Elise. 'It never tastes the same in England.'

'Our wines don't travel very well,' said Efisio gravely.

Elise laughed.

'Oh, Efisio, you only say that so you can keep them for yourselves.'

'Perhaps,' he agreed, and smiled too.

Elise listened as the couple described the work they did around the villa. They said that the owners very rarely came to visit the place now, so they were completely responsible for the daily workings of the villa.

'It seems such a shame,' said Elise.

'It isn't fashionable to be in the south of the island. There is a new development, in the north, on the Costa Smeralda, and it seems that is the place to be seen,' replied Efisio. 'Not that we can complain. The owners are good to us. We look after the place, and in return they allow us to live in the cottage and manage the rest of the estate. They pay us for looking after the tourists in the summer and in the winter we keep ourselves. But we know they are trying to sell it.'

'What do you do in the winter for a living?'

'Well, sometimes I go fishing, or if there is a large Italian party that wants to go boar hunting, I arrange it all. I have many cousins and friends who live up in the mountains and they help to organise the chase. Maria stays here and looks after the women and children. There is always work for us here; doing odd jobs in the vineyard with Beppe, or in the Cantina. The children all help. Predu always finds something to do at the farm. Sometimes he even helps the shepherds when they bring their sheep down from the Barbargia for the winter.'

'Why do they come here? And where is the Barbargia?' cut in Elise, eager for information.

'The Barbargia is the great mountain range to the north. When the snows come in the winter the feed is short and often the valleys are cut off, so they winter their flocks in the plains of the south, leaving the young and the women folk in the villages for the whole winter. They have done it for centuries that way, handed down from father to son.'

'Why don't they make hay, as we do in England, for the winter feed?'

'By July we have hardly any grass land because the sun kills it all. So they move the sheep and goats back to the macchia, the wild scrubland, up in the mountains. It makes for good-tasting meat.'

'What will you do if they sell the villa?'

'Maybe we will stay here, or perhaps we have to go back to our home village. It all depends on the new owners. Time will tell.'

'Do you both come from the same village?'Asked Elise.

'Yes.' Replied Maria. 'Efisio was the eldest son of a local olive grower. My father was the local baker and always bought his oil. We went to school together and Efisio always pulled my hair, so I brought a small fresh baked roll for him each day and he stopped.' She smiled as she looked lovingly at her husband.

'The way to a man's heart is through his stomach.' Said Efisio a broad grin spreading across his face.

Elise noticed the tender look they gave each other as he topped up the glasses again and Maria spooned out more spaghetti for Efisio and herself, realising that Elise was still struggling with hers.

'I'll fatten you up yet,' she said, laughing and wiping her hands on her apron.

'I'm sure you will, Maria. I shall go home fat, bleached and tanned, but at least I shall have had a good rest.'

'You still look very tired. You should rest a lot; take in the sun and good air, and eat well,' Maria advised sternly.

She cleared the plates and brought a wooden bowl piled high with strawberries, cherries and oranges. Elise, who adored fruit, ate an orange, and was then persuaded to have some cherries as well.

'The oranges are the last of Beppe's. You must try the cherries, they are the new crop from his land,' said Maria.

Feeling full to bursting, Elise sat back in her chair and sighed.

'Maria. Thank you. That was a lovely meal. I couldn't eat another thing!'

The genial conversation, together with the questions asked and answered by each other, made the time pass most enjoyably. Elise certainly had eaten more than was usual for her and Maria appeared to be very pleased with that.

The sea air and the good food once again had their desired effect, and it wasn't long before Elise excused herself to go to her bedroom. Her whole body ached and suddenly she felt faint; she tried to stand, but the world spun in an alarming fashion. Strong arms caught her as exhaustion completely overcame her and she fell.

CHAPTER THREE

Elise awoke to a knocking at her door.

'Who is it?' she called drowsily.

'It's Maria. I've brought your breakfast. May I come in?'

'Yes, please do,' replied Elise, trying desperately to collect her thoughts.

Maria opened the door carefully and pattered in on the tiled floor, putting the tray down on the chest beside the bed.

'It's another lovely day,' she announced as she went round the room opening the shutters. The light was bright, and the sounds of an already busy world came flooding into the room, plundering the silence.

'Whatever time is it?'

'It's about nine-thirty. I thought you might be hungry and I wanted to make sure you were alright.'

'Thank you, Maria.' Elise smiled as she pulled herself up in the bed. 'I didn't realise it was so late.'

'That is no matter. You are on holiday and it is good that you rest,' replied Maria as she poured Elise a large cup of coffee. Elise loved being pampered and the coffee smelled wonderful; although breakfast in bed was not something she would want every day, it was a real treat to have it occasionally.

The events of the last evening came back to her. She had eaten supper and then, suddenly, everything had gone blank. Someone must have undressed her and put her to bed. What would they think of her? Elise felt ashamed and embarrassed. How was she going to explain the bruises on her body? They must have seen them. She put down her cup on the table and turned to Maria.

'Did you put me to bed last night?' she asked nervously.

'Efisio carried you up, but I put you to bed.' Maria hesitated a moment, and then added gently, 'Don't you think a doctor should see those bruises and welts?'

Elise recoiled from the question and tried to draw the sheets up around her even more tightly.

'If you want to talk to me, I am here any time. Don't forget that, will you?'

'Please, Maria. Don't tell anyone, please,' she pleaded. 'Promise?'

'I promise, but you must promise to talk to me too.'

Elise looked at Maria. She could feel her emotions welling up inside her and, covering her face, she burst into tears.

Maria sat on the young woman's bed and took one of Elise's hands in hers.

'Tell me,' she whispered.

With a sob, it all came tumbling out. The loss of her beloved father; although six years ago, she had been devastated when he had died, and she still missed him. Her marriage to William, in part to get away from home and in part to have someone she thought would look after her.

'He seemed everything a woman could want,' said Elise. 'He spoke German, Italian and French, and we often spoke together in Italian. But he changed after we were married. He travelled more and more, and continued his gambling and womanising. I wanted to have children, but William was reluctant to start a family, and then he blamed me for not being able to have children. William is constantly abroad, and I have become very lonely. He does not like me to have any friends. My mother refuses to help in any way, because she feels it is my fault that my husband is always away. Up to this time, I never realised how much of a stranger William had become.'

All the time she sat wringing her hands and fidgeting with the sheet as Maria listened without interruption.

'James, my long-standing friend, came back from the States a few days ago. He had been away for two years. He called and the housekeeper refused to let him in, but he pushed his way in and found me in the house. He said he hardly recognised me; I had lost weight and had large, dark circles under my eyes, and what he called a "haunted look".'

'You certainly are pitifully thin, Elise. But, please, go on with your story.'

'James insisted on taking me out to dinner and begged me to

stay with him, but as William and I were due to come down here; I went back to the house. That night, William returned needing a lot of money to cover his gambling debts, and when I refused he tried to beat it out of me. He has always been moody and petulant but never violent. But, Maria, after a beating from him, I knew I had to get away from him. He has changed.'

'What about a divorce? Are you Roman Catholic?' asked Maria softly.

'No, but William wouldn't give me one. It has only just become possible for divorcees to go into the Royal Enclosure at Ascot. It would play havoc with his "social" life, and I have not considered such a drastic action yet,' she sobbed.

'I still think someone should see to those bruises. The skin has been cut in places. I should call in the doctor.'

'No, Maria. They will heal. I don't want to see anyone.'

Maria raised an eyebrow, but made no comment. 'And what about your friend, James?' she asked.

Elise looked at Maria and smiled. 'He's not interested in women, Maria.'

'Oh, I see. It is a very sad story, and I am glad you are here away from it all,' she said, looking at Elise.

Squeezing the young girl's hand, she continued, 'Now, eat some breakfast. Then get up and have some time out in the sun. I won't tell anyone. Efisio knows, but no one else will hear from me or Efisio. Later today, you come and see me, and I will put some healing cream on your back; do you understand.' She said patting Elise's hand. 'Now, is there anything you need in Cagliari?' Maria added. 'Efisio is going into town this morning. I told you that Beppe took Ignazio, Predu and Margherita to his brother's party. Well, it seems everything went to plan, but his mother fell down in the courtyard and hurt her foot. Beppe rang me this morning to say he is staying with her for a few days. Ignazio can't drive, so Efisio said he would drive up to Santa Cella to collect them. It seems that Beppe won't be back until Monday or Tuesday.'

'I'm sorry to hear about his mother,' said Elise as she began to eat her breakfast. 'I hope she isn't hurt too badly?'

'Oh, I don't expect so. Leila likes to keep a hold on her boys, especially Beppe, because he is the eldest. She certainly makes the most of being a widow, demanding her sons' time whenever she can.'

'It sounds as if you don't like her very much,' Elise remarked with a smile.

'Boh – we don't get on too well. The trouble is that Efisio and I recommended Beppe for the job here, and Leila is convinced I am trying to take her son away from her.'

'But that's silly; surely you were only trying to be helpful? Whatever will she do when the boy's married?'

'I don't even like to think about it,' replied Maria, her hands lifted in a gesture of despair.

'Jealousy is a strange thing,' mused Elise. 'It's always alright if you are the one making someone else jealous, but as soon as it comes the other way round, one can quickly become very sour, bitterly resentful and even murderous!'

Maria nodded, and then said suddenly, 'Well, this won't do... I must get on with some work. Are you sure you don't want to see the doctor with those bruises? And do you want anything from Cagliari?'

'No, thank you, Maria,' replied Elise, smiling. She liked this generous-hearted woman. 'And, Maria, thank you for listening.'

'And, signora – Elise – we are having dinner tonight with all the family present. Please join us if you want, or would you rather have some peace?'

'If I'm not upsetting any arrangements, I would very much like to have my meal with you and meet all the family. I feel I'm in the need of company.'

'Bene, bene. That's settled then; as long as you feel up to it. Remember, I'm always here,' said Maria as she collected the tray, backed out of the room and went clattering down the stone steps.

Elise left alone, jumped out of bed, showered and dried. She put on her bikini, tied her kikoi round her waist and put a silk top over it all, then collecting her beach towel, she went down to the terrace, where she knew Efisio would have the chairs waiting for her. She spent the rest of the morning basking in the sun, and after a light lunch, took the usual siesta in her room. She was amazed that sleep still came so easily to her. It made her realise how tired she had been when she arrived.

Elise awoke feeling refreshed and that newfound energy propelled her out of bed and down to the beach to take a late-afternoon walk in the opposite direction from that of the previous day. She had dressed in cropped jeans and a long cotton shirt to hide her bruises. The long stretch of white sand continued to a point where the beach was edged with pine trees; they smelt sweetly resinous in the gentle heat. Beyond the point, the beach led to a small, stony bay, and here the pines gave way to low bushes and coarse grasses. The area was a large salt flat from where the blue-green mountains climbed out into the hazy distance. A dusty track divided the beach from the salt flats and small fishing boats were drawn up on the sandy places among the rocks, awaiting their owner's return to venture out into the open sea once more.

She remembered how her father had once taken her for a day's fishing, and how the weather had suddenly changed. A stiff breeze had turned into a squall, and they'd had to put into a different port. On arriving home late, her mother had lectured her father on his irresponsibility. Somehow, though, it had drawn her closer to her father, and caused a slight rift between her and her mother.

At the far end of the bay, the pine trees once again took over. On the point stood another of the Spanish towers, dominating the scene; they had such a romantic quality, Elise thought, as she sat on one of the rocky outcrops and dabbled her feet in the rippling water. How peaceful and remote it all seemed, so far away from the modern world and her crisis. She was glad she had come to such a place alone, for it would have been impossible to enjoy this tranquillity with William. He had no rapport with the wonderful workings of nature. He certainly hadn't time to stop and listen to a bird singing, or to watch a butterfly lazily opening and closing its wings in the sunshine.

Elise's childhood was so completely different; she had been taught to respect and love all wild things. Her father had taken her, at an early age, to watch fox cubs at play and rabbits scampering in the bottom meadows of her grandfather's farm. How remote all that seemed now; yet strangely, here, he seemed somehow closer than he had in a long time. She sighed; he had been such a wonderful man. How had she come to marry William, so different in every way?

A breeze sprang up and made Elise shiver. The sun was already beginning to sink behind the pine trees. She walked slowly back to the villa, stopping now and again to collect the shells or stones that took her fancy. She was always rebuked by William for collecting such rubbish, but even so, she usually managed to smuggle some home to decorate boxes or picture frames or whatever else came to mind.

On returning to the villa, she put her treasures in a neat pile with those she had collected yesterday. The pebbles looked dull after a day in the sun. What a shame they couldn't keep the same shiny look they had when they were in the water.

'Buona sera, signora,' said Maria, 'another good walk?'

Elise smiled and nodded her confirmation.

'You seem to be catching the sun. It won't be long before you're brown.'

Elise was lucky that although she was fair-haired her skin was a little darker than most blondes. Years of working in the fields as a child on her grandfather's farm had given her a basic tan which she had never lost.

'All the family is here,' Maria was saying. 'They do so want to meet you. Are you sure you're feeling up to meeting them?'

'Oh, yes. That will be lovely. Thank you, Maria.'

Elise excused herself and went upstairs to shower and change.

Later she entered the kitchen where the two young men sitting at the table rose to their feet. Their eyes shone bright in their dark faces; they were just as Maria had described them, and there was little doubt that the eldest looked just like his father.

'I'm Ignazio,' said the elder as he extended a huge hand towards Elise and she shook it. 'And this is my brother, Predu,' he went on, putting Elise's hand into that of his brother's for the customary handshake. The younger brother took Elise's hand, and his vice-like grip made it feel as if her fingers were being welded together.

'And this is Margherita,' continued Ignazio.

The tall, slim, young girl rose and bobbed a small curtsey, which Elise found enchanting.

'Hello, Margherita. Well, you certainly have your mother's eyes.' She looked at all of them. 'My name is Elise, and I hope you'll call me that.'

'Thank you, *signora*,' they chorused.

Elise smiled and sat at the table with them. They began at once plying her with questions.

'Where did you learn your Italian?' asked Margherita.

'I went to art school in Florence for a year. That was nearly eight years ago now, so I am not as fluent as I used to be.'

'Did you love Florence? Was it everything you thought it would be? Beppe went to the Continent,' said Margherita excitedly. 'I have never been there, but I want to go.'

'It was wonderful, I will never forget it,' she said.

'Do you like pop music? Do you know any of the big stars that live in England?' asked Predu.

The pop scene dominated the youth of Europe, having swept in from America and with the Beatles in England, any foreigner was expected to know at least one famous personality.

'No, I'm sorry. I don't know any of them,' Elise confessed. 'I prefer classical music, I'm afraid.'

They looked at her with such surprise, she felt as if middle-age had suddenly leapt upon her.

'You will get on well with Beppe,' said Predu. 'He has been to the Continent and he loves classical music; he plays it all the time, and reads poetry. He has always got his head in a book.'

Maria came to her rescue.

'You must forgive them, Signora Elise. We have many visitors here and some have friends in the music world, so they always ask.'

'What are we having for supper, Mamma?' asked Margherita when there was a lull in the conversation.

'Fruti di mare followed by ravioli and then saltimbocca; followed by cheese or fruit.'

'That sounds good,' said Elise, adding, 'Tell me, how is Beppe's mother?'

'She's alright,' said Ignazio. 'She hasn't broken anything, just sprained her ankle – but she is certainly making the most of it.' He turned to his mother. 'He's coming back on Monday, Mamma.'

'He has to come back soon,' put in Margherita. 'We still have lots of work to do on the *traccus*.'

'He'll be back. Anyway, we can manage without him,' said Predu.

'I know we can, but I like him to help.'

'It's his brother you're supposed to be in love with, not Beppe,' teased Ignazio.

'Mamma, tell him not to be so horrid,' cried Margherita – but the noise ended abruptly when Efisio walked into the kitchen. His authority over them was, to some extent, Victorian, but he generated warmth which was lacking in many relationships between father and children.

'What is a *traccus*?' asked Elise, turning to Margherita.

'It's a bullock cart which we decorate to represent either the area or village where we live for the big *festa di Sant' Efisio*. He is our patron saint, which is why so many people are named Efisio in Sardinia,' said Margherita, and as she said this Elise notice that she looked lovingly at her father.

'Every year we have a festival in his honour,' said Ignazio.

'This year Pula is included in the villages to be represented, and we are all going,' continued Margherita, bubbling with enthusiasm. 'Mamma has our costumes. You will love them; we'll show them to you when they are unpacked.'

'It sounds wonderful.'

'Oh, it is. Everyone is there; dancing in the streets and playing music.'

'Can anyone go?' enquired Elise.

'Oh yes! You must come. We will take you into Cagliari with us, and then you can watch the whole procession. Elise can come with us, can't she, Babbu?' Margherita added, turning eagerly to her father.

'Yes, of course,' said Efisio. Then he addressed Elise: 'That is, if you would like to come?'

'I would, very much.'

'Well, now that's settled, and if you've finished being quite so excited, Margherita, perhaps you will lay the table for me?' came Maria's friendly voice.

As if by magic, papers, books and oddments were whisked off the table. A cloth was spread, and knives and forks, glasses and plates neatly arranged, each person doing his or her job. Maria certainly organised them well. A large basket of fresh bread was placed in the centre of the table, and everyone sat down. Efisio said grace in the thick Sardinian dialect, and they were ready to begin.

The fruiti di mare was fresh and delicious; appreciated by everyone as they wiped the bread around their plates to retrieve every last drop of flavour. Maria then put the steaming cast-iron pot at the end of the table, which was her usual place and served out the ravioli.

The meal passed with pleasant chatter and talk of the festa, the work that Ignazio did at the cantina and what they had done at Claudio's party. Plates were cleared and new ones laid for the main course. By the time the cheese arrived on the table, Elise had been made to feel completely at home. The family was taken by her warm, easy manner. She, too, was eager to ask questions and listen to their answers, and it became clear to them that she was genuinely interested in their island and its culture. They found the combination refreshing, for most visitors to the villa treated them as servants, a race apart.

'You're different,' said Margherita openly, 'and you speak Italian. Most visitors don't even speak to us, or mix with the local people.'

Silence fell, and they all looked at Elise, who blushed under their gaze.

'Thank you, Margherita. I find that very touching, and I take it as a compliment,' she said, and they all laughed.

'You know,' said Elise, 'you remind me of my childhood when I stayed at my grand parents. Although I have no brothers or sisters, we were a very tight-knit community. Neighbours and friends took an interest in each other, but it's not like that any more. I know you have old feuds, and they never die, even when the original wrong has long been forgotten; but here friendships are treasured, and honesty and genuine feelings seem to be accepted as the norm. If you like someone, you show it. If you don't, there is a coldness one can cut with a knife. But either way, your rules of hospitality are never broken. I know the warmth you have shown me is of genuine friendship, and I am very touched by it.'

'We have a saying here that if a foreigner makes a friend of a Sard, he has that friendship for life,' said Maria. 'I hope, Elise, you will remember that.'

Elise smiled and nodded.

The evening continued in an atmosphere of warmth and affection. The family were interested to hear that Elise came from a farming background, and promised to take her to the farm where Predu worked; also, to the cantina. She should learn viticulture, they said, perhaps then she could grow grapes on the farm in England. Margherita insisted that she must talk to Beppe because he knew much more than Ignazio about grapes and vines! The friendly argument that ensued was finally ended by Efisio demanding some peace to read his paper.

Later, lying contentedly in bed, Elise tried to read, but within a few minutes the book had fallen from her hand and she was asleep.

The storm woke her in the early hours of the morning. Darkness still hung outside, and the rain fell in monsoon proportions. The air became fresh and cooler; she wrapped herself in her kikoi and went to the window. She was met by the wonderful smell of rain on parched earth and sand, and she could hear the sea lapping gently on the beach. Lightning streaked across the sky, illuminating the whole of the sea, which was like a mill pond. Storms had a fascination for her, because as a child her father had always taken her out to watch them. She sighed; she still missed him so much. For some reason, she shivered violently; suddenly seized by some unknown fear. She returned to her bed pulled her bedclothes around her and fell into a deep sleep.

CHAPTER FOUR

The weekend passed uneventfully for Elise. The family was busy organising their *traccus* and spent most of the time at their friends' place, working on the cart. On Saturday, Ignazio went to work at the cantina, while Predu put in plenty of time at the farm. The weather continued to be hot and Elise spent the morning in the sun, her skin turning from pale-gold to a deep, honey-brown. Her tiredness gradually disappeared, and instead of taking a siesta in her room, she lay in the shade of a large parasol in a deckchair on the beach, reading the national papers or the book on Sardinia.

She also spent some time sketching the villa; it was such a long time since she had painted and she felt quite rusty, but her talent was still there. She thought back to when she left school and her father, having high hopes of her going to Art College, had sent her to Florence for a year. This had proved to be a turning point in her life. She had soaked up the art and the Italian culture, and was fluent in the language within the year.

On returning to England, the lure of London had proved too much for the country girl. A brief secretarial course had enabled her to find a good job with an advertising firm, which she had enjoyed. For the first year she had gone home every weekend, painting the ever-changing countryside, but the home visits had become fewer and fewer as her social life in London had become more and more hectic. When her father had died, her world had fallen apart. Her dear friend, James, was in Scotland and she had suddenly felt very alone.

Then she had met, and married, William. Since that time, she hadn't touched either brush or pencil. She tried once or twice to get William to sit for her when they were first married, but he had no patience to sit around 'idling time away'. Elise had decided to bring her drawing and painting materials with her, hoping to catch up on her much-neglected hobby, and was delighted to find there were subjects everywhere. Indeed, Elise thought that the whole holiday could easily be swallowed up in an endless mass of fascinating characters to sketch or scenes to paint.

On Sunday morning Elise decided to wander around the old buildings of the villa, and then out into the lane; she wanted to see the little church she had noticed when Efisio had driven her to the villa. Being so close to the villa, it appeared to be part of the estate and was probably the private place of worship for the original family.

It was a white-washed building that sat under the shade of another huge olive tree, like the one in front of the villa. It was a neat plastered building with ochre coloured tiles on the roof and above the western door was a small bell tower. She pushed open the door and was immediately met by the smell of tallow and beeswax polish. The sun fell on the small window above the door and threw odd shadows over the ancient tiled floor and the shiny wooden pews.

Devotional candles were alight in a niche beside the little altar. Elise went forward, and feeling in her jean's pocket she found a ten-lira note which she placed in the offertory box. She took a candle and lit it from one of the already flickering candles nearby, and then she placed it beside the others and said a silent prayer for her father. She was not a religious person, but she had to admit the trappings of the Roman Catholic Church fascinated her.

Elise became aware that she was being watched and, turning, she looked into the gloom and realised that an old man was kneeling in the far corner of the pews his eyes fixed on her. Smiling and nodding at him, she quietly left. Outside a chill caught the air, and she hurried back to the villa.

The weather in the evening suddenly changed, and it became quite cold. Maria decided to eat early so they could all have a long time together. Efisio lit the fire in the sitting room, and they all sat around telling stories and reciting poems. Ignazio played the guitar and Margherita, whose voice was clear and bell-like, sang with Predu. In this happy, relaxed atmosphere, Elise seized the chance to sketch Maria as she sat quietly sewing.

Margherita watched Elise, her curiosity growing until she could no longer contain herself. She came round to have a look at the sketch.

'Why, Mamma, it's just like you! Isn't it good? Elise, you are clever,' she exclaimed, and before Elise could stop her, she picked up the pad and showed it around the room. They all agreed that it was indeed a good likeness.

'It's the first time I've seen a drawing of my wife,' said Efisio, taking his pipe out of his mouth and holding the sketch at arm's length to study it.

'If you would like it, please have it,' said Elise. 'It may remind you of me, occasionally, when I have gone home.'

Efisio, unaccustomed to receiving presents, sat and fingered the picture awkwardly.

'Thank you,' he said finally, 'that is very kind of you.'

'Will you do one of Babbu and us too?' Margherita begged eagerly.

'Hush, child…' began her mother, but Elise was quick to reply.

'Of course I will; it's my pleasure, if that's what you want. However, if I am to sketch your father, I must have music and singing to give me inspiration.'

They all laughed and Ignazio once more took up his guitar. The others joined in, singing their native songs, and so the evening soon slipped away, until Maria finally announced she was ready for bed.

'There is much work to be done in the morning,' she added, 'and we must all be up early. Is there anything else you need, Signora Elise, before we go?'

'No, thank you, Maria, I shall be on my way, soon, too. Goodnight!'

They all trooped out of the house to go to their cottage across the bridge. Elise sat on her own for a while, her eyes on the fire's glowing embers. At last, she felt at peace. How glad she was that she had decided to take James' advice and come on her own. Finally she finished her drink and climbed the stairs to her room.

She was about to switch on the bedroom light when she heard a car pull into the yard. The beam of light from the headlamps swept across her room, and she drew back the curtains to see who was arriving at this time of the night. The lights from the now stationary car shone up into the huge olive tree, catching the silver grey of the leaves as they shimmered in the night breeze. In the weird half-light, she could only make out the tall silhouette of a man. He went into the small building at the end of the vinery, and a light came on. It must be Beppe, back from seeing his mother, she thought, and she closed the curtain, not wanting him to think she was spying on him.

CHAPTER FIVE

The following morning's activity woke Elise. She heard Ignazio and Predu leave for work, and then Efisio and Margherita depart for Pula. Downstairs, she could hear Maria bustling about in her usual busy way.

After breakfast, Elise settled herself outside on the terrace. The air was beautifully warm, but certainly not as hot as it had been when she arrived, so she wore a short-sleeved shirt and a pair of shorts, instead of her usual bikini and her top. She heard Efisio return from Pula, and, presently, Maria appeared.

'Efisio hasn't been able to buy any fish, so we are going to Cagliari. We won't be back until late-afternoon, but I have left your lunch in the kitchen. Margherita is with friends in Pula, and we will collect her on our way home, so you should have a peaceful afternoon. I hope that is alright?'

'Of course, Maria, have a good day, and don't worry about me; I'll be fine,' replied Elise.

She heard them clamber into the car, and listened as it bumped away along the dusty lane to the main road. She spent the morning writing letters to her mother, and sent James a note to tell him how much better she was feeling. Then, having addressed the letters, she went into the villa and put them on the chest in the hall for Efisio to post on his next visit to Pula. After that, she wandered into the kitchen to see what Maria had prepared for her lunch.

The table was covered with a large, clean cloth under which lay an assortment of dishes. Elise found a tray, helped herself to some cheese, tomatoes, olives and fresh bread, and carried it out to eat on the terrace, allowing herself the luxury of reading at the same time. Lunch finished, she laid back and idly watched the swallows darting to and fro by the river. She was just drifting off to sleep when she became aware of a constant 'clink, clink' of metal hitting against stone. Getting to her feet, Elise wandered around the small path at the side of the villa near the river.

Here, the reeds grew thick and close to the house walls. The bougainvillea that greeted her each morning at her windows had its roots here; it clambered in a riot of colour over the two walls, leaving dark recesses for the windows. Efisio must have a never-ending job trying to prevent the beautiful plant from taking over completely, she thought.

Elise could only just make out the roofline of the cottage from here, whereas from her bedroom it could be seen quite clearly. Two smaller olive trees guarded the end of the bridge over the river to the cottage. She walked past them and on towards the clinking noise that seemed to beckon to her. A small gate leading into the vineyard stood open, and she went through it, pausing to look around her. Somehow, the air seemed hotter here. The area was surrounded by dark juniper trees on three sides, the fourth being sheltered by the vinery. Without the usual breeze, it made the vineyard seem hot and oppressive.

Suddenly, above the rows of vines, she caught a glimpse of metal flashing in the sunlight, followed by the sharp 'clink' as it struck the hard earth. Elise found the row in which the work was going on, and saw there the same tall figure she had seen late last night. He stood with his back to her. He was wearing jeans cut into shorts, which showed off his long, brown legs which were placed wide apart as he swung the mattock.

Catching sight of Elise out of the corner of his eye, he turned around sharply to face her, surprised by the intrusion of a stranger. He was older than Elise expected, thinking him to be the same age as Ignazio; he was clearly in his late twenties. His long, dark, curly hair, which fell across his face and his eyes, was so brown it was almost black.

'What are you doing here?' he demanded gruffly. Then, as if realising who she was, he added, 'You startled me!'

'I'm sorry,' said Elise, flushing. 'I… I heard the noise and was curious to know what you were doing. You must be Beppe?' she said.

He smiled and nodded. 'I am the one who should be sorry for greeting you so discourteously. You must be Signora Raynesford? I have seen you already, but I didn't recognise you. You have gone quite brown. Your Italian is very good,' he said, his smile broadening.

Elise's flush deepened, for she assumed he must have seen her looking at him from her window when he returned to the villa last night.

'Thank you?' she said with a slight edge to her voice. 'And when was that?'

'When you washed your hair and dried it by the river. I was busy organising things before leaving for my village. I was going to say hello then, but you had gone before I finished.'

'Yes, I went for a walk. But I saw you return last night,' she added involuntarily, and she noticed he smiled again. 'Please call me Elise. I have asked everyone else to, although Maria and Efisio still call me *signora*.'

'And I am Giuseppe, but everyone calls me Beppe.'

'Well, Beppe, what are you doing?' she asked again, aware he was staring at her.

'I'm trying to remake the waterways so I can water the vines easily, and at the same time I am trying to get rid of some of these accursed weeds.'

'Why do you stake the vines so low?' she asked, eager to break his gaze. The vines, in their vigorous growth, seemed to be wandering pretty well as they pleased over the hard-baked ground.

'Ah – the Continentals and the French grow their vines on high wires, but here, in Sardinia, we grow them close to the ground. The heat from the sun is reflected by the dry earth and helps to make the wine *forte forte*. This is good! Have you tasted our wine yet?' he asked, opening his arms in a wide gesture.

'I have and it's good, and as you say, *forte forte*.'

They laughed, and then silence fell between them. Elise gazed at the man before her. He was tall for a Sard, with dark-brown, curling hair and his eyes were large, dark, and limpid and when he smiled at her his eyes shone with a deep inner glow that hinted of mischief. She was again aware of him openly staring at her.

'How long have you worked here?' she asked, eager to carry on the conversation.

'I came here nearly four years ago and have worked with the vines ever since,' he replied, still looking at her. Beppe stared at her openly admiring her blonde hair and hazel eyes, which fascinated him. He noticed too, with pleasure, her figure, a little thin, but her skin was clear with its deep, honey-brown tan.

He went on: 'You certainly look better now after some sunshine. You were very pale and thin when you arrived. But you are beginning to look a picture of good health now.'

Elise smiled and blushed. She wasn't used to such open admiration, and certainly not from someone so young and handsome.

'Have you... err... have you a vineyard at home?' she asked, again eager to change the subject.

'A few vines, enough for the house and family. We share a vineyard with a neighbour. We also have a small peach grove, and we grow oranges, lemons and soft fruits in the garden too.'

'Yes, I know. We had some of your oranges and cherries the other day, when you sent them back with Ignazio.'

'Did you like them?'

'Very much, they were delicious. They taste so different straight from the trees.'

Another silence threatened, and Elise went on hastily: 'Why did you come to work here? Why not work in the village?'

'My brother works in the village. He keeps an eye on my mother – she is a widow. Work is difficult to find in such a small place, so when this job came up, Maria offered it to me. I was very lucky. She and Mamma are old friends.'

'Yes, Maria told me. And how is your mother now? Her leg must be better because you were not expected back until today, I believe.'

'Yes, she is thank you. But how did you know all that? Did Maria tell you that too?' he asked, smiling.

'Well, not exactly. The family was discussing it at dinner on Saturday night, so I couldn't help overhearing.'

'You mean... you eat with the family?' Beppe asked incredulously.

'Why, yes.' She hesitated. 'I asked Maria if I could, and she said it would be alright.'

Beppe laughed, and Elise, a little nettled, added, 'What's so funny?'

'*Boh*. It's just that... well... we all had such preconceived ideas

39

of what you would be like. Married and coming on holiday on your own, no children. We all thought you would be a typical Englishwoman,' he said with his hands in an open gesture.

'And what does that mean exactly? Besides I was coming with my husband, but he had to go to America.' she retorted.

'Well...' It was Beppe's turn to look embarrassed. 'Well...'

'Come now!' teased Elise. 'You started to say something, you must finish it.'

'Well, it's just that the English are... reserved, a little cold; or so we have found. They don't really want to know much about the local people. They don't speak other languages. They sit on the beach and never go anywhere, and they are not interested in their surroundings. But you, you seem different somehow. You obviously mix with Maria's family, and you even speak Italian extremely well.'

'Thank you. I was lucky to spend time in Italy,' she added, feeling the colour rising once again in her cheeks under his constant stare.

'I'm sorry,' said Beppe. 'I have embarrassed you. Please forgive me.'

'There's nothing to forgive,' she replied, her awkwardness suddenly vanishing.

'Now, I understand from Maria that you want to know about the island. Tell me what you want to know.'

'I'm sorry Maria troubled you. I thought you didn't have time to show a lonely English woman anything...'

Beppe opened his mouth to say something, thought better of it and closed it again.

'I overheard you talking to Maria the other morning,' she continued.

Beppe put his hands up and spread them across his chest. 'I'm sorry you overheard that. All I can say is that I shouldn't have prejudged you, and you should not have been listening!'

Elise smiled and felt her heart skip a beat.

'So, tell me some of the things you want to know,' he said, staring intently into her eyes and opening his arms wide.

'Well, if you are offering, I can see Nora from my bedroom

window, and that looks fascinating. I understand there is an old town there?'

'There is. It's a Spanish tower on the point, but the town of Nora is really interesting. It goes back to Phoenician times and the ruins are well worth a visit. On calm days, we can see the remainder of the ancient city under the sea. You should go there.'

'Yes,' she nodded in agreement, 'and I also want to see a Nuraghe; they sound intriguing. I understand there are lots of them dotted all over the island.'

'Oh yes. Some seven thousand or more: some are in good order, others a mere outline on the ground. They are very old and nobody really knows what they were used for. Some say they were fortified villages, others claim that they were sacred temples. Others say that they were retreats from malaria. I doubt if we shall ever really know.'

'How do you know so much about the island?'

'I have many books on Sardinia. Also, there was a professor of archaeology who lived in our village. He is dead now, but as a child, whenever I had a free moment, I would go and see him. He would tell me about the various peoples who ruled this island, and their colourful histories. He also had many objects that he found on his digs.' Beppe gazed pensively at the ground. 'I would have loved to study archaeology and to work in that field.'

'So why didn't you?'

He looked at her, smiled and shrugged his shoulders.

'*Boh*. When my father died, it fell to me to look after my mother and brother. Childhood dreams quickly vanish with the realisation of maturity and responsibility falling heavily on young shoulders.'

'Does your mother work?'

'No. She is not very strong. She looks after the house and Claudio, my brother. Sometimes she does some sewing for the rich people in the village, but not very often.'

'What about your brother? How old is he?'

'He is nineteen and has just finished college. He works in a small vineyard and our peach grove. He also helps in the village whenever he can, turning his hand to anything and everything, but he is a trained carpenter and accountant.'

'I presumed he was older than that; aren't he and Margherita about to be married?'

'Yes. Our parents decided at their birth that they should marry,' replied Beppe.

'You mean… marriages are still arranged here?' asked Elise, amazed.

'Yes. But Margherita and Claudio are happy because it's a love match, as well as an arranged one.'

'Are you married then?' she ventured.

'No.' He laughed, but there was a hollow ring about it. 'I am, as you say, a free spirit! And now, if you can forgive me, I have work to do.'

'I'm sorry. I didn't mean to pry,' she said, turning to go.

Elise slowly sauntered back to the terrace, feeling his eyes on her as she made her way out of the vineyard and went back to her chair in order to catch the late-afternoon sun.

Efisio and Maria returned with Margherita soon afterwards, and it wasn't long before the wonderful aroma of cooking spread through the villa.

Elise was summoned to the kitchen around seven-thirty. She had showered and changed and was feeling refreshed after her relaxing day. Maria placed Elise next to Beppe, who had also washed and changed. He had combed his damp hair down close to his head in an attempt to make it look well-groomed. However, his obviously naturally, tousled hair sprung up in rebellion in odd places, and the curls were still evident at the nape of his neck.

Maria introduced them to each other, and Beppe smiled.

'Yes,' he said. 'We have met already.'

'Oh?' said Maria, surprised.

'We met this afternoon in the vineyard,' continued Beppe, politely pulling Elise's chair out for her to sit down.

'She has many questions to ask about the island,' continued Maria. 'Perhaps you will be able to help her.'

'I have already asked him,' cut in Elise, feeling rather like a child being discussed by benevolent grown-ups.

The meal passed with the usual good-humoured chatter and family teasing. Elise found Beppe easy to talk to and he was also a good listener. He corrected her Italian whenever she made a mistake, which, fortunately, wasn't too often. The more she spoke it, the easier it became. Not speaking Italian for a few years, her fluency had gone. Beppe spoke excellent Italian, with far less of a Sardinian accent than the others, but Maria and Efisio were quite content to let her carry on speaking the language without correcting her.

'You should learn to speak it properly while you are here. After all, the Sards are said to speak the best grammatical Italian because we all learned it as a second language at school. Most homes still speak *in Sardu*, so you should learn to speak it too.' He added: 'If you learnt Latin at school, you will find it easy.'

'I didn't,' she replied. 'I threw my Latin book at my teacher, so she refused to teach me!'

'I'm not surprised,' said Beppe, looking a little taken aback. 'Are you always so violent towards your teachers?'

'No. In fact, I'm really quite placid now. But if something roused me, I used to lose my temper.'

Ignazio broke up the gathering, explaining that he had to be up early the following morning because there was much work to be done at the cantina. Elise went to bed soon after they left, but found it difficult to sleep. She lay in bed thinking over the day's events, and somehow every thought, annoyingly, led her back to the same person – Beppe!

CHAPTER SIX

The sun was warm, but the morning air was still cool when Elise went into the vineyard.

'Here, this is the way to tie the low vines,' said Beppe, taking the tendrils and slipping the wire around them.

'Let me do one, and then you can tell me if it's right.'

She did as he showed her while he watched her slender, nimble fingers at work.

'Excellent,' he cried. 'Now, you go along this row, and I'll start on that one.'

Elise had appeared early in the vineyard to see if she could help, and was delighted when the offer was not turned down out of hand. Beppe was reluctant at first, saying that it wasn't her job to be working, but he finally relented when she said she would otherwise sit in the vineyard and watch him work. The sun was soon beating down, but every so often a light breeze would come fluttering between the rows of vines, giving a brief respite from the increasing heat. She watched Beppe as he started his way up the next row, working quickly. It was going to be a back-breaking job, but having volunteered, there was no way she was going to back down.

Years of working on her grandfather's farm had given her the basic training; she was quick to learn and her fingers showed great dexterity. She had dressed in shorts in the hope of getting her legs brown and, putting on her hat, she focused on the work, determined to do a good job. By lunchtime, she had completed one whole row and was only half a row behind Beppe.

Maria appeared, carrying two baskets and calling, 'Lunch!'

Beppe came to find Elise.

'I asked Maria if you could have your meal out here with me. I hope you don't mind?' he said in a matter-of-fact sort of way.

'No, that's fine!' she replied, aware she had no choice.

'Signora Elise, you must not tire yourself,' said Maria anxiously, looking at her flushed face. But Elise laughed.

'I'm fine, Maria.'

Beppe took the baskets, thanked Maria and led the way along the row to the far end of the vineyard where the boundary of reeds gave way to the slow-moving river. It was cool there with a small breeze constantly coming up the inlet from the sea.

'Sit down,' he said, spreading his shirt on the ground in the shade of an old olive tree.

She obeyed, and he set down the baskets. 'You must eat your lunch, and then have a rest,' he added, seating himself beside her. 'You have done well for a beginner.'

'It's lovely and cool under here. It is really hot out there in the sun,' she sighed watching the swallows as they dipped into the water.

They sat eating, each conscious of the other, and she was aware that Beppe was again watching her every move. Anxious to break into his thoughts, she said, 'You know I love picnics. They remind me of my childhood, when I used to help my grandfather on the farm. In the holidays, I would stay with him when my parents were away. In the summer, we'd cut the hay. With the start of the harvest, there were long days outside helping the men, and we would sit under the trees for lunch. All those days seemed sunny and golden then.'

'Does your grandfather still farm?'

'Yes. But my father went to work in the city and travelled quite a bit, so I spent a lot of time on the farm with my grandparents.'

'How many hectares does he farm?' asked Beppe, biting on a piece of cheese.

'About one hundred hectares in total.'

Beppe choked.

'But that is a big farm, surely, isn't it?'

'Not in England. Perhaps a little over average, but not much. It would not support two families.'

'What does your grandfather grow?'

'Cereals – wheat, oats and barley, with break crops of sugar beet and potatoes, and hay, of course. He has a house cow, a few hens and a goat.'

'Now you are married, you no longer farm? Your husband, he isn't a farmer?'

Elise laughed. 'No, he isn't a farmer.' The thought of William up to his ears in corn at harvest time, or up to his knees in mud in the winter, amused her. William was far too much of a 'gentleman' to do manual work. The cut and thrust of the oil business and its mental rigours were more his forte.

'Why do you laugh?' asked Beppe, intently watching her expression.

She shrugged.

'No reason!' She paused and then added, 'My grandfather and husband don't get on too well together, but... my childhood days, they were different. I used to help drive the tractor at harvest time. It was my job to look after the hens and collect the eggs. At the time, I remember, it seemed such a narrow, sheltered world, and I longed to escape; but looking back now, I know that it would have been better if I'd married a farmer rather than a Londoner.'

'Is that why you came on holiday by yourself? Did you need to be away from city life?' He asked in his direct way 'and your husband is he going to join you here?'

She shrugged again. 'Tell me about your childhood. Did you always work the land?' she said, obviously changing the subject.

'I'm sorry,' he said, smiling. 'I didn't mean to pry. As for my childhood... well... it was quite simple. We lived in a little village and my father worked hard on a small piece of land. I left school at fourteen and worked as a shepherd for a neighbour. My pay was two litres of milk a week and some cheese. In that same year my sister, Francesca, died of *impare*, which is a fever like malaria. My brother was sent to our uncle in Monastir, and I went to live with my employer; my father was afraid that we might catch the fever as well. Fran was very ill, and when she died I thought my mother would die too.'

'When I was with Maria the other day, she mentioned that your mother never really got over Fran's death.'

'She could be right.'

'What happened then?'

'I helped my father in the vineyard and the peach groves; I worked hard, very hard, and for long hours. All the watering and weeding was done by hand. I can remember breaking up the virgin soil inch by inch, and the pain of salt water on my blistered and bleeding hands made me cry out when I went home at night. I worked with my father for six years. Each year he put more and more responsibility onto my shoulders. But at twenty, I was lucky enough to go to the continent to do my national service. Then, when I was twenty-two, he died, and I was left with my mother and younger brother to look after.

'My father made me promise on his death bed that I would take care of them. Claudio was only fourteen, so he had at least two years to go at school; more, if I had my way. It was up to me to work and keep them both. So when Maria offered me this job, it was like a gift from heaven. The pay is good and my meals are thrown in, but my mother still doesn't like me being away from home.'

'Will you be content to work someone else's land for the rest of your life, though?'

'Well, I can't work our land, as Claudio will need it when he is married. If the opportunity came to work my own, of course, I would. Perhaps one day – I would like to have my own business. But I'm my own boss here, more or less, so I don't complain.'

'Efisio and Maria are certainly very kind,' said Elise, 'and they don't seem to mind that I have foisted myself on them.'

'Of course they don't mind!' he replied, looking at her with a mischievous grin. 'The Sards are very hospitable. Didn't you know that?'

She nodded, laughing.

Beppe went on, 'I'm going to look at the engine on the motor boat this afternoon, seeing as you helped me this morning. Then I shall want to try it out. If you like I'll run you down to Nora, and you can see all the ruins.'

'Are you sure about this? Have you really got the time for a lonely English woman?' she said, with mock seriousness.

'Yes, I am,' he said, smiling at her.

'Where do you keep the boat?'

'It's kept in a small boat house around the bend of the river. Have you finished your lunch?'

Elise drained the last of her wine. 'I have now,' she said.

'Well, you take the baskets back to Maria. I'll collect the boat, and you can meet me back here.'

Elise picked up the baskets, walked through the vineyard and out into the courtyard. It was cool and shady under the big old olive tree, and the loose stones crunched noisily under her feet as she crossed the yard. She passed through the arch and into the kitchen where Maria and Efisio were sitting drinking their small cups of coffee.

'I've brought everything back, Maria,' said Elise. 'Thank you for the meal. Beppe is going to do something with the boat engine and then wants to try it out, so he's taking me to Nora. I don't know how long we shall be. He didn't say.'

'Now be careful,' said Efisio solemnly. 'Don't you go leading that young man astray!' Elise, seeing the twinkle in his button-brown eyes, replied with equal gravity.

'No he is leading me.'

They all laughed and she slipped out of the kitchen, smiling to herself.

Beppe had collected the boat and was still tinkering with the engine. She climbed aboard and waited patiently while he put the final adjustments to whatever he was doing. He then picked up a long pole from the bottom of the boat and punted the craft down the slow-moving river.

'This is like being on the river at Cambridge,' remarked Elise, trailing her hand in the water. 'The undergraduates hire a punt for the day and have a picnic on the river. It's lots of fun!'

There followed a light-hearted discourse as to what a punt was, and with a number of hand signals, together with sign language, Elise hoped she managed to explain herself completely.

When they cleared the estuary, and the brackish water of the river gave way to the brilliant clear blue of the Mediterranean, Beppe started up the engine and the boat leapt forward. The wind blew through their hair and the surf flew as they raced past the little bay in which the villa was set. Once around the point the land receded, forming a much deeper bay. Beppe opened the throttle and they sped across the blue water, leaving a churning, boiling wake behind them; it was a thrilling and invigorating sensation.

They raced towards the promontory of Nora, which stretched out into the sea like a huge letter 'Y'; the tail of the letter running back to the mainland, with the haze-shrouded mountains rising up behind. In the centre of the fork was a small bay that was guarded by the Spanish tower.

Beppe took the boat in slowly. The water was crystal clear with a rocky bottom along which fish darted. He lifted the engine, so as not to catch it on the rocks below, and threw the anchor overboard. Elise watched it fall, leaving a trail of silvery bubbles. Coming in by sea made her aware of how the Phoenicians must have felt using this same port, all those centuries ago. The remoteness of the place seemed to make time stand still. At any moment she expected someone to appear dressed in ancient attire and to question their arrival.

Beppe rolled up his shorts and slid over the edge of the boat. The water was thigh deep, and he insisted on carrying Elise. He lifted her in his strong arms and she became aware of his closeness, but with her arms around his neck, she suddenly felt very safe. She remembered being carried like this by her father when she had been thrown from the beautiful chestnut horse he had given her. Her ankle was sprained and he had carried her back to the house; she had felt safe then. It was the last time, she realised, that she had felt really safe.

'There's nothing of you. We will have to feed you up on some good Sardinian food,' Beppe said, smiling and looking at her.

He didn't release her until it was shallow enough for her to walk without getting her shorts wet. She held on to him momentarily until she found her balance. The big rocks were surprisingly smooth under her feet and not at all painful to walk on. Smiling, he took her hand and the two of them paddled ashore and trudged up the beach.

Before them lay the old Roman forum; to its left, Beppe pointed out the foundations of the early Phoenician houses. They admired the wonderful Roman mosaics, and she marvelled at the ruins as they walked along the magnificent roadway which had lain there since early Roman times. It was still possible to see the remains of the drainage and underground heating systems that had been in the houses. Standing proud above all else was the theatre, and in front of it lay two large amphorae, just as they had been found during the excavations. Elise gazed at the raked rows of stone steps built in a semi-circle around the stage. The backdrop for the plays would have been the open sea; she could imagine the whole of history taking place before her eyes.

Elise climbed the stepped, stone seating and turned towards the sea. She closed her eyes and, placing her hands together as in prayer, she recited in English: '*Romeo, Romeo, where for art thou, Romeo?*'

'I am here, Juliet!' replied Beppe, laughing.

'You know Shakespeare?' she asked, climbing down from the seating again.

'A little, but then everyone knows Romeo and Juliet.'

'Do they?'

'Elise, all the world loves a lover,' he said, taking her hand, and they laughed.

'It's all remarkably well preserved,' she said, 'and what a beautiful setting, with the mountains behind and the calm waters of the bay in front giving perfect shelter for all their trading vessels.'

'The Phoenicians are supposed to have jealously guarded this island, with its silver and salt deposits. So if, when sailing near the island, they happened to have strangers onboard, they would kill them and throw them overboard so that they would not tell anyone else about this prize in the Mediterranean,' said Beppe.

'It's still an unknown island,' she replied, adding with a giggle: 'Do you still get rid of tourists like that when it's time for them to go? Are you planning to do the same to me?'

'Who knows?' he said, smiling.

They walked towards the Roman temple from which one could see across the huge bay that fell away from the point.

'If you look over there, towards Cagliari,' said Beppe, pointing, 'you can see the outline of streets and houses now in ruins under the sea. It's not as calm today as it can be, but when it's like glass, usually early in the morning, it is possible to see them quite clearly.'

Elise followed his direction and gazed into the clear blue depths. It was certainly possible to make out a variation in the colour and smoothness of the water. In the distance, a single rigged fishing boat glided across the bay, watched over by another small Spanish tower on the island of San Maccino.

'Do all the points have towers?'

'Most of them, the idea was that you could stand at one tower and see another on either side. They were used as warning beacons when the Spanish held the island under King Phillip. They were built for protection against the raiding Mohammedans.'

They strolled round the site, looking at more of the beautiful mosaics and the wonderfully preserved footings of the ancient dwellings. It hardly seemed possible that they had once housed Phoenician traders or Roman generals, people who may even have travelled as far as England and traded with, or ruled over, that cold, green, distant land of the north.

'Our patron saint was beheaded here,' Beppe remarked. 'Efisio was a general, but he became a Christian and preached throughout the island, turning the heathen towards Christianity.'

'Is that why you have the festa this week?' asked Elise.

'Yes. The image of the saint is carried through the streets of Cagliari, then on out here to Nora. It takes them four days in all to come from the town and return again.'

'Has it always been like that?'

'A long time ago there was a terrible plague in the old city of Cagliari, and all the people prayed to Saint Efisio for help. The plague went away and ever since we have all given thanks to him for his great favour.' Beppe paused for a moment in silent thought, and then added, 'Are you coming to see the festa, Elise?'

'I am and I'm really looking forward to it. Will you be there too?'

Beppe nodded. 'We shall be going early in the morning. Ignazio, Predu and Margherita are on the *traccus* with their friends. I'm riding with my cousins.'

'Will you be in costume, too?'

'Yes, I have the costume my grandmother made for me, and Claudio has my father's. I had to have a new one; my father's was too short for me! They are usually handed down from father to son.'

'It all sounds so exciting,' said Elise, her eyes bright with anticipation.

'It's quite a spectacle. If you watch the procession with Efisio and Maria, we can all meet afterwards.'

They sauntered towards the water's edge as they talked and took in the scenery.

'Have you seen enough?' asked Beppe. 'Are you ready to go back?'
She nodded.

'And I can walk to the boat myself,' she said, laughing, as he moved towards her. 'You don't have to carry me.'

She waded out, clambered into the boat and sat dripping all over the seat. Although the water was not as warm as it might be, it was still a good deal warmer than the English Channel in midsummer. Beppe pulled himself up on board with alarming agility and then turned his back on Elise to do something with the engine.

Elise, eager to help, went forward and climbed onto the bow of the boat. She leaned over to pull up the anchor.

Beppe turned to see her, and called out desperately, 'Lean back, Elise!'

She glanced at him and at the same time felt the boat slowly slip away from under her. Beppe dropped the engine, hoping it would give the boat some stability, but it was too late. As if in slow motion, and still holding onto the anchor rope, Elise went headfirst into the water. Beppe looked over the side of the boat to see Elise rising in a mass of churning water and bubbles. She looked up at him to see his concern turn to mirth as a broad grin spread across his face.

'It's not that funny,' she cried. 'I was only trying to help!'

'Come here to the boat,' he said, leaning out to catch her hand. He turned her so that her back was against the boat, put his hands under her arms and, with ease, lifted her onto the deck of the boat. She turned to him and shivered.

'You are so light, there's nothing of you,' he said as he went to the locker under the bow, pulled out a large sweater and put it on her. She sat in the boat on the seat and watched him, feeling wretched. She gazed as the sea water trickled down Beppe's long, muscular, brown legs and formed little puddles on the deck, and she sat hunched in the sweater he had given her, admiring his lithe body. He glanced up, saw her eyes fixed upon him and he smiled.

'Are you alright now?' he asked, looking at her quizzically. 'You shouldn't have done that, Elise. It's my job to look after you.'

'But I just wanted to help. Did you throw me overboard so that I would not tell anyone about the island?' she replied, looking miserable.

'I did not throw you over, Elise. Are you warm enough?'he said gently touching her on her shoulder.

She nodded. She felt something stir inside her; a longing, a fear, a thrill – she wasn't sure.

Beppe went to the front of the boat, opened up the engine and the boat raced back across the vivid blue water towards the villa.

CHAPTER SEVEN

The family was gathered round the table when Elise entered the kitchen, and the babble of voices hit her as she opened the door. Margherita patted the chair next to her and asked Elise to join her. Ignazio was chatting to Beppe *in Sardu* and laughing; Predu and Margherita listened, and then looked first at Beppe and then Elise.

'What's the matter?' asked Elise.

'Nothing,' said Margherita. 'Come and sit down here next to me and tell me what you did today. Beppe said you went to Nora, did you like it?'

Elise looked around the table. All eyes were on her except Beppe's, he was looking at Margherita.

'Yes, it is such a lovely old site. I suppose Beppe has also told you that I managed to fall in trying to lift the anchor.'

A burst of laughter erupted around the table.

'Well, it wasn't that funny!' said Elise.

Margherita took Elise's hand and looked at her squarely in the face.

'Did Beppe ask you to lift the anchor? Think carefully.'

'No. Why? I did it because I thought I could help. He was busy with the engine, so I thought I would go forward onto the bow and lift the anchor. What is all this? It was only a silly accident, nothing serious.'

Ignazio leant forward to Beppe and asked him something *in Sardu*, and when Beppe replied they all laughed and clapped.

Elise turned to Beppe, suddenly feeling unsure of herself.

'What have I done? What happened?'

'Elise,' said Margherita, 'when Beppe or Ignazio take the clients out in the boat, they always try to tip someone into the water. It's the oldest trick in the book. The boat is really unstable when in the water with the engine lifted out; any sideways movement will destabilise it. So when you leaned over and pulled on the rope, the action of you pulling on the anchor pushed your weight forward and so the boat went away from you, dropping you in the sea.'

Elise looked at Beppe throughout the explanation and watched him as he refused to look at her.

'Ignazio asked what number you scored,' continued Margherita, 'and it seems you scored an eight, which is really good. Most clients only make a two, so you must have fought well.'

Elise looked around the table and met all the smiling faces, but was not willing to look at Beppe. She had been so convinced it was an accident, but now she wasn't so sure. Had he dumped her in the water on purpose? Were all men untrustworthy and stupid? She felt cross with herself that something as trivial as this should affect her so much. She spent the rest of the meal chatting to Margherita, and later she excused herself to go to bed early.

She was about to climb the stairs when Beppe approached her and grabbed her hand. He looked at her with a wistful smile.

'Do you really think I would do that after wanting to carry you out to the boat? I could have dropped you then – why would I wait until you were in the boat?

'I don't know. It just seems rather childish to try and drown your clients.'

'Elise, you have to believe me. You know I didn't ask you to lift the anchor.'

She pulled her hand out of his and started to walk away.

'Please come and help me in the vineyard tomorrow.'

Still unsure of herself, she turned away and walked up the stairs without looking back. She suddenly felt she was not capable of making any judgments about men.

In the morning, Beppe was in the vineyard again. It was late before Elise arrived. During the night, she had played the scene in her mind repeatedly and now knew, for certain, that it had been an accident and that the family had just enjoyed having a joke at Beppe's expense.

Beppe came to meet her when she entered the vineyard and asked her if she would like to work with him. She smiled and agreed. This time he worked beside her, enabling him to answer her unending stream of questions about the island and its strange customs.

In the afternoon, he took her in the boat to Chia, another promontory guarded by a Spanish tower, with the promise he would carry her out if necessary. Elise assured him that she would not touch the anchor, and they both looked at one another and laughed.

It turned out to be a glorious afternoon, the hottest so far, and so they decided to take a swim in the small bay. The water was surprisingly warm and crystal clear. Elise insisted on keeping her cotton shirt on in the water, which Beppe thought strange, but put it down to shyness and so he didn't remark on it.

Suddenly, Elise began to laugh.

'What's so funny?' asked Beppe, splashing her playfully.

'Maria said that locals never go swimming before the first of May unless they're mad!'

'Well, signora, that just about sums us up,' he replied, laughing.

He began to dive for sea urchins and came back to the beach holding a number of the shellfish. Elise returned to the beach, wrapped herself in a large towel and started to dry herself.

'Mmm! Delicious,' Beppe said as he opened an urchin and scooped out the star-like fleshy piece inside with his penknife. The orange-coloured flesh fell limply over the blade, which Beppe pointed towards her.

'Try it, it's really very good.'

Elise shuddered and made a face and Beppe laughed openly and chided her for her squeamishness.

Later they climbed to the top of the hill, and from there they went up the outer iron stairway to the winding stone staircase of the Spanish tower. The view was awe-inspiring in its remoteness. Below them, the turquoise sea lapped gently against the sheer rock face that was topped by windswept grass. To the left was the bay of Chia, where the boat lay at anchor. The water was so clear that the boat appeared to be suspended. To the right, a vast stretch of white sand swept across a wide bay washed by the gentle, blue waters of the Mediterranean.

'Below this tower, under the grass mounds lie the ancient ruins of Bithia where the Semitic people used to worship their demi-god, Bes. He was the finder of husbands and lovers for all the young maidens,' said Beppe, pointing to the wild scrubland below.

'There isn't a soul in sight; it's like being on a deserted island. Such isolation in the modern world seems unbelievable, and the water is amazingly clear,' she replied, gazing around in wonder.

Later, on returning to the villa, Elise found that excitement was building up to fever pitch with the preparations for the festa on the following day. After supper, Elise was quietly reading in the sitting room when Margherita burst in from the kitchen.

'Do you like it, Elise?' she cried. 'Oh, say you do.'

Margherita pirouetted, showing off her costume to its full advantage. Her long, black hair was crowned with a delicate white lace mantilla that swung as she turned. Her blouse was of fine, white cotton with intricate embroidery around the neck and down the wide sleeves, which were gathered in at the wrist and held by gold filigree buttons. A stiffly starched lace collar stood up around the neckline, forming a frame for the mantilla. Over the blouse, Margherita wore a tight-fitting, black velvet waistcoat adorned with several gold necklaces, and there were numerous gold rings on her fingers. Her scarlet skirt, of hand-woven linen, was finely pleated and was edged with an intricately hand-embroidered border. Over this she wore an apron which matched the border, edged with gold thread. Even her shoes were made of the same material.

Elise stared at the young girl. 'Margherita,' she said, in all sincerity, 'you look absolutely beautiful. And, yes, I love the costume. I don't think I've seen anything quite so exquisite. It's stunning.'

'It belonged to my mother,' said Margherita with obvious pride. 'She made it all before she was married.'

'And look at all your beautiful jewellery.'

'That goes back for generations,' said Margherita, stepping forward, eager to show off her treasures. 'The necklaces belonged to my great-grandmother and my grandma. The buttons were a present; one from an uncle when I was christened, the other from Babbu when I was confirmed. I hope I shall have another when I'm married,' she said with a shy smile.

Ignazio and Predu came into the room at that moment.

'Mamma and Babbu said you would like to see our costumes,' said Ignazio proudly as they stood before her to be inspected. They were wearing similar full-sleeved blouses to Margherita's, but with less embroidery and closed at the neck with small gold buttons. Ignazio sported a red waistcoat, while Predu's was black velvet, like his sister's. They were both wearing short, black, tunic-like skirts tied at the waist with red bands, and under the tunic skirt, a pair of baggy white trousers, tucked inside black, cloth gaiters bordered with red bands. Predu was also wearing a long, stocking-like hat.

'You both look so romantic,' sighed Elise. 'I like your hat, Predu. It's very dashing.'

'Thank you. It's called a *berrita*,' said Predu, glowing with pleasure.

Maria came into the room. 'And what do you think of them, Signora Elise?' she asked, clucking at her brood.

'I think they look very handsome indeed. I never imagined they would be so colourful and elaborate,' she replied, smiling.

Maria sighed. 'In the south, we don't wear the costume as often as we should. In Cagliari, you can see the old women wearing it occasionally, and the young wear them for their weddings – but in the Barbargia, they still wear them every day. Not so elaborate as those worn for festivals or weddings, but just as colourful.'

'It seems such a shame when the old traditions die,' said Elise sadly. 'Customs that have been adhered to for generations, just cast aside for modern ways, and it's even worse when the customs and music are adapted to "civilised" tastes, or to entertain camera-happy tourists because they lose all their original meaning.'

'Our young people wear jeans, but some still guard their traditions jealously,' replied Maria. 'In Sardinia, we say you can't have a custom without a costume, because the words are the same. They always go hand in hand.' She turned to her daughter. 'And now young lady off to bed with you please there's a busy day ahead of you tomorrow.'

They said their goodnights.

'You are coming tomorrow, aren't you?' asked Margherita, ducking under her mother's protective arm.

Elise laughed. 'I wouldn't miss it for the world.'

'You must come with us,' said Maria. 'Efisio and I are leaving by car. The children are going early, as they have to put the final touches to the *traccus* and collect their friends.'

'Is Beppe going to be with you, Margherita?' asked Elise.

'No, he's gone to his cousin's, just outside Cagliari tonight, and will be riding in tomorrow. We are all meeting at Viale Ignazio, near the hospital.'

'The procession starts at eleven o'clock,' said Maria, 'so we shall plan to be there about nine-thirty. That means we must leave here at about a quarter to nine at the latest.'

'I'll be ready,' Elise assured her.

Later she lay in bed, thinking idly. Had it only been a week? So much seemed to have happened in that time, and she felt so at home amongst these gentle people.

CHAPTER EIGHT

The following morning she was awakened early by the excited chatter of the family in the the courtyard below her window as they prepared to leave. Showering and dressing hurriedly, she went down to see them before they left.

'*Buon giorno*, Signora Elise,' they chorused.

'*Buon giorno*. It looks as though it will be a lovely day for the festa,' said Elise, looking toward Nora where the sun was already up and the sky a clear, brilliant blue.

'We'll see you with Mamma and Babbu in Cagliari,' said Ignazio.

'Bye,' added Predu, waving his *berrita*.

Margherita took Elise's hand. 'You'll love it, I know you will, for you are *simpatico* with the Sardinian people,' she whispered. 'We'll see you later.' And she ran off to join her brothers.

The journey into Cagliari was a repeat performance of the outward drive Elise had endured just over a week ago. Only this time she was sitting in the back of the car and could close her eyes if the oncoming traffic seemed to be on the same side as they were.

At Cagliari, Efisio parked the car near Via Buoncammino. The walk down to Viale Ignazio took them past the Roman amphitheatre, which was carved out of the white rock. Wild flowers and weeds grew in profusion among the now silent terraced steps, softening the hard outlines, but the shadows of the passageways from which the gladiators had emerged to fight the Christians, each other or the animals, still looked dark and menacing.

They continued along the street, joining others walking in pairs or small groups. The sound of music could be heard in the distance, and when they rounded the corner by the hospital, the sudden sight of milling crowds, the people in varied-coloured costumes and the magnificently decorated *traccus* took Elise's breath away. People were everywhere. Some were holding horses, while others put the final touches to their manes and bridles. One young girl was cupping a horse's nose in her hands and giving it a kiss. Other young girls were arranging their costumes.

Old men helped their families with their carts, and old women were making sure everything was perfect. The smell of animals and the fresh flowers from some of the *traccus* mingled in the morning heat and filled the senses. Young children in costume sat perched on the carts and babies, in miniature costumes, rested or slept in proud parents' arms. The whole scene was a heady mass of colour, music and smells, and Elise breathed it all in with pleasure.

'There they are!' exclaimed Efisio, pointing to a group standing near a large stone wall, their colourful costumes contrasting vibrantly with the greyness of the massive stone edifice. He led the way through the chattering throng to the group of familiar faces. The cart was beautifully decorated with homespun rugs, and a delicately woven tapestry formed a canopy over it. The supporting poles were a riot of both fresh and paper flowers, as was the plate bearing the name – PULA – on the front of the *traccus*. Two large oxen stood patiently between the shafts, their horns topped with oranges, and the tack was covered in multi-coloured ribbons which seemed to cascade over the animals like a rainbow, all interlaced with fragile crepe-paper flowers. The whole effect was dazzling and resplendent.

Efisio stood looking with pride at his children's handiwork and Margherita came forward to greet her parents and Elise. She hugged her father and mother, and was happy to receive their praise.

'What do you think Elise? Do you like it?'

'I love it. You have worked so hard,' said Elise, admiring their handiwork. 'I think you have done a wonderful job.'

'Thank you,' smiled the young girl with obvious pride, and then turned to her companions. She spoke to them *in Sardu*, and as they came forward, she took Elise's hand.

'These are our friends,' she said. 'Luigi, who works on the farm with Predu and is a great friend of Beppe's; Gavinu and Stefano, who work in the cantina with Ignazio and Rita; and her brother, Paolo, and sister, Bianca, who all live in Pula.'

They all shook hands and exchanged greetings. Elise complimented them on their appearance: how handsome the men looked in their costumes and how wonderful the girls looked too. She was much taken by the artistic result of their work on the *traccus*.

It was well-deserved praise, which clearly pleased them all very much.

In the next moment, there came a clatter of hooves drowning their conversation, as four men, in costumes of white shirts topped with embroidered waistcoats of gold and red, rode up to the Pula group. Their horses were festooned with flowers which had been entwined in their bridles and round the saddles under which were brightly coloured, hand-woven saddle rugs.

One of the men leaned out of his saddle and touched Elise on the shoulder. 'Are you coming for a ride with me?' he whispered.

She swung around, annoyed by this familiarity, and found herself looking up into a familiar pair of laughing dark eyes.

'Beppe! I didn't recognise you,' she exclaimed with a pounding heart.

He smiled down at her, repeating the invitation, which she eagerly accepted. Hitching up the loose skirt she had donned in preference to jeans for the festa, she put her foot in the stirrup which Beppe had freed for her. His strong arms pulled her up behind him, and she sat sidesaddle, clasping her arms around his waist.

'Are you alright?' he asked over his shoulder. 'You have ridden before, no doubt?'

'Yes, I'm fine, and yes, I've ridden before,' she replied, giving him a playful squeeze.

He introduced her to his cousins, who had ridden in with him, then called to Margherita: 'We are going to see if there is any dancing.' Then he urged his horse down the heavily thronged street to the narrower roads below.

Elise held on tightly; she wasn't afraid, but was surprised how good it felt to feel his strong body move in rhythm with hers as they swayed together on the horse. Everywhere people were making last-minute adjustments to their dress, or chattering among themselves. Old friends greeted one another and families, separated by miles across the island, had emotional reunions. Elise found the whole atmosphere electric. Its vibrant feeling was contagious, sending shivers of excitement up and down her spine.

'I never imagined it would be quite like this. The whole island must be here. There are so many different costumes,' she said in Beppe's ear.

'We all enjoy ourselves on our special festive days,' he replied over his shoulder, raising a hand yet again in salute to someone he knew. 'And the costumes here are only a small representation of the entire island. They do it by ballot each year.'

At the bottom of the road there was a small junction. People were gathered around an old man who was wearing his *berrita* at a crazy angle on his head. His gnarled fingers moved with ease as he played a three-reeded pipe. The onlookers – men and women, boys and girls – were dancing or clapping to his doleful, wailing music, and as his fingers moved over the stops, his eyes twinkled in his brown, wrinkled face.

'He's playing the *Launaddas*,' said Beppe. 'It is a very old instrument and goes back to the time of the Nuraghi people. In the museum, there are little bronze statues of the men playing the same pipes.'

They watched for a few minutes and then, hearing a band strike up in the distance, Beppe turned the horse's head to return up the road.

'It's time we went back,' he said, 'then you can join the others.'

Halfway up the Viale Ignazio, they saw Efisio and Maria fighting their way down through the crowd.

'I'll let you down here,' said Beppe, 'but look out for us in the procession, won't you?'

He helped her down, momentarily holding on to her hand. Then, while Elise joined Efisio and Maria, he raised his hand in salute and rode on.

CHAPTER NINE

Efisio, Maria and Elise, deafened by the babble of voices, pushed their way along the crowded narrow streets into the Piazza Matteotti. On either side of the route, backed on one side by the municipal building and on the other by the gardens, were the canopy-covered seats. The local dignitaries were already in their places, some dressed in the full uniform of the service they represented while others wore the costume appropriate to their civil position.

People jostled and pushed one another in their effort to find a good vantage point. The music grew louder, and a cheer went up from those in the wide street of Largo Carlo Felice. Children were lifted onto their father's shoulders, while young men clambered up lampposts or hung from windowsills in order to get a better view of the oncoming procession.

Maria pulled Elise toward the maroon-covered stands; all three of them were short enough to stand there without blocking the view of those seated behind, because it was built up on staging. Just as they reached their places, the band of the Carabiniere came into view, followed by the first of the decorated carts.

The ox-drawn *traccus* lurched precariously with each turn of its great wheels, rocking all the people on board in a camel-like motion. The girls, all decked out in their fine jewellery, looked lovely in their colourful skirts and blouses. The men, too, were resplendent in their costumes; waving and smiling as they threw sweets called *dolci Sardi* to the eager crowd. Cart after cart followed, each one distinctive in its own way, displaying hand-made rugs and home-spun tapestries. Hand-turned pots rocked uneasily while newly beaten metal pans and bells jangled discordantly together. Each cart had the name of its town on the front, and as the people from the town saw their cart a great roar would go up. All around there was the buzz of the crowd; some applauding, while others called to their friends.

'Look!' called Efisio, pointing to the line of oncoming carts. 'There is our *traccus*; doesn't it look fine?'

They all waved frantically. Maria called to Margherita, who waved back on seeing her mother and father. Ignazio and Predu were playing their guitars together with Gavinu and Stefano, accompanying the girls, who were singing a traditional song. Another group in the crowd, obviously from Pula, roared and whistled at the *traccus*, and Margherita and the two other girls threw them some sweets. More music filled the air; this time the rasping notes of an accordion rose above all the chatter of the crowd. Elise craned her neck forward to see what else was following.

Behind the last *traccus* came groups of people on foot, each representing their village. The first ones carried a small banner announcing that the following dancers and players were from Sinnai. The men's costumes were similar to those of most of the men throughout the island, but these tied their *berrita* around their forehead with a large, red-spotted handkerchief. The women's dresses were of heavy brocade, topped with an elaborate waistcoat with a jewelled front over which spilled the fine, white cotton, lace mantilla. Representatives of Osilo had intricately embroidered, silk borders to their red, velvet capriccio or headdress; while those from Gavoi wore heavily-pleated red skirts bordered with brocade and embroidery, with boleros in matching brocade.

'There is Desulo,' said Maria, eagerly pointing. 'I think they have the most beautiful costumes in the whole island. You can still see the women wearing them every day in their village.'

Still, the procession continued with a riot of colour under the increasing heat of the sun. Once more, the music changed and the group in front of where they were standing formed a circle, dancing with tiny steps that traced out stories and movements handed down through the generations. The Ollolai group, dancing in front of Elise, wore the most beautiful costumes, rich in embroidery and brocade. They were a startling contrast to the women of Tempio, whose black-and-white costumes made them look like novice nuns, the severity of their clothes adding a mystic charm to the wearer and giving them an air of dignity. People came forward and threw rice and rose petals at the dancing groups of girls and young men. Soon the road was covered by rose petals and their scent hung in the late morning air.

Fishermen came after the dancers; carrying nets or models of the rush boats used in the Nurra area of Sardinia. A couple of them proudly carried fish on the ends of their spears. Then there was the man from Cabras with a green bow tied around his big toe.

'Not so poor that he couldn't afford something on his feet,' whispered Maria.

Girls followed carrying bowls or baskets on their heads, in which were the *dolci Sardi* or local Sardinian bread made in various shapes especially for the festa. After them came the shepherds, one carrying a little white lamb slung around his neck like a small woolly scarf, contrasting with the black fur of his coat. Elise noticed that the lamb was quite content to be held in place by its four feet, and was surveying the noisy, colourful scene with wondering eyes.

'The woollen waistcoat he is wearing is called a *mastrucca*,' said Efisio. 'The shepherds wear them a lot in the mountains.'

But Elise wasn't listening. A number of horses had come into sight, all beautifully decorated with their colourful trappings, and she was looking for Beppe. The men looked dashing riding their carefully groomed mounts. Some had young girls up behind them, either riding sidesaddle, as Elise had done earlier, or astride the horse with their pleated skirts spread out over the animal's rump.

Suddenly, Beppe was there, at the corner on Elise's side of the street, his eyes searching the crowd. Efisio and Maria called out and waved to him, but Elise could only gaze in breathless admiration. He looked splendid, so handsome, with his horse's coat gleaming in the sunlight; like a character out of the Sard book she had been reading. Beppe reined his horse momentarily, took a rose and some sprigs of rosemary from the bridle, and handed the small token to Elise. He was wearing his *berrita* at a jaunty angle and it made him look more mischievous than ever.

'*Per te, signora,*' he said his dark eyes alive with laughter.

'*Grazia a te,*' she replied, inclining her head.

It was the first time he had used the familiar form of address to her in Italian, and she had used it to thank him. She watched him wave and ride on, aware that her heart was pounding and the dazzling colours around her seemed to be spinning. The noise that dominated everything suddenly died away; people were talking in whispers.

The military passed, and then a procession of young men in pale-blue robes with white cassocks came into view. Each one was carrying a magnificent silver-gilt lamp in his hand, and they were followed by the priest carrying a large, silver crucifix that glimmered and shone as it caught the brilliant sunlight. The crowd pressed forward as a gilded coach, drawn by two decorated oxen, came round the corner. The effigy of their beloved saint was inside the ornately decorated carriage, and as it passed, the devout onlookers crossed themselves.

The crowd pressed forward again and people threw flowers before the carriage. A woman dressed from head to toe in black pushed past Elise and went to touch the coach. A young man laid some lilies on its side; others knelt in the street turning their rosaries. Many of the older people were in tears. Elise, completely overcome by the emotion of the day, also found she was openly weeping.

Efisio pushed a large, red handkerchief into her hand and said gruffly, but kindly, 'You're becoming like the Sards. You say nothing, but all your thoughts show in your eyes!'

'Come – let's find the others,' called Maria and they crossed the still busy road and slipped up the cool side street. The carriage having passed; many onlookers had fallen in behind it to follow it to Nora, where they would spend the night in prayer before returning with the effigy on the fourth day.

Elise, Efisio and Maria climbed the steep road to Viale Ignazio. The milling crowd of spectators dissolved under the midday sun. Elise looked around her; everyone was there – all of the Fozzi family, with their never-ending line of cousins and friends – chattering ceaselessly amongst themselves.

'You did enjoy it, didn't you, Elise?' enthused Margherita. 'I can see you did, you've been crying.'

'Oh yes, I did. It was wonderful,' replied Elise, smiling at the young girl's obvious delight.

'I knew you would! And now, please, I want you to meet Claudio, Beppe's brother.'

Elise looked at the young man. He was certainly not going to be as tall as Beppe, but he had the same kind, profound eyes and pleasant, friendly expression.

'I've heard a lot about you,' Elise told him. 'Tell me, how is your mother?'

'She is much better; thank you for asking. Are you enjoying your stay in Sardinia?'

'Very much! I seem to be meeting so many people.'

'I hope you will meet many more,' said a familiar voice behind her.

'Beppe,' said Margherita.

'Ciao,' he replied, and then, turning to Elise, he added, 'We're all going to a party at the farm in Pula tonight. Ignazio, Predu, Margherita, Luigi, Claudio and all those you met here today will be there. There will be dancing and we are having porcheddu.'

'What's that?' enquired Elise.

'Suckling pig, roasted over the open fire. It's very good. I can recommend it,' replied Beppe.

'Will you all be in costume?'

'I expect so. I doubt whether we shall change. But you are wearing a skirt, so you'll be fine. It's only a friendly do,' he explained.

She smiled and nodded in agreement.

They all agreed to meet at the farm at whatever time suited them, because the food would not be served before nine o'clock at the earliest.

'Where have Efisio and Maria gone?' Elise asked, anxiously looking around.

'Oh, they went home,' said Beppe. 'They're going to help with the party. Ignazio and the others are going in the *traccus*, which leaves you and me. I told Maria that I would take you home. Do you mind?'

'Should I?'

'I hope not. You see, my car is at my cousin's house, and I have to take his horse back there. Then we can drive to Pula,' he said with a wide smile on his face.

'Where does your cousin live?'

'Just outside Capoterra; it's between here and Pula. So if you're coming with me, you'll have to ride behind me.'

'The poor horse; do you think he'll manage both of us?' she asked, smiling.

'Of course! He is used to being ridden by my uncle, a really big man; bigger than both of us and Margherita put together!'

Elise and Margherita laughed as he blew out his cheeks and pushed out his stomach, trying to make himself look fat. Then he mounted the horse in one easy fluid movement and bent to help Elise up behind him.

'Are you going to follow us?' called Margherita.

'Until we get to the turning to Capoterra,' replied Beppe.

They moved off at a slow pace and soon reached the outskirts of the city on the road towards Pula. The others in the *traccus* sang traditional songs and people waved and cheered as they passed by and they all waved in return.

Elise was once again conscious of the thrill of having her arms around Beppe's waist. She rested her head on his shoulder and felt an ache in her heart; she delighted in the warm glow as her cheek came into contact with him. Beppe felt her close to him and smiled contently to himself.

After about an hour, they reached the turn-off to Capoterra, and with waves and yells Beppe turned the horse towards the mountain road. The afternoon sun was warm and the cicadas chirruped in rasping harmony with the grasshoppers in the breeze-blown grasses. The movement of their bodies swaying, together with the rhythm of the horse's gait, lulled her into a deep contentment. He felt so strong in her arms, and a great longing for him filled her soul.

'What are you thinking about?' Beppe asked softly, turning his head so that it touched hers. He found himself savouring the closeness of her body, and smiled.

'Oh… just how peaceful it is, and what a lovely day it's been.'

'Happy?'

'Very,' she sighed, 'very happy indeed. I could ride like this forever. Don't they say that the breath of heaven is that which blows through the ears of a horse?'

He laughed, put his arm back and around her and drew her close to him.

Elise sighed again; she was truly at peace at last. Her world, she thought, could never bring such divine tranquillity. This man had a tender quality; he was gentle, caring, thoughtful and romantic, and what was more, he was hers in this brief moment of time.

CHAPTER TEN

They returned the horse to Beppe's cousin and helped to brush him down and feed him, and, were then welcomed into the house by his cousin and given refreshment before making their way back to Pula.

The party was in full swing when Beppe and Elise arrived that evening and a short, plump, round-faced man came forward beaming from ear to ear.

'I'm so glad you've come,' he said, shaking Elise warmly by the hand. 'You must be Signora Raynesford. I'm Franco Piras, the father of Paolo, Bianca and Rita. Will you have some wine?'

He ushered her toward the long table that had been set up under a rickety-looking bamboo roof. Paraffin lamps threw a soft light over the table. Nearby, in a barn-like building, Efisio was busy refilling the earthenware jugs with homemade wine from the huge vats. A large woman with a jolly expression came forward, wiping her hands on her apron.

'Madelena,' said Franco, 'this is Signora Raynesford. She is staying at the villa with Efisio and Maria. This is my wife, signora,' he said, turning to Elise.

'How do you do?' said Elise. 'Please call me Elise. Everyone else does.'

'Your Italian is excellent. Are you enjoying your stay on our island?

'Thank you, and yes, very much.'

'Have a drink then, Elise,' said Franco, handing her a glass of dark-red wine. 'Salude.'

'Salude,' she replied, and took a sip of the dark, full-bodied wine. It proved to be strong, but surprisingly smooth.

'It's good, yes?' asked her host.

'Very,' she replied.

'Elise you should get Beppe to take you up into the interior of the island. They have bandits up there, and it's all very romantic. I think...'

Just then Beppe joined them. 'Ciao, Madelena,' he said to Franco's wife, then turned to Franco, 'how is the farm?'

'*Boh*. Ground is hardening up, but I can't complain. Have some wine?'

'I have some, thanks. I've come to collect Elise before you start to fill her head with your wine and those wild stories about the island.'

'He was just about to tell me about the bandits,' replied Elise, her curiosity aroused.

'The bandits in the mountains who kidnap people and hold them for ransom,' replied Franco, laughing.

'It's only the shepherds in the winter,' said Beppe. 'When they run short of cash, they kidnap a leading citizen, and when the ransom has been paid, they let him go.'

'They don't kill them then?'

'No. Not as a rule. Not unless it's a family vendetta,' said the older man.

'Well,' said Elise gravely, 'I wouldn't mind being kidnapped, especially when it's time to go home. Another couple of weeks in the mountains with some dark, good-looking Sards might prove more than educational!'

Franco and Madelena looked momentarily taken aback, then seeing that Elise and Beppe were struggling to suppress their laughter, they joined in, Franco's large stomach jiggling up and down in unison with his laughter.

People in costume from the *Sagra* mingled with others in casual clothes, a wonderful mix of men, dark-skinned and swarthy, women with dark hair and fascinating eyes together with lots of children of all ages. Elise took it all in, savouring the happiness shared by people who lived and worked in a community and knew each other well.

The meal began with vast amount of anti-pasta of local meats and olives, followed by huge bowls of spaghetti and then *porcheddu*. The young pigs, which had been cut in half lengthwise, had been placed on long spears and cooked near the fire. This had been done by the men on their return in the late afternoon. The roasted piglet was accompanied by salad, and rounded off with fresh fruit; all washed down with copious amounts of wine.

'Are these your cherries, Beppe?' asked Elise.

'Yes,' he replied, and once again she became aware that he was watching her every move.

'I shall have a terrible headache tomorrow morning with all this wine,' she said, grimacing and laughing at the same time.

'Not on Sard wine, you won't. It goes to your legs, not to your head,' he told her.

The meal over, Ignazio played his guitar and Franco played the accordion while the rest danced until the early hours of the morning. Tomorrow was Friday, still a workday for most, but in the country areas the four days of the festa were kept as a holiday. The evening passed all too quickly, and finally, when the time came to say goodnight and for all the friends to go their different ways, Beppe drove Elise back to the villa.

'Would you like a drink before you go to bed?' he asked. 'Just a small Vernaccia; it will make you sleep well. Quick, it's starting to rain.'

Beppe opened the door to his large room at the end of the vinery. The room was neat and attractively furnished, with terracotta tiles on the floor on which was thrown a beautiful hand-woven rug. At the far end of the room a big tapestry hung on the wall beside the great hand-made bed, which was covered with a home-spun bedspread. Above the bed was a huge wooden crucifix with an agonised Christ carved in white wood. Hanging from the large bedpost was a mother-of-pearl rosary. Elise noticed that the Bible lay open on the table beside his bed, together with a book of Italian poetry.

One wall was covered with shelves that were filled with a great collection of both Italian and French poetry, little objects and stacks of records lay by an old record player. There were numerous copies of books on Sardinia. Modern ones with their gaudy covers, contrasted with the old leather bindings of others; some on costumes and numerous ones on the archaeology of the island.

Two chairs were set near the end of the bed, and a writing desk stood in the corner on which sat a notebook and a table lamp. There was a door at the side, near the bed, that was ajar, and Elise realised that there was a bathroom beyond.

Beppe went over and lifted the arm on the record player, and dropped the needle on the record, and the room was filled with the sound of a Rachmaninov piano concerto.

'You have some lovely books,' she said, running her hand gently over the bindings. 'I love books; they seem to have a life of their own. There is nothing quite like the feel of one in the hand, or the smell of a new edition.' she turned to him, 'have you ever wondered what will happen to all these wonderful thoughts and words when our civilisation has gone? And how many beautiful works and words have been lost from past civilisations?'

Beppe drew in a deep breath and looked at her tenderly.

'Do sit down,' said Beppe, with a smile.

She sat in one of the large chairs and watched him as he produced two glasses and poured from the bottle he had taken from a small cupboard in the corner. The rain beat down outside and the wind whined through the buildings. Elise shivered.

'Your religion means a lot to you, doesn't it?' she said.

'It does indeed. It has always stood me in good stead. Although I'm not as devout as my mother and my priest would like me to be. I live my life according to the code of the church and the traditions of my people, in as much as I'm able – and you – are you not a practising Christian?'

Elise looked up at Beppe. 'No. I have no such faith. I believe in Christ and his teachings, but I'm not a committed Christian.'

'But did you enjoy the *sagra* today?'

'I did, and if I'm honest, I find the pomp of the Roman Church very moving. Perhaps I envy those who have such blind faith.'

Beppe smiled again and sat down beside her. 'I shall always remember you riding behind me on the horse. We were like Elias and Madelena,' he said, looking straight into her eyes.

'Who are they?'

'Characters in *Elias Portolu*; it's a book written by Grazia Deledda. She was a famous Sardinian writer. I have the book here somewhere. I'll find it, and you can read it.'

He rose and searched through his collection of books, adding, 'they both rode together up to the mountain area of the Barbargia... she was married too...' He broke off. Then, as if to change the subject, he said, 'Would you like to go to Cagliari on Sunday evening to see the saint returned to his church?'

'That would be lovely, thank you,' she said. She drained her glass and stood up. 'Thank you for a lovely evening, and for such a wonderful day. I must go now. It must be nearly dawn.'

Beppe turned to face her; the book he had been searching for in his hand. His dark eyes searched her face. 'It's been a long time since I have been able to share my love of the arts with someone. I hope we can share a lot more.'

The rain had stopped, and he walked her to the bottom of her outside staircase. She paused and looked at him, saying softly, 'I shall enjoy sharing things with you. Goodnight Beppe, and sleep well. Thank you again for everything.'

'Goodnight,' he said, squeezing her hand as he gave her the book. He was about to say something else, but changed his mind, turning away quickly and disappearing into the darkness.

CHAPTER ELEVEN

The next day was bright and sunny; all signs of the rain had vanished. With all the family at the villa, Maria was extra busy, but she would not hear of Elise helping in anyway.

'You go down to the beach; they are all there. Go and enjoy yourself.'

Ignazio, Predu, Beppe and Margherita were already on the beach. They had collected the boat and were getting organised to go water-skiing.

'Elise,' called Beppe, coming to meet her, 'we are going skiing. Have you skied?'

'Snow-skiing yes.'

'This is much better,' said Beppe, taking her hand.

'Oh, this is going to be another drowning then?' she said as she neared the others. They turned and laughed.

'No, we will teach you,' said Ignazio. 'With your score of eight you must have good balance.'

'You ski first, and I'll watch. Then you can teach me after you have all had a turn.'

They all nodded in agreement, and Elise watched, fascinated, as they readied themselves for the sport.

Beppe drove the boat and Margherita sat in the observation seat. This was the passenger seat turned around to face the back of the boat so that she could 'observe' the skier and relay any signals to the driver. Ignazio put on his ski, pulled on his life jacket and walked into the water. He pulled a long slack of the towrope so that it lay in the water beside him and nodded. Beppe put the throttle down and the boat leapt forward. A good couple of seconds passed before the rope started to take up the slack, and when it was taut Ignazio hopped on the ski and leant back. He took off across the water in a wonderful, sweeping arc of spray where the ski cut into the water as he turned, crossing the wake made by the engine.

'Wow,' said Elise, laughing as she turned to Predu, 'I hope I'm not expected to do that.'

'Not yet,' he said, returning her smile. 'We'll start you off on two skis and see how you go from there.'

The boat must have gone to Nora and back before Ignazio signalled to go in. Elise watched as Beppe bought the boat in towards the beach and then turned sharply out to sea again. Ignazio dropped the ski rope, which danced off after the boat, leaving him free to glide toward the beach. When he came close to the shore, he hopped off his ski to stand on the beach.

Elise watched in amazement.

'It's great out there. You'll love it, Elise,' said Ignazio, pulling off his life jacket and handing it to his brother.

Beppe took Predu next, but he started in the water, his ski upright in front of him. He nodded and the boat took off again, and he was up in a short space of time. Margherita went next; she did it the same way as Predu. Elise watched, admiring their skill. Next to go was Beppe, with Ignazio driving the boat; he called to Elise to sit in the observation seat. Beppe skied the same way as Ignazio, straight off the beach. Elise was thrilled to watch him cut across the wake, throwing up a huge arc of spray which caught all the wonderful colours of the spectrum. They went to Nora, turned, and then returned to the beach.

'Your turn now,' said Margherita to Elise. 'Take off your tee-shirt and put the life jacket on.'

Elise hesitated; she didn't want to remove her shirt. She had her bikini on underneath, but Margherita had already lifted the tee-shirt up to help her. There was a silence and then a gasp from Margherita as she saw the bruises and welts on Elise's back and the top of her arms; they were still black and blue from the beating she had received from William before she left. Margherita stared in horror, and then quickly pulled down the tee-shirt as Beppe approached them.

'I think you would be better to keep the shirt on,' she said quickly, and handed her the life jacket with a nod and a knowing smile.

Elise took the jacket gratefully, hurriedly putting it on over her tee-shirt, and returned Margherita's smile.

'You'll be cold with that on when it gets wet, and it will drag,' said Beppe turning to Elise.

'She'll be alright,' said Margherita. Then, turning to Elise, she said, 'The one golden rule is not to bend your arms. Whatever you do, keep them straight.' She made Elise sit on the sand and put her knees up to her chin. 'That is how you want to be in the water. We will hold you to begin with. Now hold the bar.' She handed Elise the bar from the ski rope while she held the other end. 'Now, with your arms straight, pull on the bar and push down with your feet. Don't bend your arms,' she stressed.

Elise tried it a couple more times until she felt she knew what Margherita wanted her to do. Ignazio put on the skis for her. Predu was the observer, and Beppe was to drive the boat. Elise shuffled into the water and sat back while Margherita held her and Ignazio held the rope. Beppe trawled the boat out slowly until the rope tightened, and she felt herself being dragged. She felt a frisson of fear as Ignazio called, 'Okay,' and with Margherita's words of straight arms ringing in her ears and her heart beating as if it would jump out of her chest, she put into practice what she had been shown on the beach. To her amazement, as she pushed down with her legs, she felt herself rise out of the water and skim across the surface. The wind caught her hair, and the feeling of exhilaration flooded her whole body; this was skiing, and skiing at its best.

They had gone halfway to Nora when Beppe turned to look at her. The concentration on Elise's face was a picture, and Predu called out to her and put his two index fingers on either side of his mouth.

'Smile,' he called.

Elise distracted for one moment caught her ski on the wake, and before she knew it, she went head-first into the water. Immediately, the boat was beside her and Beppe was lifting her up by the life jacket.

'Oh, that was wonderful,' she laughed, spluttering and coughing from the rush of water. 'Can I do it again, please?'

'Are you sure?' said Beppe.

'Oh, yes.'

Beppe saw the look of determination on her face that he had seen once before when she helped with the vines. Predu helped her get her skis on, and she lay back in the water to put her skis together.

'Try to look as if you are enjoying it,' said Predu, laughing.

'I will, but don't distract me,' she replied, her face a picture of happiness.

Beppe trawled the boat out again, and Elise flipped the rope between her skis as Ignazio had done. She nodded to Beppe, who put the throttle forward once again. Margherita's words to keep her arms straight sounded in her head, and she was thrilled to find that as she pushed down with her legs again she popped out of the water with relative ease. Beppe took her back to the shore where he stopped the boat and let Elise drop gently into the water.

Margherita rushed forward with Ignazio; they were smiling broadly.

'Well done, Elise,' said Ignazio.

Margherita hugged her. 'I knew you could do it,' she said, smiling.

They all decided to have another ski, but Beppe came to sit beside Elise while the other three skied. 'You did really well, Elise. I'm proud of you. Not everyone manages to get up first time. You should be very pleased with yourself,' he said, looking at her in his usual disarming way.

'I had a good teacher. Can I go again?'

'Not today. Give up on a high, and then you will be ready next time. There will be plenty of time. I promise you if you go out now your arms will be tired, and you will struggle. Better to go out fresh another time. After all, I might drown you this time,' he said, giving her a sideways grin, and she laughed at him.

Later, Beppe showed her how to fish for small octopus with a spear-like harpoon while Ignazio, Predu and Margherita lay on the beach. Beppe and Elise soon joined the group and they sat chatting together.

'Well done, Elise,' said Ignazio again, 'I was impressed.'

And the others all agreed and said that it would not be long before she could go mono and ski on one like they did. Elise smiled; she was pleased with the praise, and thanked them.

'Do you realise you've been here for ten days now?' said Ignazio.

She nodded. 'I know. I was thinking that only last night. But somehow I feel I have known you all much longer than that. But even so, the time seems to have flown!'

'Do you like it here, Elise?' asked Margherita, moving and plonking herself next to Elise.

Elise smiled at the young girl. 'Why do you ask?'

'I just wondered. Do you think you will come back again next year?'

'I don't see why not.' Elise paused. So much could happen in a year, and she might even be free from William by then she thought to herself.

'What are you thinking?' Beppe asked, looking concerned.

'Nothing,' she said, giving him a reassuring smile.

'Race you to the sea!' he said suddenly, leaping to his feet.

She pulled back. She had put on a new dry top, not wanting to expose her skin to everybody. Ignazio and Predu took up the challenge. Beppe grabbed Elise, pulled her up and put her over his shoulder and sprinted across the beach. Elise begged him to stop, but Beppe was deaf to her pleas. She thumped him on his back with her fists, desperate for him to put her down. Her top fell down over her head as they ran towards the sea. Margherita watched anxiously as the bruises were revealed down Elise's back and across the top of her arms.

Predu hit the water at about the same time as Ignazio, but Beppe was already swimming away, having released Elise. She swam underwater for a bit and then surfaced. The two brothers were splashing in the water when she suddenly felt something grab her ankles. She let out a surprised shriek as she felt herself being pulled under the water. She struggled, but the water rushed over her face and she cried out, taking in a mouthful of water. Beppe, realising she was fighting, brought her to the surface. She was choking and crying at the same time as Beppe gathered her up into his strong arms. He carried her to the shore, where he put her down carefully.

'I'm sorry,' he said, looking concerned, 'I didn't mean to scare you.'

'Please leave me,' she spluttered, still coughing, 'please, just leave me. I will be alright in a minute. I do believe you are determined to drown me.'

He pulled her towards him and put his arms around her, patting her gently on the back. Looking up into his eyes, Elise suddenly felt secure again; they were so dark – so profound, with an expression that was both intense and tender at the same time.

Margherita handed her a towel, and, smiling, gave her a quick nod.

'Thank you,' Elise said gratefully.

As the men dried, Elise went to sit with Margherita.

'Thank you for that.'

'Are you alright?' asked Margherita.

'Yes, I'm fine. The bruises are nearly gone. They are much better. Your mother kindly put an ointment on them.'

'Who on earth did that to you?' she asked, looking concerned.

Ignazio and Predu came up to her, laughing.

'You looked really funny, Elise,' said Ignazio. 'You were so surprised when Beppe grabbed you.'

'So would you have been,' she retorted. 'Still, with luck, I'll get my revenge.'

Eventually, Ignazio, Predu and Margherita said they were going back to the villa and would see them soon.

Elise took Margherita's hand and smiled at her.

'Thanks,' she said, grateful for the young girl's discretion.

They climbed into the boat and left to put it back in the boathouse further up the river.

Beppe and Elise stayed on the beach and talked together about the island, discussing the many facets of its history. They found they shared an interest in farming and wildlife, and the time slipped by as they also spoke of their love of poetry and music.

CHAPTER TWELVE

When, Sunday evening came Beppe and Elise, left together to watch the return of the saint to Cagliari. Maria, Efisio and the family went down separately because they had planned to visit Maria's cousin in Cagliari afterwards. Beppe seized the opportunity and arranged to take Elise out for a meal.

In no time at all, they were again mingling with the crowds in the Largo Carlo Felice. The streets shone out brightly against the blackness of the night sky. It had turned colder and an earlier shower had made the streets gleam, the water reflecting the coloured lights. Young and old were once more gathered together: the women in their long skirts and heavy woollen shawls, and the children wearing fur boots, thick coats and balaclavas to protect them against the chilly, night wind. They were a little early, so Beppe took Elise into a cafe on the Via Roma for a cup of hot chocolate.

Later, they made their way through the crowd to find a good vantage point.

'Don't get lost!' he said, taking her hand.

She smiled back at him, thrilling at the contact as their fingers entwined.

From the Via Roma, at the bottom of the Largo Carlo Felice, they could see the outline of the men on horseback. The star-like lights that half-illuminated the street played weird tricks in the semi-darkness; the brightness was more subdued now, with a warm, incandescent quality. The Carabiniere, with their big horses, striking uniforms and two-cornered hats with feather plumes of red and white, came past first. They were followed by the civil police in green uniforms; they too were on horseback, looking splendid, with either a rifle or a sword in their hands. They had all decorated their horses with lilies and carnations, winding the flowers through the harness, which in some cases was delicately hand-tooled and ornamented with leather tassels and jangling silver bells.

Behind them came the councillors in tall black hats, black suits and bright-blue sashes denoting their officialdom. They doffed their hats to the crowd as they passed, and the people replied with a tremendous cheer. The priests followed with the lamp bearers, trailed by a priest on a small donkey, looking more like a figure from Don Quixote. Behind him came another priest carrying the huge silver crucifix held above his head. It caught the light from the lamps and flashed and glittered as if emitting a light of its own.

Lastly, there was the beautifully ornate ox-drawn carriage, containing the image of the saint. There were rows of candles on either side of the carriage, illuminating the saint's face and giving the whole figure an ethereal effect.

People surged forward to pay their homage to the saint. Elise watched as Beppe took his mother-of-pearl rosary out of his pocket, crossed himself, kissed the small crucifix and returned it to his pocket. The procession went on up the street and turned left up the wide Largo Carlo Felice. Then it wound its way back to the church interior to reinstate the image, in its proper place, for another year.

'Are you hungry?' asked Beppe, turning to Elise. 'I know a nice place to eat and the fish is excellent. You do like fish?'

Elise smiled and nodded.

They made their way to the car through the throngs of people that still filled the streets and alleyways. The magic of the candlelit procession had vanished, and rain had started to fall in a fine drizzle.

The restaurant was only a short drive away, and was on the bridge over the *stagni*, on the coast road back to Pula. They parked outside and went in through the plastic curtains. It was warm inside and they were immediately welcomed by a young waiter. Beppe said something *in Sardu* and the young man showed them to a small table in an intimate corner by the window.

'It doesn't look a lot, but the food is excellent,' said Beppe as he took her hand.

'What a lovely view!' Elise exclaimed. 'Look – you can see the whole of the *Golfo di Angelli,* and Cagliari dominating it all with the lights of the city reflected in the night-black sea.'

Beppe held her chair for her, and then took his seat opposite her.

The waiter returned with a bottle of red wine and two glasses.

'I ordered a wine which we, in Sardinia, are rather proud of,' said Beppe. 'It's called *Perda Rubia*. I hope you don't mind drinking red wine with fish? We drink what we like best, rather than what is considered correct.'

'I prefer red wine anyway,' she replied.

'Good. Now what would you like to eat?' he asked, spreading the menu on the table.

'I'd like a typical Sardinian meal, and I'll leave the choice to you,' she replied, smiling at him.

He nodded and pursed his lips as he studied the menu and then looking up, beckoned to the waiter. The two men chatted cordially *in Sardu* with many gesticulations of the hands; the waiter repeated what he had painstakingly written down on his pad, and after a nod of agreement from Beppe, he picked up the menu and left.

'Well? What are we having?' asked Elise eagerly.

'Mussels to start with, followed by *anguilli* roasted on an open grill rounded off with *burrida*.'

'*Anguilli* are eels, but what is *burrida*?'

'*Burrida*, well – I don't know the name of the fish in Italian, so goodness knows what it is in English. But it's a big fish cooked in a sauce of oil, pine nuts and seasoning.'

'Sounds good to me,' said Elise.

The mussels arrived piled on a huge oval plate with a tomato sauce, sprinkled with fine parsley and smelling deliciously of garlic. The waiter gave them a plate each and a basket of freshly baked bread, then, wishing them '*Buon appetito*', he went away, returning with a bowl of warm water and lemon.

'I didn't realise I was so hungry,' said Elise as she spooned some mussels onto Beppe's plate and then on her own. The two of them sat eating in silence, each covertly watching the other and acutely aware of the fact that they were engrossed in one another. His dark eyes hardly left her face and she was again conscious of their deep intensity and found herself blushing.

'What are you thinking?' he asked presently.

'I was thinking how beautifully dark and deep your eyes are,' she said with disarming honesty, and then paused, searching his gaze. 'I believe I can see down to your soul. Tell me, Beppe, why haven't you ever married? You said your brother has a chosen wife, and he is the second son. Surely you, as a first son, would have had an arranged marriage too?'

He hesitated for a moment before he replied.

'I was to have married Grazia, a girl from our village, but she didn't love me; she loved one of her cousins, and he loved her. They had an affair and when it was discovered she was carrying his child, the immediate family insisted that they marry. In Sardinia, if a woman is compromised by a man, they are as good as married. If they sleep together then they are married in the eyes of God and Man!'

'Do you believe that, too?'

'Yes, I do. If a man takes a woman, then he must be responsible for the consequences,' Beppe replied gravely.

'Go on with your story. Did she marry her cousin?'

'The wedding day came. Her brother was so fired up with shame at seeing his sister marry a man to whom she was not originally betrothed that he shot at the groom. But the bride ran between them and was killed instantly, right outside the church.'

'Oh, my God Beppe how tragic!' Elise shuddered.

Beppe shrugged.

'Revenge was swift. Someone from the groom's family knifed the brother. The vendetta will probably go on for years.'

'I think that's terrible,' said Elise. 'All because a young girl gave her love to the man she loved. Surely, Beppe, you wouldn't have been happy, married to a woman you knew was in love with another man?'

'*Boh*. She was mine by right. But no, I was happy to let her go to the man she loved. What life would it have been, knowing she loved another?'

'And you, did you love her?' she asked softly.

Beppe sighed deeply.

'That doesn't come into it. The laws of the Sard people and the church are strict, and must be adhered to.' He said vehemently adding, 'not always for the best.'

'Have you… have you never found another woman?'

Beppe reached across the table and squeezed her hand.

'There is plenty of time for that. At the moment, I'm more than happy,' he said quietly.

'But since we are sharing secrets, I know why you always wear a top. Tell me, how did you get those bruises on your back? Margherita told me; she is very concerned about you. Why couldn't you have told me?'

Elise looked down at the table and toyed with a piece of bread.

He took both of her hands in his. 'Who did that to you?' he asked gently.

'Please, Beppe. Not now. We are having a lovely meal don't spoil it.' Her mood had changed and Beppe knew he would have to tread carefully.

'Just tell me, was it your husband?'

She nodded slowly and then said, 'I will tell you, but not now. Now is our time.'

The waiter arrived to take away the plates and returned bearing a large dish with two delicately-twisted *anguilli* on a long skewer, which had been roasted over the open grill. They were accompanied by a green salad and another generous helping of bread.

'These *anguilli* are really delicious,' she said after taking a rather cautious mouthful.

'People eat them jellied in England, but I've never tried them; they always look so horrid! but they're lovely roasted like this.'

Beppe wasn't listening. His thoughts were miles away as he stared at her intently. She gave the appearance of being weak, but he could see there was an inner strength to her character which she tended to keep to herself. It had a habit of showing itself, though, when he least expected it.

He sighed and said, 'I'm ahead of my work thanks to your help, and Efisio doesn't need me much at the moment. Will you come to Barumini with me tomorrow?'

'That's the ancient building called a Nuraghi, isn't it?'

He nodded impatiently.

'I know you'll find it interesting. We could have a picnic. Please, Elise, say you'll come.'

'Are you sure?' she said, smiling. 'I'd love to Beppe!'

The *burrida* was brought to the table; a sensational mixture of coarse-grained fish with oil and sweet pine nuts.

'We'll make an early start tomorrow and then we can have the whole day to ourselves,' continued Beppe.

'It sounds wonderful,' she agreed, 'and this fish is marvellous, too. Thank you, Beppe, for this lovely meal.'

They drank coffee, black and unsweetened, and talked of the coming day.

When they left the restaurant, the rain had stopped, and by the time they reached the villa the clouds had cleared. A full moon was sailing high in the blue-black, star-shaken sky and it made a silver pathway across the sea.

Everything was very still. Maria and her family were obviously in bed – and the wash of gently-lapping waves against the silent beach sounded like the whispering of a million sea nymphs.

'Let's go for a little walk along the beach, just to the river,' Elise begged. 'It's such a lovely night now.'

'Won't you be cold?'

'No, of course not,' she laughed.

They walked as far as the river, each with an arm around the other.

'How slowly the river is moving! It looks like molten silver,' murmured Elise.

'It's strange; when the sand is cold and the night still, it has a language of its own,' replied Beppe quietly.

The rasping of the cicadas, the croak of frogs calling to one another, the sea lapping on the shore and the wind whispering in the nearby reeds filled Elise's senses.

She looked at him.

'Thank you for a wonderful day, Beppe. It's something I shall always remember: the festival by candlelight, the lovely meal and now the smell of rain on the dry earth and the sea by moonlight.'

He gazed back at her intently, saying nothing. She shivered and he pulled her close to him, his body warm and strong.

'We should go back now,' he said.

They walked slowly to the foot of the outside staircase leading to Elise's room.

'Thank you again,' she whispered.

Beppe again gazed at her, holding her at arm's length. Meeting his hypnotic stare, Elise felt a longing stir in her body. She leaned forward, kissed him quickly on the cheek and whispered, 'Goodnight – see you in the morning.'

Then, before he could answer, she ran upstairs to her room.

CHAPTER THIRTEEN

Elise was woken from a deep sleep the next morning by a constant rapping at the door.

'What is it?' she asked, stirring lazily.

'Wake up,' came Beppe's voice. 'It's six-thirty. We promised ourselves an early start.'

'I'm coming!' called Elise, sitting up and trying to rub the sleep from her eyes.

'Don't be too long,' he replied. 'I'll be downstairs.'

She heard Beppe clatter down the stone stairs and cross the hall to the kitchen. Lying back in bed, she allowed herself a moment to collect her thoughts. Of course, last night she had agreed to go to Barumini. She rolled out of bed, walked to the window and threw open the big wooden shutters. The shaft of sunlight illuminated the whole room reflecting against the white paintwork on the stippled walls. The vibrant colours of the oleander and bougainvillea flashed in greeting, making her shade her eyes against the light. Below, the sea looked like a sheet of blue glass and the early sun was already reflecting on the glistening white sand, promising another hot day. She quickly washed her hair and showered.

Downstairs, Beppe was greeted by Maria, who was busy in the kitchen baking bread. The scrubbed table was laid for breakfast with earthenware plates, and at one side was a large basket full of rolls fresh from the oven.

'Those smell good,' said Beppe. 'Can we take some with us today for a picnic?'

'Where are you going? Somewhere nice?'

'I'm going to take Elise up to Barumini for the day. She wants to see some of the ancient buildings, and it will give her a chance to see a bit of the island too.'

'She'll like that. I'll pack a picnic for you with fresh bread, salciaccia, olives and your favourite; pecorino cheese,' said Maria, with a broad smile.

'And we'll stop somewhere and buy the wine,' replied Beppe.

'*Buon giorno*, Maria,' said Elise from the doorway.

'*Buon giorno* Signora Elise.' Maria came forward. 'Come – sit down and have some breakfast,' she said as she cut the bread.

Elise went to take her place at the table next to Beppe.

He rose and pulled out Elise's chair and then moved his closer to her.

'Did you enjoy the procession yesterday?' asked Maria, handing Elise a slice of bread.

'Very much,' replied Elise, and she eagerly described what she had seen and the meal they had together afterwards.

'You were quick getting dressed,' said Beppe, changing the subject. 'Don't all women take hours to organise themselves?'

'Ah well, I'm not all women!' she laughed in reply.

She looked so fresh and cool in the blue linen dress she was wearing. Her blonde hair, still damp from the shower, was now bleached even fairer by the strong sunshine, contrasting beautifully with her deep, golden, honey-brown tan. Beppe could hardly take his eyes off her. How different she looked now from when she had arrived; then she had been so thin and pale, Beppe thought. She had gained a little weight, and it suited her.

'Wake up, dreamer!' laughed Maria, placing a large slice of bread on his plate.

Beppe poured out coffee for them all, and tried hard to prevent his eyes from straying to Elise's face. She, in fact, was aware of his attentions. An understanding had grown between them, intensified by last night, and it was something they both wanted to build on. William never had the time, or the inclination come to that, to listen to nature or the sounds of the night as they had done last night. William saw it all as nonsense and stuff for romantics, whom he despised. Elise felt a deep happiness that she had, at last, found someone with the same interests. Someone who wouldn't laugh at the things she liked. It was like discovering one's sanity; or better still, a kindred spirit or a soul mate.

After breakfast, Beppe took the basket and put it in the car.

'We won't be back until very late, Maria,' said Beppe, 'so don't wait up for us.'

'I won't. It's alright for you young things – you don't mind late nights. When you reach my age, you will change your mind.' She laughed, and then added as she gave Elise a hug, 'Now have a good day – and mind you don't get lost!' She frowned at Beppe. 'And make sure you take good care of her, young man.'

'Naturally,' he replied, patting Maria's arm and at the same time giving her a broad smile and a wink as he passed.

The drive to Cagliari was not as hectic as the one Elise had taken with Efisio. On this occasion, she had time to take note of the passing scenery. The mountains of *L'Accundas* had clarity about them that she had never noticed before; they stood out like cardboard cut-outs against the violet blue of the sky. The sea, the trees, the plants – everything had an aura about them. She sighed – a deep, deep sigh.

'My, Elise that was heartfelt!' said Beppe.

'Yes. Oh, Beppe, it's going to be really hot today, just ideal for a picnic.'

He looked at her and smiled. The look of her filled his senses and he was happy.

As they neared Cagliari, the tangy smell of the salt flats filled the air; making it fresh and invigorating. The fishermen were already busy with their early-morning tasks. Some sat on their boats mending nets, or sorting the fish from the previous night's catch into boxes ready for the market. Others laid their nets out on the quay, in order to inspect the damage from the previous night's work.

'I want to take you up to *Casteddu*,' said Beppe, 'so you can see our lovely city in the morning light. We've plenty of time.'

Cagliari was already busy. The Via Roma looked clean in the morning sunlight, as if it had been washed by the sea and dried in the sun. The nearby port was deserted except for the fishermen unloading their catch. Their boats festooned with nets of brown, ochre and green. The huge white ferry that plied between the island and the continent lay peacefully at anchor, awaiting the jostling passengers and cargo for her next journey.

Beppe pulled in by the port so that Elise could see the rising city. The town began in the port with its sparkling, moving water reflecting the cloudless blue sky. The palm trees in the centre whispered in the warm breezes from their native Africa, while the wide Arcade of the

Via Roma, looked cool and shaded from the mounting heat. Elise noticed a small church caught between the neighbouring shuttered buildings; and a tree-filled square opposite, the impressive filigree-towered municipal building. The total unity of the port and the city was ageless, and the marriage between the two was a wonder to behold, giving Cagliari an air that was unique to Sardinia.

They drove on around the large old magnolia tree-filled square, past the municipal building and turned up the Largo Carlo Felice where only last night they had watched the carriage of the saint return by candlelight. They continued up to Viale Buoncammino, where a number of cars waited impatiently, as in all Latin countries, for the lights to change and allow the single line of traffic to pass through the massive arched gateway. Once through the gateway, Beppe took a sharp right through another smaller archway and parked the car in the Piazza Independence – a wide, sunlit square with trees set against the imposing grey buildings which dominated the piazza. To the side, a large pink-washed building stood out against the other grey buildings.

'That is the National Archaeological Museum. They have finds there from all over the island,' Beppe told Elise proudly as he helped her out of the car.

The stone steps up to the impressive doorways had low, smooth-concrete walls on either side, and two young, dark-haired children were taking it in turns to clamber up the steps and slide down the wall to the accompaniment of much shouting and giggling. Beppe grinned and ruffled the tousled hair of one of the youngsters as he went by.

'Some mother will be sewing patches on those trousers and laying a hand on their bottoms tonight!' he said, laughing.

Beppe took Elise's hand as they walked across the piazza and down the narrow street to the Piazza Palazzo, which was dominated by its massive Pisan-style cathedral of Santa Maria. Elise paused to look and admire the magnificent building. Steps ran up to the three doorways through which a steady stream of people came and went. Above the middle and largest door was a painting of the Madonna and Child, outlined in gold leaf, which, on catching the sun, appeared to come brilliantly alive.

They carried on down the narrow streets, hemmed in on either side by the old buildings which towered five or six stories above them. Strung from each side were washing lines; some already full, catching the morning breeze and looking like regal ships in sail. Others were in the process of being filled, and the dripping water splashed and pattered onto the streets below, making it necessary to look upwards, rather than in front, in order to avoid being caught by a sudden downpour.

Dark doorways opened into small shops or cool hallways, where apparently unending marble staircases wound themselves to the very top of the buildings leading to their warren-like rooms and apartments; all adding to the character of this ancient part of the city.

Suddenly, they emerged from the shadows into a wide, open square.

'This is bastion San Remy,' said Beppe, squeezing her hand.

Elise followed Beppe across the first small square, down the old stone steps to a larger area below. Pine trees grew in neat round gardens and their dark green was in striking contrast to the uneven grey paving stones. They walked to a large archway at the far end of the area, through which they could see the terracotta-coloured roofs of Cagliari. Elise looked back from where they had come. She could see up the steps to the domed roof of the cathedral, which perched precariously over the reeling drop of San Remy, and onto the tree-lined Viale Regina Elena. Below, a number of brown-skinned children ran and shouted; some playing football, others were in hot pursuit of a darting alley-cat. Here, the old part of *Casteddu* jutted out like a rock, defiant and proudly overlooking its ever developing surroundings.

'That's Monte Urpini and Villanova, and to the left over there is the basilica of Bonario,' said Beppe, pointing out each to her. 'Long ago, there was a shipwreck, and the sailors had to throw everything overboard in order to save the floundering ship. One casket wouldn't sink and when it finally washed ashore it was found to contain the statue of Our Lady. The sailors believed that it had helped to make the waters calm, so they built a small shrine here in honour of Our Lady. That small shrine has since grown into that large church.'

'What a lovely story!'

'Look,' said Beppe, taking her hand again and drawing her close to him. He put his arm around her and, bringing his head down to rest on her shoulder, pointed with his left hand. 'Over there, next to Bonario, in the dip of the cemetery with the palm trees, that is the oldest and most important Christian monument on the island.'

They stood close to one another, surveying all that lay before them. Elise became aware of his closeness and was surprised to find it made her feel slightly weak. The smell of his lemon cologne filled her senses. She turned to him and smiled, and realising he was watching her and smiling too.

By now, the city had begun to come alive. People were arriving at work in the shops and offices. The streets were full of the clamour of traffic and bustling people. Men called greetings to each other or whistled cheerfully as they busied themselves with their daily tasks.

Elise and Beppe wandered back up a street parallel from that which they had descended. Similar tall buildings dominated the cool, narrow streets and the washing, which was now out in full abundance, waved and dripped water, stirred by the passing sea breezes. Fleeting courtyards with florid cascades of geraniums contrasted with the sombre greyness of the stone.

On creaky-looking balconies, pots of geraniums and assorted flowers flourished in profusion. The air was full of an incoherent babble of sound as the noisy occupants of the apartments exchanged daily gossip with one another across the narrow ravine of buildings. Outside many of the windows were placed little cages containing gold and brown canaries, hopping and twittering, adding their sound to the morning confusion.

Halfway to the piazza, where they had left the car, two small streets crossed; one ran down towards the Pisan tower, and the other climbed up to the steps of the cathedral. By the side of the alley was a communal tap used by all the local tenants. Someone had left it dripping, and a crowd of children had collected around it. A few had made little rivulets on the dry road and were trying to sail small pieces of paper down them. Others merely splashed in and out of the puddles, enjoying the sound of the water and the cool feel on their bare feet. The half-darkened street was lit by brilliant shafts of sunlight which played on the water and the shiny brass tap, turning it to silver and gold. Elise tried to take it all in, but it had such a dreamlike quality; she was afraid that at any moment she would wake up to find the whole vision had evaporated with the heat of the morning sun.

The excited shouts of the children still playing on the steps of the museum, now joined by more friends, could be heard as Elise and Beppe walked back to the car. Watching all this was an old woman, sitting motionless in a corner of the square. She was dressed from head to foot in the traditional widow's black; when she turned her head to watch them, Elise noticed her parchment skin was crisscrossed with countless wrinkles.

'Well? What do you think of *Casteddu*?' asked Beppe, breaking the silence. Elise looked at him blankly for a moment, and then gathered her thoughts.

'It's medieval and overcrowded, with poor living accommodation, but it has an enchanted, magical quality that I don't really understand,' she replied, as they reached the car.

'It's very old,' said Beppe, unlocking the car. He slipped inside and leaned across to unlock her door. 'And do you know that it's ten o'clock already? We should leave now if we want to be in Barumini for lunch.'

CHAPTER FOURTEEN

The road to Barumini passes through the *Campidano*, a fertile plain that runs up the centre of the island. It is flanked by rows of vines, and peach and citrus groves; the leaves of which shake and shimmered in the gentle breeze always present on the island. Finally the groves give way to open fields of waving corn.

Beppe and Elise soon reached Monastir. They travelled in relative silence, each content with their private thoughts. It didn't seem necessary to speak; the occasional glance between them said volumes.

A few minutes out of Monastir, Beppe suddenly stopped the car.

'What's the matter?' asked Elise, surprised.

'Look over there, in that field. See? They are picking the early peaches. Do you want some?'

Before she could reply, he climbed out of the car and clambered down the bank to the grove. A number of men were busy watering the fruits, while others were collecting and stacking the fruit into large wooden crates; but they all stopped and crowded around to speak to the stranger. Beppe shook hands with the largest and apparently the oldest man in the group before greeting the rest. While they talked, a young lad fetched a piece of paper which he rolled into a cone and screwed up at the end, making it into a neat bag.

Although Elise couldn't hear what they were saying, she watched with great interest at their various gesticulations; it was like watching an opera. Beppe was shown the early varieties of fruit and then invited to pick what he wanted. A price was agreed, followed by more hand shaking and a final verbal discourse. Beppe returned to the car, clutching his prize and smiling with satisfaction.

'There,' he said, giving them to Elise, 'these peaches are lovely. They are a new early variety called *Fiori di Maggio*. Try one. These are good. But wait until you taste my peaches; they will be ripe soon.'

'Do you know those people?' she asked, selecting a large, ripe peach. Beppe shook his head, waving to the men as he drove off.

'No, I don't know them. But it seems that the big fellow's wife is the sister of one of the men in my village, which isn't very far from here. So he knew me by name.'

'These are lovely. Have one,' she said, holding out a large peach, its skin warm against her palm. He took it, squeezing her hand as he did so, making her smile broadly at him.

They continued to talk about family matters and friends, Elise questioning him from time to time about the villages they passed through, and he chattered about his relatives who lived in the area and how he had helped his cousin buy a tractor from a local farmer.

Suddenly, rounding a bend in the road, Elise saw the plain stretch away before them. To one side of the road there was a huge mound which dominated the whole area. It was crowned with the ruins of an old castle, which was precariously perched on the top.

'Las Plassas,' said Beppe, anticipating her question and at the same time beaming from ear to ear.

She laughed aloud. 'You know, you remind me of that Phoenician mask that was found near Cagliari when you smile,' she said. 'It has a wide, open smile like yours. Not the sardonic grin you are all supposed to have.'

He laughed too.

Las Plassas towered over the landscape; its graceful sloping sides made it look as if someone had poured it from a great height. The land around laid in neatly cultivated patchwork fields, some outlined by dry stone walls, others left open, their boundaries known and guarded by generations of farmers. At the foot of the impressive mound was a small church, half hidden amongst the sentinels of Cyprus trees. It was surrounded by a white-washed wall that gleamed in brilliant contrast to the brown and pale-green landscape.

They continued in silence up to the next village.

'Barumini,' said Beppe at last. 'The Nuraghe, which is the largest in Sardinia, is just outside the village. I want to stop and collect some wine for our lunch first,' he added as he stopped the car outside a small cafe. 'Do you want to come in?'

'No, I'll wait here,' Elise replied.

She watched him as he pushed through the beadwork strips

which appeared to hang in all Sardinian doorways in a vain deterrent to the flies. Elise sat quietly and looked around her. The main street was concreted over, but the side streets were rough, stony. Large potholes were filled with fine dust, so typical of sun-dominated lands. On the other side of the street there sat five old men on a low stone wall. Elise became uncomfortably aware that she was, herself, being watched and discussed. She tried not to mind; after all, it must be obvious she was a foreigner, and in any case she, too, was fascinated by the odd assortment of characters and studied them surreptitiously.

Two of the men were wearing black berets instead of the Sardinian *berrita*; one was like the French beret, worn at the usual angle over one ear; the other looked more like an English cloth cap. All five sported moustaches of various sizes. The man wearing the cloth cap was leaning forward on a stick with both his legs sticking straight out in front of him. Curled at his feet, lay a sandy-coloured mongrel, fast asleep and completely indifferent to the strangers. The two wearing caps were of a thin build, while the other three were large, portly men, their white-shirted stomachs sagging ponderously over their belted trousers and straining at the buttons. They chattered amongst themselves, casting furtive glances at the car from time to time, and when they laughed they revealed broad, toothless grins.

Further on down the road, Elise noticed that the women were seated outside their houses doing their various household tasks: preparing the vegetables for the midday meal, knitting or sewing. Some were dressed in black from head to toe; others wore long skirts of varying browns and greens. The old women in black sat hunched like crows over their needlework, and Elise was struck by the division of the sexes. There was little doubt that Sardinia was still a man's world; for the older generation at least.

Beppe returned carrying two bottles, which he placed beside the picnic basket.

'What's the matter? You look very pensive,' he said as he climbed back into the car.

'Nothing, I was just looking at the old men and women. Do they always live such individual lives?'

'Here, women don't have the freedom of other European countries. Their place is in the home. Even now, in many villages there is very little contact between men and women. Marriages are arranged by the parents from an early age. In the mountain villages, it's still the same as it was when I was a boy: the evening promenade is taken with the boys on one side of the street and the girls on the other. All are very closely watched by the old people of the village. A boy can catch a girl's eye, smile at her, even turn his head to watch her go by, but he never crosses over to talk to her, and woe betide him if he touches her.

Most of the mountain people are illiterate. But people travel more now; they have learnt to read the newspapers. The young watch television – they have much more freedom than when I was a child. But when I marry, I shall want to do everything with my wife,' he said. 'I believe they should be as one together.'

'And what happens if things don't work out between them? If they find they are not suited?' asked Elise. 'It does happen, you know. Sometimes a greater force takes over. I know what it can be like. What then?'

'The Church sees that they stay together here. It's impossible to break away.' He sighed. 'Yes. They always stay together... always,' he repeated quietly and sighing. He turned the key in the ignition and set the car in motion.

Elise noticed the change in the tone of his voice. 'What's wrong? Have I said something to upset you?' she asked anxiously.

'*Boh*. It's nothing,' he replied, looking straight ahead, and she refrained from pursuing the subject.

There was that word again, that expression, so Sard and so expressive, she found it fascinating. *Boh* seemed to mean I don't know; I suppose so, in fact – whatever you wanted it to mean. She smiled to herself.

Beppe turned left in the village and carried on a little further, past a small restaurant that had been opened in the hope of catching the tourist trade. Turning into a walled area, he parked in the shade of a clump of trees; the sun was, by now, very hot. A guide came forward to greet them, but Beppe told him that he had been before. The two men chattered together in the local dialect, while Elise listened, fascinated, trying hard to understand the odd word here and there.

The guide was a slim, young man in jeans and a tee-shirt, and he had a tatty piece of rope tied around his waist from which dangled a key.

'What is the key for?' asked Elise when there was a lull in their conversation. Beppe put the question to the young man.

'Come,' said the young Sard, pulling her by the arm. Elise looked anxiously at Beppe, who smiled encouragingly.

'Go on,' he said. 'He's going to show you.'

All three of them walked over to the base of the large Nuraghe tower where there was a maze of small roofless buildings, walkways and storerooms. In the floor of one of the round buildings there was a wooden trap-door which was secured by a padlock. The young man took the key, opened the lock and carefully lifted the trap-door. Elise lent forward to peer into the gaping hole. Cool air came up to meet her as she stared down into the depths of the ancient well.

'Goodness. How old is it?' she asked.

'About two thousand years,' said the guide in a matter-of-fact sort of way.

He took a rope attached to the underside of the trap-door and hauled up a shiny aluminium bucket. The water inside was crystal clear. Each took it in turns to drink from the bucket, and the water was indeed sweet and very cold.

'We keep it covered so that it stays clean,' explained the young man. 'It can be thirsty work showing people around here.'

He lowered the bucket, slammed the trap-door shut, replaced the padlock and started back to his little hut, as a new group of tourists had just arrived.

'Let me know if you want any information,' he said over his shoulder.

Beppe took Elise's hand and led her round to the far side of the tower, where an iron staircase had been placed to allow visitors to reach the high tower; they climbed up the staircase, then onto the tower itself. From the top, the whole of the area known as *Malmilla* could be seen. To the south was the all-dominating mountain castle of Las Plassas in the distance and between the castle and Barumini were countless fields; some already harvested, their matchbox-sized bales scattered where the baler had dropped them, and other fields that were still under their mantles of waving corn.

'Up there is the *Giara Gesturi*, a huge plateau where the wild horses still graze,' said Beppe, pointing behind her; she turned and followed the direction of his gaze. The ridge stood out in a blue-green haze and there was a strange, dream-like remoteness about the area, Elise stared out across the wild panoramic landscape.

Beppe watched the wind lifting her hair, which gleamed golden in the strong sunlight. Keats came into his dreamy mind: '*Thee sitting careless on a granary floor, Thy hair soft-lifted by the winnowing wind.*'

'What was this nuraghe originally used for?' Elise asked, turning to him. But Beppe had a faraway look and made no reply. She took his hand and repeated the question.

'*Boh?* Oh… err… I don't really know,' he stammered. 'There's quite a lot of speculation. It's still a mystery. Some say it's a temple, while others say it's an early form of castle or walled fort. Some say they were lookout towers, as the land would have been covered in forest and you could see over them, others say they were a defence against malaria because they are high. I'm not sure. Here come with me.'

He led her to a narrow opening, and they picked their way down a dimly lit stairway with treacherously uneven steps. Out in the daylight once more, they found themselves at the top of a rough flight of wooden steps which led to the inner courtyard. Descending the rather rickety ladder, Elise couldn't help wondering if it had been there for as long as time itself.

The enclosed courtyard had an old disused well in the centre, and several doorways leading into the four round towers, the first of which was open at the top, where the stones had fallen away. The shaft of sunlight that poured in lit up the stones, making it possible to see how each ring of stone had been neatly graded or corbelled so that the top ones rested on each other; held together by their weight and without the use of mortar, and highlighting the ingenuity of the ancient builders.

Passing through to the next tower, Beppe took Elise's hand as the darkness enfolded them. His grasp was warm and strong, and her hand felt very small within his.

'Are you alright?' he asked softly.

'Yes. I'm fine.'

The air was cool and Beppe slipped his arm around her waist as he drew her close to him. She could feel the warmth of his breath on her face, and the scent of his lemon-based cologne once more sent a thrill of excitement through her body in anticipation of his kiss – but the sound of voices approaching through the darkness made him pull away. He took out his lighter and produced a small flame that flickered against the massive walls. It highlighted the lower part of his face and reflected in his deep, dark eyes.

'Come,' he said, turning to lead the way. 'There's light further along. I think it's the doorway.'

Outside, the air was hot after the coolness of the stone building, and the sunlight appeared to be even more brilliant in contrast with the ancient darkness. More people had arrived, and the guide was busy explaining about the massive stones and how they were laid. Looking up at the tower Beppe touched one of the large stones.

'If they were built by a Sard then I'm truly proud of being a Sard,' said Beppe gravely.

She looked at him and they both laughed.

'Race you to the car,' he called.

Each picked a different route through the small alleyways, but Beppe leapt over a low wall, giving him the advantage.

'Hey – that's not fair! Your legs are longer than mine,' cried Elise.

He reached the car first and opened the door. Elise panted up behind him, flushed and laughing, her eyes sparkling.

'God, it's hot!' she gasped, leaning against the car. 'Let's have lunch here by the ruins, overlooking Las Plassas.'

'Alright, if that's what you want.'

Beppe collected the picnic basket and the wine from the car, and they strolled back to the small square ruin standing by itself at the foot of the nuraghe. As they passed along the walled walkways for the second time, Elise was aware of the greenness of the grass near the stones. Bees hummed noisily as they visited the wild flowers that grew in every nook and cranny of the great stone edifice and the small surrounding ruins. The wild oats in nodding profusion and the waving, scarlet poppies made her think of all the Sard blood that must have been shed here over the ages, in the constant battles against tyranny and oppression.

She threw herself onto the ground in the shade of the square ruin, breathing in the dry, sweet perfume of the grass and enjoying the little breeze that cooled her face.

'How beautifully quiet it is here,' she said as she watched the windblown grasses that crowned the charmed, magical stone circles.

Beppe opened the basket and untied the big, white cloth in which Maria had wrapped everything. Inside was another freshly laundered cloth which he spread on the ground, placing on it a carved wooden platter on which he placed salciaccia, olives, bread and cheese. Then, opening the wine, he poured it into two earthenware beakers and passed one to Elise.

'*Saludi e trigu*,' he said, raising his beaker.

'*E tappu e ottigu*,' she replied, with a grin.

'Whoever taught you that?' he asked, surprised.

'I said *salude* to Maria the other day, and she told me that whenever one says that in Sardinia, the correct reply is *e tappio ottigu*. I believe it goes on, but I can't remember any more.'

'It does,' he said, raising his eyebrows. 'But it's not terribly polite,' and they both laughed.

After the picnic, they lay back in the grass and watched the birds circling and wheeling on the thermal currents of the cloudless sky. The food, the wine and the heat of the afternoon made them both feel drowsy.

'Elise,' said Beppe, taking her hand, 'would it be so terrible if we didn't go back tonight? We could stay with my cousins who live in Aritzo for the night. I could show you the Barbargia and we could return to the villa tomorrow, in the evening.'

'What about Efisio and Maria? Won't they worry?'

'I'll ring them. There is a telephone in the shop where I bought the wine.'

'What about your cousins? They may not have room for us.'

'We always have room for relatives and friends in Sardinia,' he replied confidently. He raised himself on one elbow and looked into her eyes.

'Well – if you think it will be alright. I'd love to,' she said, melting under his velvet gaze.

'Good, that's settled then,' he cried, springing to his feet with renewed vigour. 'I'll ring Maria from the village.'

He busied himself packing the basket, humming happily. Elise lay there watching him, taking pleasure in the movement of his lithe body. When he had finished packing everything away, he put his hand out to help Elise up and they made their way back to the car, waving farewell to the young guide as they drove through the gate.

Once more they stopped outside the shop and Beppe disappeared through the beaded doorway. The women and men she had observed before were all gone; the street was now completely deserted. Suddenly, Elise felt very alone.

'It's alright. Maria is quite happy,' said Beppe as he clambered back into the car. He restarted the engine and swung the car around. He put his hand out and touched hers. 'Are you alright? Your hand is very cold,' he asked, looking a little concerned. Then, smiling at her reassuringly, he added, 'It's a beautiful drive to Aritzo, you wait and see.'

CHAPTER FIFTEEN

It was indeed a beautiful and very picturesque road that wound its way through the unspoiled countryside. At Nuragus, a tiny village en route, they waited while a local shepherd, wearing a flat, black cap at a jaunty angle and sporting a rakish-looking moustache, herded his sheep along the road. He sat, perched precariously, on the back of his donkey, his feet nearly touching the ground. A cloud of fine dust rose into the air, thrown up from the dry road by the trampling of many hooves as the herd wandered on its way towards new pastures, the bells around their necks, clanging discordantly as they hurried past.

'Each flock has a different sounding bell so that the shepherds know which herd is theirs.' he said with a wide grin.

Bend after bend in the road revealed scenes of breath-taking beauty. Elise was fascinated by the cork trees. The men had not yet started their work after the siesta, but the already stripped trees looked strangely naked with their red trunks gleaming against the golden grass and brilliant blue sky; others that had been stripped for some time were a darker red, contrasting with the browning vegetation. Nearby were piles of the ochre-coloured cork which had been taken and stacked neatly, waiting for collection.

'This is Larconi,' said Beppe. 'Saint Ignazio was born here in this village to of a very poor family. He became a lay brother for the Cappuccine brothers, and in later-life begged alms for the brotherhood. He is Saint Francis of Sardinia. The church has many saints, but it's good to have a Sardinian one, and therefore he is very special to us.'

'Is the street where we met for the festa named after him?' she asked.

'Yes and the Cappuccine monastery is there also.'

The views across the *Birissariu* valley were of a boundless wildness. The road crossed and re-crossed the railway tracks, which wound alongside it, many times before the narrow-gauge railway disappeared on its own meandering journey to Meana Sarda. Beppe took a right-hand junction and started to climb to the Barbargia Belvi, watched over by the mountain range of the Silver Gate, the Gennagentu. When they reached the top he stopped the car, and without a word Elise got out. Below where she stood lay a patchwork of wild vegetation of every hue, from green flecked with yellow to brown peppered with orange. The grasses had begun to change colour from the lack of rain and the constant, unrelenting sun.

In the distance, stone walls ran for miles, seemingly going nowhere, but dividing lands and families.

'All that work just to say "this is mine and that is yours",' she mused.

She was aware of the constant movement as the breeze shook the grasses and whispered in the tangled, sweet-smelling macchia. Birds twittered in the myrtle bushes and bees hummed in the nectar-laden flowers. The cicadas and grasshoppers added their small grating noises, and butterflies fluttered in the cloudless sky. The air was heavy with the scent of the dry earth, countless flowers and anticipation.

Elise drew a deep breath. She felt a lump rise in her throat, and tears stung the back of her eyes and fell silently down her cheeks. Beppe approached, pointing out the different landmarks as he came towards her.

'From this point, you can see nearly the whole of the Belvi Barbargia and over there…'

He broke off, seeing her tears. He understood instantly. Elise was totally enchanted, bewitched by his island's magic, the wonderful peace of this place. He put his arm around her and gave her his handkerchief.

'You must think me incredibly stupid,' Elise sniffed, half sobbing, half laughing, 'but it's not often I'm so moved by anything. Since I've been here that… that's all I seem to do.'

'Everyone experiences the Barbargia in their own way. I remember the first time I saw this view; I couldn't talk to anyone about it. I felt it belonged to me, and was mine and mine alone.' He pulled her gently towards him, and his strong arms enfolded her. He felt her heart pounding as she looked up into his face.

Elise stared into his eyes. They were dark brown, but there was just a fleck of green in them, making them look like the macchia. Beppe took her face in his hands and gently stroked her cheeks with his thumbs, and then he bent down and kissed her gently on each eye. Such a tender gesture, and she was surprised at her reaction: it made her feel like a child again, and even a little shy.

A warm wind whispered through the nearby trees and fluttered with the butterflies in the grasses of the macchia. Elise shivered. Gathering her in his arms, Beppe kissed her cheek and, feeling her melt against him, his mouth at last found hers.

When Beppe released her, he steadied her gently as she swayed a little. Then, kissing her on the tip of her nose, he said, 'Come – we must get to Aritzo before it gets dark.'

They drove in silence. Elise watched the passing scenery, trying desperately to understand her feelings and to gather her thoughts. Why did she feel the way she did? She wondered. She had known other men before William, but none had ever had such a profound effect on her. He was the same age as her, but in many ways he was older and even worldlier; but then he could also be like a young boy, full of the joy of living and with all that boundless energy.

'I'm sorry,' said Beppe, breaking the silence at last. 'I shouldn't have done that. I've offended you. I know you are married...'

'Oh yes, you should have!' Elise interrupted quite vehemently.

'Then you're not offended? But you're so quiet I...'

'No – not offended. It's just that I've... I've never before felt quite as I do now. Not about anything or anyone. I find it difficult to understand myself.'

Beppe stopped the car and turned to her; his eyes were dark and deep with an inner fire.

'I know you're married, Elise,' he said in a low, husky voice. 'I know, too, the feelings I have for you are wrong, and the things I want to say to you should never be said. But how can it be a mortal sin to feel as I do about you?'

'Shush,' she said softly. 'We have such a short time together; let's not spoil it by worrying about whether it's right or wrong!'

He smiled and covered her hand with his for a moment, gently squeezing it. The wind whispered through the grasses again, and Elise sighed in deep contentment.

The fire crackled welcomingly in the grate, and the glass of Vernaccia that Elise was drinking warmed her, making her feel happy and relaxed. Angelo and his wife, Giuseppina, Beppe's cousin and namesake, had greeted them with open arms and shown their English guest typical Sardinian hospitality. Elise was introduced to each member of the family. Because, like many Sards, they spoke Italian, she had no difficulty understanding them, even though the dialect sounded harder and coarser than that of Cagliari.

Elise sat with Beppe by the fire, watching the inner flames dance among the outer, glowing embers. A kerosene lamp, hanging from a hook in the sooty ceiling, cast a soft light over the room that served as both sitting and dining room. A wooden stairway at one side of the room led to the small bedrooms upstairs. Off the main room was the kitchen, and further on there was a doorway to the bathroom; a recent addition and a sign of increasing prosperity in the family. The familiar smell of cooking filled the room, and Elise took in the family as they sat around the fire.

Giuseppina, or Beppina as she was called, had the same dark hair as Beppe, and although hers was largely confined in a knot at the back of her head, the tendrils that had freed themselves curled round her neck and face. She, too, had dark eyes and a rich, olive-coloured skin, and was fairly tall for a Sard. Although her body was thickening, she still retained a good deal of her former beauty; walking with the graceful, erect carriage of a woman accustomed to carrying water containers or washing baskets on her head. She wore a long, linen skirt which was gathered at the waist and covered with an apron. She was only in her mid-thirties, but clearly Beppina would soon go the way of most Sardinian beauties: worn down by the constant demands made upon women, by long hours working in the fields for small rewards, together with years of child-bearing.

Angelo, shorter in stature than his wife, was stocky and strong, with wiry hair and earth-stained hands. He worked a small vineyard and two fruit groves. He also kept a few sheep for the two boys, Franco and Beppino, to care for, grazing them in a neighbour's olive grove. In return, Angelo supplied the neighbour with milk, and occasionally some homemade cheese. Angelo was also a skilled carpenter by trade, and was kept busy in the area by making and repairing doors and shutters for the villagers, or making coffins for the deceased.

Franco and Beppino were two young lads in their early teens, and both bore an astonishing resemblance to their father. Elise was amazed by their insular existence, and the way they all accepted their roles in the large jigsaw of daily life. She also noticed that there was no television set in the house to influence the young people – but an abundance of crafts and books to keep them occupied in the long winter evenings.

Soon they were all summoned to the table. Angelo said grace and they sat down, the babble of chatter going on around the table making it a warm and friendly meal. They ate pasta, pane fratau, salciaccia and salad; all washed down with Angelo's very palatable homemade wine. There was newly baked bread accompanied by Casu Marzu cheese – rather akin to stilton, but made from ewe's milk. Elise took it all in her stride when they offered her the cheese complete with the maggots, said to be the best part and reserved for special guests. Her father's training of 'eat it and think of something you really like' always came in handy at times like this. The meal was followed by numerous glasses of Vernaccia. Finally, the table was cleared and they sat around the dying fire to sing songs or talk among themselves

It wasn't long before the good meal and the warm fire took their toll, and everyone was ready for bed.

Beppina left the men to talk and she placed the boys head to toe in one bed to give Beppe a room on his own. Elise went to sleep in the small room at the far end of the landing. Angelo and Beppe sat by the dying embers and finished their wine.

'She is nothing like they say,' said Angelo, looking down at his feet.

'Like who says?'

'Well, the family of course. The gossip is rife about you and a married woman. Beppe, you must take care; your mother is not in favour of this relationship. She is dripping poison into every ear. Please take care.'

'*Boh.* News travels fast, but gossip even faster. I have done more than my fair share for the family. If my mother can't accept Elise then she will lose me. But she is married and I don't even know if she will leave her husband.'

'Look, Beppe, I'm on your side, but again all I say is take care. But I understand foreign girls are easy; is that right?'

'I wouldn't know. I haven't touched her,' said Beppe, draining his glass.

'God, it is serious then,' replied Angelo, looking stunned.

'Thanks, Angelo. It is,' he said, and made his way up to bed.

That night, try as he might, Beppe couldn't sleep. He tossed and turned, going over the day's events. He knew now that he was in love with Elise and couldn't stop loving her and needing her, even if he wanted to. But adultery he knew, too, was a mortal sin. He had been taught that since childhood. The taking of another man's wife… even thinking about it was surely sin enough. He had checked in his Bible and found no comfort there. Confession would be out of the question; a sinner had to be contrite before he received absolution from the church or forgiveness from God. If he made love to Elise, he would glory in it, rather than repent. When at last he fell into a fitful sleep, he dreamt he saw Good and Evil casting lots for his soul.

Beppe woke with a start to find he had only been asleep a couple of hours. After a while he climbed out of bed, wrapping his towel around him toga-fashion. He walked quietly to Elise's room and noiselessly opened her door. A shaft of moonlight from the tiny window fell across the bedroom floor, bathing the room with silver light. Elise lay sleeping peacefully, her blonde hair lying in profusion on the pillow, and Beppe, bending over her, felt in his heart a melting tenderness. He wanted so much to wake her, to lie beside her, to tell her how he felt about her and most of all to hold her and make love to her; but his courage failed him. The words of one of the songs they had sung that evening came back with a poignant meaning:

Aberium sa yanna frisca Rosa…
Standing at your doorway, sweet rose,

I tremble like the reeds.
While you in your bed are sleeping,
I am left outside waiting!'

Quietly closing the door, he returned to his room. He remembered the way he and Elise had clung together that afternoon; remembered the warmth and softness of her kiss. He wanted her, needed her, was willing to face hell for her; he knew that now. Having faced this and accepted it, he felt a sudden, peaceful calm wash over him and he fell into a deep, dreamless sleep.

CHAPTER SIXTEEN

Angelo and Beppina were up early attending to their normal morning chores, and Elise was woken by the sound of the two boys herding the ewes into a small pen, ready for milking. Sitting up, she saw the early morning sun was lighting up the massive mountains of the Gennagentu, with their distant snow caps somehow looking out of place. The soft breeze flowing through the open window came from the valley, bringing with it the fragrance of the countless wildflowers that carpeted the mountain slopes. Here, everything was still green and lush, for summer comes late in the mountains. A hawk hung overhead on the upper air currents, gliding now and then to a different spot. Elise watched it for a few moments, envying its freedom, and then dressed quickly and descended the stairs to wash in the now vacant bathroom.

Beppina was busy organising breakfast when Elise went into the kitchen. They greeted each other, then Beppe came in from outside, carrying a large pail that was brimming over with frothy white milk, and was followed by the two boys.

'Beppe has helped milk the ewes, Mamma. He's really quite good!' said Franco.

'So he should be,' she replied, smiling. 'He used to do it at your age, too.'

'Where do you want this, Beppina?' he asked, lifting the pail onto the table and smiling in his usual disarming way.

'In the small room off the kitchen, please. We're going to Tonara today, Beppe. Are you coming with us?'

'No, cousin we are going back to Pula after I have shown Elise some of the Barbargia,' he said, giving Elise a broad wink.

Beppina indicated for them to sit down and have their breakfast, while Beppino put his head out of the door and called 'Babbu' at the top of his voice. Angelo appeared and settled himself at the table. He said grace and then smiled at Elise.

'Did you sleep well?'

'Yes, thank you very much. I was very comfortable,' she replied.

'I'm making a picnic basket for us, so I'll fill yours, too,' said Beppina.

'Can I help at all?' asked Elise.

'No. Thank you, my dear. Eat your breakfast and then get Beppe to take you to see the village. I'll lend you a shawl.'

The morning air was still a little chilly and Elise was grateful for the extra warmth as they wandered through the narrow streets of the sprawling village which clung so lovingly to the steep mountainside. The surrounding area was robed in trees of walnut and sweet chestnuts, and rose like a backcloth to the village and overshadowing the whole area was an impressive, sheer-sided mountain.

'It's Monte Texile,' Beppe said smiling, anticipating her question. 'It's where Sant' Efisio is said to have preached to the barbaricini and converted them all to Christianity. They say that when the people heard the good news, they fell to the ground in homage and gave thanks for their new faith. The whole valley bloomed with trees at that moment and that's why there are so many trees in this area.'

Elise was surprised by the number of legends that the church still held as gospel and how many of the Sards believed, without questioning; and she found herself thinking what a rarity such faith was in this day and age.

The main street of Aritzo was busy with women going about their daily tasks, many of them wearing the local costume.

'It's the women who cling to the traditions,' said Beppe. 'They find it difficult to adjust to modern living. The men leave the villages in search of work, going to Cagliari, or perhaps abroad to the continent, and they see the changes in the outside world. True, the women welcome TV if they have electricity, but most of them cling to the old ways, and many still do the household washing together in the communal wash-houses or in the river.'

'It must be difficult for them,' remarked Elise. 'They try so hard to keep the old traditions and family ways alive – and they have every right to be afraid of change, for it may not bring them the peace of mind they once knew!' she added sadly.

'Change comes to all of us; however welcome or unwelcome,

whether for the better or worse. You can't stop progress,' he replied.

'But can you really call it progress? After all, when small village communities are broken up and have their ordered way of life changed, all that happens is a demand for material possessions like radio, television, telephones, motor cars – and with all this comes greed and envy.'

'You can't hold them back all the time,' he said. 'But it's the men, I feel sorry for. They come back from the continent and find things difficult. The closeness of the family becomes claustrophobic. Morals are looser abroad, and the family is shocked at the free-and-easy life of the foreigners. When you meet men who have been away, they tell you how much they long for their native villages and the security of the family; their longing to return to the land of their birth – but the reality is a closed society with a lack of privacy and freedom. I have seen it happen many times. When they go into the army, they learn to read and write, and a whole new world opens up to them; something that is denied to most of their families. Resentment comes between father and son, and it opens up deep rifts in families. I think the Sards are locked in a battle. They are frightened to look outward, but afraid of being inward; frightened of change.'

'Is that how you felt and feel after coming back from the continent?' she asked.

He sighed, lowering his head.

'I've seen it all happen in England, too,'said Elise, 'where you have small, pretty villages with a way of life that has carried on for centuries in its own rural rhythm; then the Londoners or towns' people move in with their money, developments, big cars and materialistic ideas. In no time at all, cattle can't even walk along the street without someone complaining about the mess they make. Workers leave the farms and go for higher wages and boredom in the factories, crime increases and...'

'There I agree with you,' cut in Beppe. 'I've seen it happen in neighbouring villages. They say you even have to lock your door in Cagliari when you go out now as there are so many strangers around.'

'Now you're teasing me!' said Elise, a little nettled.

'No. I'm not, really, Elise. As a child, one could walk into any house in Cagliari and the door would be open. We still leave ours open in the village, but it won't be long before we too start locking up, I suppose. The sad thing is that the *Sardu* language is no longer taught in our schools as a rule, and the children don't hear it in the home as much. Soon our language will go because everyone is taught Italian instead. Perhaps in years to come they will realise what they have done, but by then it will be too late.'

'That is sad,' replied Elise.

He sighed again. 'No more profound talk. I want to take you to Desulo; it's such a beautiful and picturesque village.'

They returned to the house and found Beppina and her family all ready to leave.

'What are you doing today then?' she asked Beppe.

'We're going to Desulo, and then driving home.'

'Well, you keep the shawl until you return,' said Beppina to Elise. 'It can be a lot colder in Desulo. It's very high – nearly five thousand feet; nearly the highest village in Sardinia.'

Angelo came round from the back of the stables leading a donkey with a large pack on its back. Franco and Beppino followed behind.

'Are they going for a week?' asked Elise, astonished.

'No,' said Beppe, laughing, 'they are taking food and provisions up to Tonara. Angelo's father is a shepherd and stays up there, so they all go to see him and make a day of it.'

'I've put the basket in your car, Beppe,' said Beppina. Turning to Elise, she added, 'I hope you will come and see us again next year, when you return. You will always be welcome.'

Angelo stepped forward and handed Elise a wooden platter, ornately carved by hand.

'This is for you both,' he said. 'Whenever you eat together, you can use it and remember us.'

'Did you make it yourself?' enquired Elise.

'Yes, I carved it last winter,' he replied with honest pride. 'It's made from the wood of the sweet chestnut that grows in this area.'

'It's lovely; we shall treasure it, won't we Beppe?'

Beppe nodded and, smiling, he shook hands with Angelo, who put his large hand on Beppe's shoulder and nodded back to him.

They held each other's gaze for a moment and then Angelo pulled away.

Beppe then kissed his cousin. She said something to him *in Sardu*, which Elise didn't catch, but she noticed Beppe squeeze her hand and smile. Then the young boys came forward and hugged Beppe.

Angelo kissed Elise's hand in farewell, as did the boys, but Beppina embraced her and kissed her on both cheeks.

'Take care of each other,' she said, 'and good luck.'

Desulo, Elise discovered, was another village that clung lovingly to the mountainside in limpet-like fashion, like so many of the villages in the Barbargia. Houses with balconies overlooked steep roads, which in turn overlooked the falling valleys. Parking proved no problem, and she and Beppe wandered along the main street where young children played five stones with small pebbles, while old women scrubbed the stone steps to their houses. The young women walked through the village carrying heavy loads of washing or water on their heads with a natural poise and dignity.

In one place, where there was a beautiful and uninterrupted view down into the valley, three women sat catching the warm sunshine. They were wearing their traditional scarlet costume, edged with blue and decorated with yellow, and were all busy sewing a new one. Beppe stopped and talked to them for a while, and from the way the women kept glancing at her, Elise knew they were talking about her. Finally, Beppe turned to her.

'They are making a traditional dress for one of their daughters who is to marry soon,' he said.

One of the women, who was wearing a small bonnet decorated in the same colours as the rest of her dress, beckoned to Elise to come closer and proudly showed her all the intricate stitching that was involved.

'But it's beautiful!' she breathed. 'Look at all that delicate embroidery around the neck and the sleeves!'

The white cotton blouse was being embroidered in white, every stitch lovingly worked in minute detail. The woman smiled at Elise's obvious admiration, and then asked her in broken Italian: 'Don't you have a traditional dress in England?'

'The Scots have a kilt, and the Irish and the Welsh have their own dress, but it tends to be clans and a national dress, not an area or village one, as here. Perhaps,' Elise added, 'it's because we haven't anything like this that we appreciate your traditional dresses so much.'

The women beamed approval and shook hands cordially with them both.

The morning slipped by and they decided to head back to Pula, calling in at Aritzo again to leave Beppina's shawl at the house. Beppe decided on a different route home, to give Elise a chance to see more of the scenery. So they took the small road that twisted its way down to the valley, where everywhere appeared to be totally deserted.

'You can drive for miles on this island and never see a soul,' she remarked.

'It's always like that up here. This land seems to belong only to the shepherds and their flocks,' he replied.

He pulled off the road and stopped the car in the shade of some eucalyptus trees, then beckoned her out.

'This is the boundary between the two great Barbargi. On one side is the Barbargia Belvi and on the other is the Barbargia Seulo,' he explained, pointing out the difference. He looked at her, but she obviously wasn't listening and was looking at the meadow that lay before her.

'Everything is so wild,' she exclaimed. 'And the flowers are beautiful, and it's much greener up here in the mountains compared with the *Campidano*. And look at the butterflies! I haven't seen so many in ages!' she said, running into the long meadow grass and dragging her hands across it, disturbing all the insects and butterflies. She turned and called to him.

'Oh look, Beppe – there's a stream down there. Do let's have our picnic here! It's such a lovely, peaceful spot.'

Beppe nodded in agreement. His heart was aching and beat uncontrollably as he watched her in the meadow. The light shone in a halo around her, and he found it mesmerising. She looked so lovely. He sighed and finally pulled himself together. He went back to the car to collect the basket, but when he returned, Elise had disappeared. He looked anxiously around, at the same time calling her name, but there was no answer. He walked on towards the stream, quickening his pace and calling again.

'Elise! Where are you?'

'Over here!' she called.

Beppe looked around and saw her sitting on a low bough under the branches of an overhanging willow tree. He hurried to join her.

'You shouldn't do that!' he exclaimed crossly.

'Do what?' she said with a melting smile.

'Hide like that!'

'I wasn't hiding, Beppe. What's the matter? Did you think I'd been kidnapped by one of Franco's handsome bandits?' she teased.

She had removed her sandals and was dabbling her feet in the cool water; her dress was pulled up around her shapely, sun-tanned thighs, and a froth of white lace petticoat spilled from under her skirt. Beppe drew in a long breath as he stared at her; he was aware that his heart was beating uncontrollably and time was suspended as he took in the scene. His love for her had grown over the past weeks, and as she sat there in the shade, he knew he would love her forever.

'Isn't it lovely here with the stream chattering over the stones and reeds growing by the water? It's so cool under the shade of this old tree,' said Elise, splashing her feet in the water.

'Here,' said Beppe, tearing his eyes from her, 'put the wine in the stream. It will be nice and cool when we want it.'

Elise slipped off the branch and took the bottle from him and put it in the water, carefully banking stones around it to keep it in place.

'Come and join me,' she said, sitting down and patting the bank invitingly. He shook off his shoes and sat down beside her, slipping his arm around her waist. After a while, he turned to her.

'Elise,' he said quietly, 'tell me: why did you come on holiday alone? Tell me about William?'

'I told you, we were supposed to come down together but William had to go to America on business,' she replied, 'and I don't want to talk about him. He has hurt me.'

'Do you usually take separate holidays?'

'Yes. He's always working...' She broke off. 'But we were coming here together, because he was going to work at Sarroch. Beppe, you've asked all this before. What is it you really want to know about William?'

'I know there is something wrong between the two of you. No man beats his wife if all is well. Before, I didn't think it was any of my business to pry too deeply, but now I want to know for sure.'

'Why now?'

'Well, you never mention him or your family, and as far as I know you haven't written to him or phoned him since you've been here, and neither has he bothered to contact you.'

'We have no family – no children – and as I told you, William is in America. He's travelling around. I don't know his address, and I don't care.'

Beppe reached down into the water and took out the wine bottle. He pulled the basket closer and found two beakers and a corkscrew. He opened the wine.

'If I were him, I certainly wouldn't let you go wandering off on your own,' he said slowly, handing her the wine.

She took the beaker he offered her and looked into his eyes.

'Perhaps if I was yours, I wouldn't want to go off on my own,' she said, and then added, 'He has his life, and he's happy.' She shrugged.

Beppe took out the wooden platter Angelo had given them and began piling on the bread, mountain sausage and olives that his cousin had put in the basket.

'What did Beppina say to you when we left?' asked Elise, anxious to change the subject.

'She said that you were beautiful and that I was a lucky man, and obviously very happy too,' he replied, not taking his eyes off the bottle he was holding.

'And... Are you happy?' she asked.

'What more could I ask for?' he replied. 'It's a beautiful day, the wine is good and I have you. I couldn't ask for better company. *"Here with a Loaf of Bread beneath the bough, A Flask of Wine, a Book of Verse – and Thou,"'* he quoted.

Elise smiled, lay back in the shade and watched the sun as it flashed and flickered through the constantly moving branches of the willow. The reeds along the water's edge rustled and quivered in the breeze, while the stream chuckled and gurgled as it tumbled over the stones. Beppe turned toward her and, resting on his elbow, gently stroked her hair away from her face. He remembered her lying in the bed at Aritzio.

'You lie like that when you're asleep,' he said softly.

'How do you know?' she asked, laughing.

'I saw you last night. I couldn't sleep, and I came to your room. I wanted so much to talk to you, but you were sleeping so peacefully I hadn't the heart to wake you, so I left.'

'What did you want to talk about?'

'About you, about us and about the way I feel about you…'

'And how do you feel about me?' she whispered.

'Like this.' He brought his face slowly down to hers, giving her a succession of tiny kisses; then he kissed her soft mouth, gently at first, but with a growing passion. He felt her put her arms around his neck as she drew him closer to her and he buried his face against her breast.

'Oh Elise,' he said, his voice deep and husky. 'I can't help how I feel. I've tried to fight it, but I can't. It's wrong, I know. The church teaches us that adultery is a mortal sin. I know I shall pay dearly for loving you, but I don't care any more! Surely, God and the Blessed Mary will forgive me for wanting and loving you the way I do?'

'Hush, darling. If we share the sin,' she whispered, 'we can share the punishment.'

'If only things were that simple,' he sighed. 'I don't mind if you don't feel the same way about me as I do for you. I have never felt like this about anyone before. I want you so much it hurts. I want to hold you and to show you how much I love you, darling Elise. Life is a loan, a gift, but a loan even so; we must live it to the full. We have no idea of the time allotted to us; we need to take all that it has to offer us.'

She stared up into his eyes, and a feeling of longing washed over her.

'Don't look at me like that, please Elise.'

'Why darling?' she whispered.

'Because when you look at me like that I want the world to stand still, and I want to hold you in my arms forever. I want to feel your breath against my cheek, to smell the scent of you and hear your heart beat against my chest.'

'I love you, Beppe Zedda.' she breathed.

He turned away, the emotion rising within him. She turned his face gently towards her. He was looking into her face now, and she could see herself reflected in his deep, limpid, dark eyes.

'I love you too,' he said, drawing her closer to him.

Tears fell down her cheeks, and he kissed them away.

'Salty tears,' he said as he gently ran his hand across her cheek and down her neck.

Her skin thrilled to his touch, and her body began to sing. She felt breathless and Elise noticed that Beppe trembled when he touched her.

'I love you, Elise, more than life itself. I think about you all of the time, and you are always in the background of my mind.'

She raised herself and kissed his nose, and then his lips. She kissed him repeatedly, pulling him closer to her as she did so, knowing that from this moment on their relationship would be totally different. It would either blossom into an affair with all its problems, developing into something neither of them could, nor would want to control; or he would end up despising her, or, worse still, himself.

Elise pushed that thought out of her mind. What could be more natural than two people in love sharing that love in the sweet-scented grass, to the sibilant murmur of the breeze as it passed through the willow leaves and whispered in the reeds?

She remembered another verse from Omar Khayyam. *'The Moving Finger writes: and, having writ, Moves on: nor all thy Piety nor Wit Shall lure it back to cancel half a Line, Nor all thy Tears wash out a Word of it.'*

And she surrendered to their passion, completely.

CHAPTER SEVENTEEN

The lovers, enraptured by each other, were unaware of the afternoon slipping by, and it was not until they felt the first chill of the evening and saw the rapidly darkening sky that they realised how late in the day it had become.

'We should get back before it's too dark,' said Beppe, reluctantly drawing Elise to her feet and kissing her on her forehead.

They collected their belongings and walked hand in hand back to the car.

Elise's face was still flushed and her eyes shining and Beppe's dark hair tousled when they walked into the warm kitchen at the villa.

Maria was there and gave them a quick, close glance as she greeted them.

'Did you enjoy your trip?' she asked.

'Oh yes, Maria. We've had a wonderful time,'said Elise. 'You have a beautiful country; so wild, so free!'

'Where is Efisio, Maria?' asked Beppe, putting the picnic basket on the table.

'He's in the vinery,' she said and, smiling, added, 'He's alone.'

Efisio was filling the earthenware jugs with wine for the house, and greeted Beppe without looking up.

'Had a good time at your cousins? Are they well?' he asked, carrying on with his task.

'Yes, thank you – they are… Efisio, there's something I want to ask you…'

'We have a lot of work to do in this place, Beppe, but Predu is willing to do an extra bit and so is Ignazio. You are always helping them out…' continued Efisio.

'Yes, I know I've been away today, but…'

'Don't interrupt me when I'm talking!' said Efisio, standing up slowly and looking Beppe straight in the eyes. 'You know what you are doing is wrong and against all you have been taught. Your mother is strict and a disciplinarian and a strong believer in the faith. She has tried hard to impart those same standards into you boys, but I'm not here to be your moral judge. What you do is between you and your maker. What I'm trying to say is… you can have all the time off you want while she is here.' He patted Beppe on the shoulder. 'Just mind you don't get hurt, that's all. Remember, she is a married woman and she has a husband to go home to!'

In the kitchen, Maria turned to Elise. 'Elise – while we are alone, I want to have a word with you,' she said gently.

'What is it, Maria?'

'Efisio and I have been talking about you and Beppe while you were away. We have seen how happy he has become in your company. I can see a change in you both since you came here. You have had time to get to know one another better away from us, and I can see the result in both of your faces. But I…'

'Maria, I know what you are going to say,' Elise interrupted, taking the older woman's hands in hers. 'I promise I won't do anything to hurt him. I didn't come looking for a holiday romance or a bed-partner; far from it, I can assure you. You know what a state I was in when I arrived here. What has happened has been completely outside my, or Beppe's, control.'

'I know,' said Maria with a smile. 'But listen to me, Elise. Efisio is talking to Beppe, because you know his mother will never accept you. Not even if you were free to marry him. Not even if you were single and had never been married. He is also telling Beppe that he can take whatever time off he wants so that he can be with you. Beppe has worked many, many times for us when the children have wanted to do something. Now it's his turn to be free.'

'Thank you, Maria. I won't let him down, I promise. I think he's very special, you know.'

'Have you told him so?' asked Maria.

'I have, but will he believe me, married as I am to another man? Will he believe me?'

'Why don't you ask him?' said a voice from behind her. Elise turned to see Beppe standing in the doorway and went to hold him.

'Will you believe me?' she repeated, looking up into his eyes and losing herself in their deep gaze.

'Yes, Elise,' he said, softly and smiling, 'I might.'

He tilted her head and kissed her gently on the forehead. It was a small gesture, but one Elise always found deeply moving. She looked into his eyes and smiled; his eyes said everything she needed to know about him.

She reached up to kiss his cheek and gently whispered, 'I love you.'

He kissed her on her cheek and whispered, 'I love you too.'

Efisio entered the room and placed the flagon of wine on the table.

'Do you want anything to eat for supper? Before we go back to the cottage?' asked Maria.

'No, thank you, Maria,' said Beppe. 'If we do, we can help ourselves.'

Later, Elise crossed the yard to Beppe's room. She felt refreshed after showering and changing. The door to the vinery was open, and she stood at the doorway, taking in the scene before her. Beppe was sitting at his desk; the metal-shaded lamp cast a pool of light on the paperwork, his arms and part of his face. His hair, still wet from his shower, glistened in the light, and Elise was reminded of a Rembrandt painting. She took in the rows of books along the wall and became aware of the music. He was again playing the *Rachmaninov piano concerto,* and the arm of the record player was pulled up so that it would repeatedly play the record. She entered slowly and gently rested her hand on his shoulder. He rose and gathered her in his arms in one continuous movement.

She put her arms around his neck and felt him hold her tight as he backed into the door to close it behind them. He carried her across the room and gently laid her on the freshly made bed. She looked into his wonderful, dark eyes and thrilled at his touch. He undressed her slowly, savouring the touch of her closeness to him. He made love to her, and she was happy to surrender to him completely. It was not the violent, all-consuming lust of the afternoon by the river, but a gentle, seeking love, with the need to know one another, body and soul. Later, a tender and complete fulfilment finally washed over them, and they fell asleep in each other's arms.

It was Beppe, who awoke with a start. He looked at his watch. Two o'clock in the morning. Elise was asleep beside him and he was starving. He watched as she lay in the bed where they had shared their love; she was lovely and his heart went out to her. He loved her so much. He sighed and then grabbed one of the kikoi by the bed, which Elise had given him to wear instead of a dressing gown and wound it round his body and, turning off the record player, he slipped out of the room to raid the fridge in the main house.

He returned to the vinery carrying the tray of food.

'Wake up, sleepy head,' he said, kissing her forehead. 'I've brought us something to eat. I'm starving, how about you?'

Elise stirred, sat up and covered herself in the cotton wrap he had passed to her. 'What is the time?'

'Early.'

He laid the tray on the bed. There was a selection of bread, olives, cold meats and cheese, a bottle of wine and one of water, with glasses and napkins.

'What a feast,' she said, smiling and looking into his eyes.

They sat together, propped up by large pillows, and helped themselves.

'Tell me about yourself. I want to know everything about you,' said Elise. 'Tell me about your time in the army on the continent.'

Beppe smiled as he thought back to those carefree days. He remembered how lucky he had been.

'I arrived late, and at the same time as four others from all over Italy. They were all from well-to-do backgrounds. After staying in the barracks for the first three months, they had rented a large flat in the neighbourhood and asked me to stay with them. It was a turning point in my life.'

He sighed. 'Gianni was tall and dark, and came from Milan. He was studying music. His main instrument was the violin, but he played the piano too. He introduced me to all the romantic works; hence, the *Rachmaninov*. The flat was always filled with music and an endless stream of adoring women.

'Then there was Stephano: short, stocky, from Naples and a wonderful painter. He was studying art and architecture. He was always pointing out the finer details in the buildings and having loud discussions with all of us on the merits of various paintings. And then there was Gabriele, dark, brooding and Byronic, who was studying European literature. I learnt my love of poetry from him.

'And finally, there was Matteo.' He paused and, sighing again, pulled Elise into the crook of his arm, gently kissing her hair. 'Matteo,' he said, 'he was the most talented of them all. He played the piano like a dream. He could draw and loved all literature. He was forever reading and listening to music; he spoke French, Latin and Greek. Opera was his great love, and when we were on leave, he took me to Verona to see *Madame Butterfly:* needless to say, I was totally overcome by the experience. He opened my eyes to another world.

'He was also a very keen sportsman. He came from a very wealthy family in Venice. Everyone loved him, and he was always there for us if we needed him. He never despised my lack of knowledge, and encouraged me to look at, love and listen to everything. We became very close friends.'

'Are you still in touch with him?'

'No. He died of a brain tumour during his second year in the army. His family was devastated. He was their only son. When my father died, and I came back here, Matteo's father tried to persuade my family to let me go back to Venice with him; he said he wanted to put me through university. But there was no way that was going to happen. In the end, he took their daughter and went to live in America. The last I heard they were in Canada.'

He looked at Elise as she took his hand.

'How very sad, and what about the others?'

'At the time of Matteo's death, the others had finished their national service. We all went our separate ways. It was a wonderful time, and I am truly grateful for the experience, but it was over and any dreams of becoming an archaeologist were finished. My father's death meant that my mother needed me, and I was determined that Claudio should stay on at school, at least until he was sixteen, and maybe more if I could manage it. It worked out too; he has just finished college and qualified as an accountant, so all is well. He is also an extremely talented carpenter.'

'But he still works in the garden?'

'Yes. He will never give that up. He loves it,' Beppe confirmed. 'Elise, the one thing I miss, more than anything, is being able to talk about music, books or art. People in the villages haven't time for anything like that, because many are still unable to read and write. So you are like a breath of fresh air.'

'Didn't any of your other friends go abroad for their national service?'

'No, they all did their service at Macomer or Teulada. Only Paulo Canno, but he went to live on the continent; and now Gino Garcia has gone to study medicine in Milan. It was just luck that I went to the continent. People here find it difficult to understand how I feel. But, I think you do.'

He put the tray on the chest of drawers and climbed back into bed. Drawing Elise toward him, he gently nibbled the back of her neck.

'What are you thinking, darling?' Beppe murmured in her ear.

'Just how lovely your body feels so close to mine,' she said, putting her arms around him. 'Tell me Beppe when did you know you loved me?'

He looked at her and a broad grin spread across his face.

'When you sat in the back of the boat dripping wet and wrapped in my old sweater.'

Elise smiled.

'And you?' asked Beppe.

'When you stood before me trying to explain what a typical English woman was.'

They laughed and he pulled her closer, settling her head in the hollow of his shoulder. It felt wonderful having her so close. Her perfume filled his senses, and he felt at peace with the world.

'Maria wants some things from Cagliari tomorrow and Efisio has to go to Pula, so I said I would go. Will you come with me? I'll show you the market.'

'What day is it tomorrow? I've lost all track of time.'

'It will be Wednesday.'

'I'd like to do some shopping too. Will you take me shopping in the centre of Cagliari?'

'Of course, what do you want to buy?'

'I don't know yet,' she laughed. 'I'd like to window shop and see what takes my fancy, but I do want to go to a record shop.'

'Alright, but we will have to leave early,' he teased.

'Goodnight, darling,' she said, and turned away from him.

He cuddled up to her again and gently kissed the nape of her neck. Their love-making was more confident, more passionate, as they became in tune with one another. Finally, sleep overcame them both as they lay in each other's arms.

CHAPTER EIGHTEEN

The market at San Benedetto was a large, redbrick building which stood in a huge square, dominating the area. Cars parked all round the square, using up every inch of space, and small stalls stood close together, laden with all manner of goods for sale.

'The building is on two floors,' said Beppe. 'Upstairs is the meat, vegetables and cheese market, while all the fish is downstairs.'

Elise glimpsed the meat market. A cut of every joint of every animal lay on bunches of rosemary and myrtle. It all smelled so clean. As they descended the stairway, the noise from the men calling about their wares hit her unexpectedly. It echoed around the tiled walls, which were decorated with coloured pictures depicting every imaginable kind of fish. In the market, buyers wandered from counter to counter, looking over the different varieties or examining the quality. She was aware that the usual smell of the fish markets at home was not here; instead it smelled salty, like the sea.

'What does Maria want?' asked Elise.

'A good selection of fish for frying.'

She followed him around the numerous counters, watching him as he bargained over the prices. Baskets of crabs stood side by side, and some of the more lively occupants clambered their way over the edge and scuttled sideways across the tiled floor, chased by young boys who had their work cut out to catch them. Squid squirmed their way round glass enclosures, eels slithered in other containers and fish flapped against the marble slabs when prodded by shoppers searching for the freshest buy. There were fish of every colour, from dark-silver through to pink and red, and every size from large tuna, down to small silver whitebait; some laid out in neat rows, others piled on top of each other.

Solitary widows in black argued over the prices, along with young wives surrounded by their black-haired, brown-skinned broods. Beppe went to buy the fish and Elise wandered along the counters; she stood out from the other women with her golden-brown skin and sun-bleached hair.

'*Que bella!*' said one of the men, leaning admiringly across the counter – but Beppe was soon at her side, glaring, before Elise realised what had happened.

'Are you coming shopping?' he demanded, steering her away from the counter.

'Now, darling,' she teased, 'he only paid me a nice compliment.'

'He should keep his mind on his fish!' Beppe retorted, pretending to scowl.

He took the fish he had bought, which was wrapped in a plastic bag with smashed ice and layers of newspaper, and steered her upstairs to the street.

Outside the market an old woman sat at her stall under a huge umbrella, selling fresh herbs to go with the meat or fish. Her face was wrinkled and her small, dark eyes were soft and kind. She offered Elise a bunch of basil, rosemary and thyme, indicating the price with her fingers, and beamed a toothless smile. Elise gave her the money and took the bunch of herbs.

'You've paid too much,' declared Beppe.

'Maybe, but don't they smell lovely? I'm sure Maria can find a use for them.'

'I'll put the fish in the car, and then we can walk around for a while. Here – give me the herbs as well,' he added.

Hand in hand, they strolled along the sun-soaked streets, Elise pausing every so often to point out something she liked or to ask Beppe about some building or statue. Soon, they found themselves at the busy junction of the Piazza Costitutzione. Two sets of steps climbed to San Remy; roads led off in all directions, and one, the Via Mazzini, climbed in a meandering fashion towards the old part of the city.

There was an old herbalist shop on the right with its carved shutters and large heavy wooden doors. The iron balcony above the shop sign was filled with a riot of colour from the cascading flowers. Further on expensive shops filled with fine Italian shoes stood next to exclusive-looking dress shops; obviously, this was the Bond Street of Cagliari.

Between some of the buildings small stairways led up to the streets above, whilst on the other side little roads ran down towards the port. A large, grey dome of the church stood above the roofs on the left. The great doors to the church were dominated by the huge portico where there was a little statue of Sant'Antonio Abate.

Next to the church, Elise noticed a shop full of beautiful hand worked table linen and handkerchiefs. While on the other side was a small jewellery shop and then the road fell down towards Piazza Yennes.

'Ciao, Beppe,' said a young man, taking Beppe's arm.

The two stood and talked together *in Sardu* while Elise sauntered on to the next shop and stood staring in the window. Inside, religious articles of every kind filled the window. On glass shelves were the Sardinian gold and silver buttons, from big ones which dangled from the sleeves down to the small ones for the cuffs and buttons for the shirts. Rings and other traditional jewellery were also displayed in the window. On one shelf was a beautiful green velvet lined box in which lay a most unusual crucifix made of a dark-pink coral decorated with gold filigree work.

Elise pushed open the shop door, wrinkling her nose at the musty smell that met her which reminded her of old bookshops in England. The shelves were lined with religious statues of every conceivable saint, along with crosses, crucifixes and figurines of the Madonna and Child. Hundreds of rosaries, in assorted beads and metals, hung from long, wooden pegs fixed to the walls.

'Can I help you, signora?' enquired the plump, round-faced man who emerged from behind a bead-draped doorway.

'The crucifix in the window; how much is it, please?'

'It is expensive, signora – fifty thousand lira – but it is exquisite. It is very old. You won't find another like it in the whole of Sardinia. It is an antique, you understand,' he added, reaching for the cross.

Elise peered out of the window; Beppe was still chatting with his friend and hadn't noticed where she had gone. She took the crucifix from the man and examined it carefully.

'It certainly is beautiful,' she said. 'I'll take it, but I want a strong, gold chain to go with it and I want the cross engraved while I wait.'

'What kind of chain do you want, signora?' asked the man,

bringing out a selection for her to look at. She chose one with a heavy link to take the weight of the crucifix. The old man weighed the chain, and they bargained for a few minutes over the price until, finally, Elise gave him a handful of notes.

'I'll give you half now and the other half when I collect it on my way back, in about an hour,' she said.

'Very well, signora. Now, what do you want engraved on it?'

'Just the letters E, G and O. One letter at each point of the cross on the flat piece at the gold tip of the cross.' She said and chose the design for the lettering.

'Certainly, signora. I'll have it ready. I will engrave it myself.'

'Thank you.'

At that moment, Beppe came into the shop.

'What are you buying?' he asked.

'Just a little something. It needs altering. The signore is going to do it, and I'll collect it later,' she told him as Beppe opened the door for her.

'Who was that you were talking to outside?' she asked when they emerged into the sunny, bustling street.

'He is a friend of Claudio's. They are having a small festa on Saturday night. All our families will be there, and he has asked me to bring you so that they can all meet you.'

'It sounds fun. I'd love to go. If that's alright with you?' she added.

'Of course, silly!'

They wandered on down the narrow street of the Via Manno, which suddenly opened out on to the Piazza Yennes at the top of the Largo Carlo Felice. Towering above them was the ancient, Pisan tower, while below them, at the bottom of the tree-lined street, lay the Via Roma, running parallel with the wide, blue harbour.

'I know where I am now,' exclaimed Elise. 'This is where we saw the candle light procession, and we drove up here to park near the museum.'

Beppe nodded and took her hand. Dodging the traffic, they crossed to the island in the centre where three twisted trees gave shade to a green, wooden kiosk that sold newspapers and magazines. A number of people were resting there from the heat of the midday sun.

Passing the large statue of Carlo Felice, they darted across to the other side of the road. Beppe led Elise into a big bookshop called *Libreria Cocco*. A tall, rather distinguished looking man stepped forward.

'Can I help you, signore?'

'Yes. I would like a well-illustrated book on Sardinia,' said Beppe.

'Follow me, please,' said the man, leading them to a tall set of shelves in the corner.

'You will find all the books on Sardinia here, signore.'

They spent a long time browsing through the numerous books; then Beppe, looking up, said, '*Sardegna Quasi une Continente*, this is the one. It is all in Italian, all the illustrations are good and there's lots of information about the whole island. You will love it.'

'It certainly is a beautiful book,' she agreed, looking over his shoulder.

'The author lives here, in Cagliari, and is very well known and loved throughout the island,' said Beppe, taking the book to the counter where he paid for it.

'Here you are, darling,' he said, handing it to Elise. 'You'll be able to look up everything now. I expect you to be an expert on Sardinia.' He smiled. 'It even has a picture of the mask in the museum that you said reminds you of me.'

She laughed.

'Oh, Beppe, thank you!' she said reaching up, she kissed his cheek. He hadn't shaved that morning and the touch of his skin sent a thrill through her. 'You didn't shave.'

'My pleasure, signora,' he said and, smiling, added, 'And no, because I thought you liked me unshaven. Now – have you finished your shopping? The shops will be closing soon for the siesta. Give me the book to carry.'

Elise blushed under his dark stare and laughed.

'I must find the record shop, please.'

Beppe took her to a large shop that seemed to stock all the records ever made. He wandered around and bought a copy of *Desperado Logudorese*. Elise found and bought the one she wanted and joined him at the shop door. They made their way up the Via Manno again until they reached the jeweller's shop.

'Wait here,' she said. 'I won't be a moment!' And releasing her hand from his, she went inside, where the proprietor recognised her at once.

'Ah, signora – I have the crucifix.' he beamed, showing her the engraving.

Elise nodded in approval and thanked the man for his trouble. Then she reached into her shoulder bag for the remainder of the money she owed him while the man put the crucifix into its original green, velvet-lined box and placed it in a small cream carrier bag and tied it with ribbon.

'Thank you again, signore,' she said, taking the bag and putting it in her handbag and at the same time handing over the money.

'Thank you, signora. It has been a pleasure doing business with you. I hope I shall see you again.'

He came forward, opened the door for her with a flourish and bowed her out of the shop.

'My goodness!' exclaimed Beppe. 'Such attention! Have you bought the place?'

'No, of course not,' she retorted, but refused to say any more.

On returning from Cagliari, and having unpacked, Elise suggested going for a swim. The sea proved delightfully refreshing after the heat of the town and later, she showered and washed her hair, and joined Beppe in the sitting room. They were alone as the rest of the family had retired early after their supper.

Beppe sat on the floor beside the smoldering fire, leaning his back against the cushions from the sofa. He felt content and at peace with himself.

'Come and sit beside me,' he said, holding his hand out to Elise. She obeyed and he put his arm around her, drawing her closer to him.

'More wine?' he asked.

She held her glass out, and he filled it for her.

'Do you realise, Elise, you've only been with us for a month, and yet I feel I've known you all my life. Fate brought us together and for that I shall be eternally grateful.'

He buried his face in her hair. 'You smell lovely, what perfume are you wearing. It's wonderful?'

'*Shalimar*.' She said smiling and snuggling closer to him.

'Saturday,' he said, 'when we go to Santa Cella for the festa, you will probably meet my mother.'

'Does she know about me?' Elise asked apprehensively.

'Of course she does!'

'But does she… does she know I'm married? Isn't that going to be a problem for you?' she hesitated.

'Some kind soul has told her.'

'Won't she mind? After all, it's not exactly the situation she would choose for you, is it?'

'I know that, Elise. I faced that from the first time I knew how I felt about you,' he said gravely. 'Efisio and Maria turn a blind eye because they are not such devout Catholics as my family. Worst of all, you are Church of England. A heathen and a non-believer; a heretic even,' he said, smiling at her.

'What about your brother? How does he feel?'

'Well,' sighed Beppe, 'he is in love with Margherita, so he has his own problems. Mamma does not accept Margherita as completely as she might, because she is not as devout as Mamma would like her to be.'

'My God, Beppe. If she won't accept Margherita, what chance is there for me, for pity's sake? Tell me, could it be that… that your mother is jealous of Margherita?' ventured Elise. Then, adding as an afterthought, 'Or perhaps of anyone who might take her sons away from her?'

'I don't think she's jealous,' Beppe replied slowly, 'but I think she may be afraid of being lonely.'

'Aren't we all?' Elise paused, and then added in a low voice, 'Perhaps it would be better if you went to the festa on your own, and I'll stay here?'

'You'll do no such thing, darling. I want to take you. I want people to meet you. I don't care what they say. I have my own life to lead.'

'Brave words now, my love, but what about when I've gone away, back to England?'

'You'll come back to me, Elise. I know you will. It is just a matter of time, we will have to be patient, but I know you will come back, and we can be as one forever.'

She placed her fingers against his lips.

'Don't say that, Beppe. I'm not free to come back to you, and even if I did, what sort of life would it be for you? You would be cut-off from all your family and friends. How would you do business with people if they didn't accept you?'

'I don't care, Elise, if I have to wait all my life. Because whatever life is like with you, it would be a living hell without you! I love you.'

He pulled her to him and kissed her, making her lips part under the searching pressure of his tongue. She felt his hand as he slowly undid her blouse and kissed her breasts.

'So smooth – so soft,' he murmured, putting his lips to her silky skin. He was aware of his passion and desire rising for her, as he tenderly kissed her fading bruises, and she heard him sigh deeply.

She ran her fingers down his shirt, undoing the buttons. His skin was brown and hair lay black and flat upon his chest. Looking into his dark, luminous eyes, she whispered,

'Beppe… darling. I want to say I love you, but it doesn't tell you how I really feel about you. I do love you, but it's more than love. It's a completeness I've never known before.'

'We call it a union of souls, a joining of spirits,' he said softly. 'They have become as one. I am yours and you are mine, joined forever in a spiritual union; one soul living in two bodies, as Shelly said *'When soul meets soul on lover's lips.'* Promise me, Elise, there will never be anyone else for you. I know you're married and you belong to William, but your soul belongs to me now, just as mine belongs to you, whatever happens. Promise me, Elise. Promise.'

'I promise, Beppe. I promise that no one else will ever own my soul. I swear it.'

It was a solemn moment of declaration as they searched each other's faces intently, then Beppe took a small box from his pocket.

'I want you to have this, Elise,' he said, opening the box and taking out a ring. 'It's a Sardinian wedding ring, and it belonged to my grandmother.' He handed her the gold ring which was delicately engraved with a heart encircled by flowers and mystic-looking signs. There were three rings in one which when opened revealed a small heart inside. 'You don't wear your wedding ring, so perhaps you will wear this for me.'

'Beppe – I can't take it,' she said softly, giving it back to him. 'Not if it belonged to your grandmother. It belongs in your family.'

'Don't you like it?' he asked, looking anxious.

'I love it. I think it's beautiful. But I can't accept it.'

'Elise, there is little enough I can give you. Please take it and wear it always to remind you of your promise to me, and the love I have for you.' Taking her left hand, he slipped the ring on to her third finger, adding in a low voice, 'If we can't be bound together in the flesh, at least our souls are united.'

'Oh, Beppe, please hold me. I love you so much.'

They made love with passion and tenderness, later he carried her over to his room and laid her gently on his bed. She kissed him and, sliding from his grasp, went to fetch her shoulder bag from which she took the present and the record she had purchased that morning. Beppe was already in bed, and she sat beside him.

'First, I have this record. Will you play it? It's one of my favourite pieces, and I see you haven't got it. It was my father's favourite piece as well. I remember him playing it in his study. I have never shared it with anyone before, because it is so very special to me, but I want to share it with you.'

He did as she asked, and they sat quietly listening to the sound of Jasha Heifetz playing *Bruch's violin concerto*.

Then handing the little cream bag to Beppe, Elise said,

'I have something for you, too. I was going to give it to you tomorrow, but it must be early morning already. Anyway, please take it with all my love.'

Beppe took the bag, undid the ribbon and took out the green box and opened it slowly. His fingers trembled as he took out the antique crucifix. He felt his heart drumming against his chest as he fingered the beautiful cross.

'Is this what you bought this morning, in Cagliari?'

'Yes – and I had it engraved, as well. See – on the three points of the cross?'

He turned it over.

'E, G, O,' he read aloud. 'Ego. That means one in Latin.'

'Yes – I know – and as you have already said, we are one. It's made up from E for Elise, G for Giuseppe, and O, which, as you know, in Latin, is an expression of both joy and sorrow. I'm sure we shall have our share of both!'

He stroked the coral crucifix, and when he spoke there was a break in his voice.

'I don't know what to say, dearest Elise. Thank you. It's beautiful. I'll always wear it as an everlasting token of your love and our vow. You will only have it back when I die...'

'Hush – don't say such things,' She begged. 'Here, let me put it on for you. Beppe, you've not only captured my heart, but you've stolen my soul. You know George Elliot put it into words: *"What greater thing is there for two human souls than to feel that they are joined to strengthen each other, to be at one with each other in silent unspeakable memories?"'*

Beppe put his hand out to her and she bent to kiss him, and then slid into bed beside him.

The coral cross with its gold crucifix and heavy, gold chain looked splendid resting on his hairy, brown chest, and later she felt it pressing against her breast as he tenderly made love to her while the music washed over them.

Elise fell asleep in the crook of his arm, but Beppe lay awake, thinking about their time together. How it had flown by, with such long, happy days of being together. In the mornings, they worked in the vineyard, and after lunch they swam or, if the others were at home, they went water-skiing. Elise had improved greatly since her first pull and was now progressing well on the mono; although she still came out of the water on one ski and slipped her trailing foot into the binding once she was up. She had begged him to teach her to start from the beach, but had taken so many tumbles trying that even she had given up, putting it down to the lack of strength in her arms to pull her out. He smiled to himself and pulled Elise closer, kissing her gently.

He thought of the cool evenings when they sat on the terrace listening to classical music, reciting poetry, sharing the poems or books they loved and knew by heart, or strolling together along the beach. He thought of Matteo, of how he had taught him to love all the things that Elise loved. He thought of Maria and Efisio who had both turned a blind eye to the fact that there were nights when Elise didn't sleep in her room, or he in his. These were balmy nights spent in love making which brought them closer together.

He felt it was a gift that someone as wonderful as Elise loved him and that he could share his love of music and literature with her, but most of all, her love. He put his arms around her and nestled into the softness of her sweet-smelling hair and silently thanked God for all his blessings.

CHAPTER NINETEEN

Darkness had fallen when Beppe and Elise arrived at the house where the festa was being held. Beppe, parking in the narrow street, pointed and said.

'My home is just along the road there. I'll take you to see it later, and show you where I was born.'

She squeezed his hand.

'I should like that.'

They had walked a few yards when Beppe paused beside a huge pair of closed wooden doors; he unlatched a small door which was let into the big one and stood back to allow Elise through. They blinked in the sudden brightness of the lights that were placed all-round the large courtyard. Outhouses led off on one side of the courtyard, running back to the wall dividing it from the street in which was set the door through which they had come.

In a far corner, in a gap between the outhouses and the wing of the L-shaped house, a charcoal pit glowed, throwing out a great deal of heat. There were stakes on either side of the pit on which were impaled small suckling pigs, slowly roasting. The house had a wide veranda running along its full length under which was set a long table spread with white cloths and place settings for a great number of people. Many guests had already arrived and there was a friendly hum of conversation; in addition, someone, somewhere, was playing a guitar and singing.

'That's Ignazio, isn't it?' said Elise, pointing in the direction of the house.

'Yes, with Claudio and Margherita.'

They went to join them, and after greetings were exchanged Margherita turned to Elise and said eagerly, 'I'm so glad you came; I know you'll enjoy it. There will be dancing and poetry reading, and the village dancers are here, too. You know, I can't believe what you have done for Beppe; you have changed him completely. He is so happy now he is with you.'

Elise smiled and took Margherita's hand and squeezed it.

A young man came forward carrying a couple of glasses and a flagon of wine. He filled the glasses and smiled at Elise.

'You remember Luigi, don't you?' said Beppe.

'Yes,' said Elise, returning the smile, 'we met at the *Sagra di Sant' Efisio*.' She raised her glass to both of them, '*Salude!*'

'*Salude!*' they chorused.

Beppe turned to Claudio.

'You've done a wonderful job, brother. Tell me, how many people are coming?'

'I think nearly everyone is here now. Perhaps some will come later after the meal when the dancing starts; there should be about fifty or so.'

'Is Mamma here?'

'No. Not yet. She said she wanted to see father Guido about something, and would be along later.'

Suddenly, there was a blast from an accordion and a bell rang. A man dressed in local costume stood on a chair and made a brief announcement *in Sardu*.

'What is he saying?' asked Elise.

'He says he hopes we all have a good time, and that we should take our places at the table.'

Margherita called to Beppe and beckoned him to join her. He put his arm around Elise and led her to where all the people she knew were sitting. The babble of voices was deafening, but then it suddenly died away as the sound of wailing music took over. A man in traditional dress playing the *Launaddas* walked around the table, followed by another, similarly attired and carrying a large, carved wooden platter on which were piled the *anguilli*.

After a quick tour of the courtyard, the platter was placed before the women, who cut up the eels and served them to everyone at the table while young girls in traditional dress carried around the wine and the bread. This procedure was to be carried out for each course, with only slight variations. As the meal progressed, the babble became more subdued as people nodded to one another, enjoying the eating rather than talking. Finally, the suckling pigs came, lying on a bed of myrtle leaves. Beppe helped Elise to some and then himself. Everyone was concerned for his or her neighbour, making sure that they had everything they wanted.

'This is delicious,' said Elise, pulling the succulent meat apart with her fingers and eating it in the same way as everyone else.

'Look, Elise,' said Margherita, 'the dancers are here.'

A large, jolly-faced man began to play the accordion, while others, four men and four women, danced. The women looked graceful in their delicate costumes, the men proud and handsome in theirs. When the dance was over, there was tumultuous applause and much calling for more; several of the guests joined in the words as they followed the song, or conducted with sticky fingers which they licked noisily from time to time, obviously enjoying every moment.

As the fruit came piled high in bowls, Beppe said, 'these are our peaches; you must try one,' as he held one out to her.

He squeezed her fingers gently as she took it. She bit into the fruit, which was sweet and juicy, an early variety with an extremely delicate flavour.

'Mmm, this is wonderful, Beppe.'

'I'm glad you like it.' He looked at her with a proud expression.

'*Tra la la lerra*,' called a voice from the far end of the table.

The man with the accordion nodded and smiled, then struck up the tuneful song, signalling to everyone to join in. Elise found herself tapping out the beat, and although she couldn't understand a word, the song made her so happy that she laughed along with the rest of them at the comical faces pulled by the singers.

Shouts of approval went up when the singing came to an end. Then, there was more dancing as couples left the table to join in.

'Don't you want to dance, Beppe? There are a number of girls free,' said Elise as Claudio took Margherita onto the floor.

'No, I don't. I'm quite happy sitting here with you. Anyway, I've eaten too much to go jigging about like that,' he added, laughing.

At last, the dancers took a rest, and people stood talking in the centre of the courtyard; everyone, it seemed, knew everyone else, and again Elise became aware of the feeling of loneliness she had experienced at Barumini. She tried not to mind as she noticed that the older people avoided her gaze and stood huddled together, obviously talking about her because they kept casting glances at her. Beppe reached across to take her hand.

'Are you ready for a short walk, darling? No one will miss us for a while. I want to show you where I lived and spent my childhood.'

'Won't your mother mind?'

'Why should she? Are you alright, Elise?'

'Yes, of course.'

'You seem very quiet.'

He took her hand and gently led her to the door.

The street outside appeared darker after the brightly lit courtyard, and it was difficult to see the potholes and loose stones in the unmade road. After a short walk, stumbling along near a high wall, Beppe stopped and pushed against a small door, similar to the one at the house where the festa was being held. The walls of the houses and courtyard were made of white-washed, dried mud and straw, and reminded Elise of the cob cottages in England. The courtyard inside was dimly lit. A well stood at one side of the L-shaped house, which loomed dark against the deep, blue-black night sky.

'One day I shall build a house here for the family, like the people two doors along,' said Beppe. 'I shall demolish this and build a two-storey house with storage underneath. You can see the house silhouetted against the sky over there,' he added, pointing to the stark, square outline of the new concrete building; then, leading the way into his own house under a small veranda, he pushed open the door.

'Mamma,' he called, and then said something *in Sardu* before switching on the light as he beckoned Elise to come in.

She found herself in a surprisingly spacious room, which served as both sitting and dining room. The walls were white-washed and the furniture, though sparse, was traditional. On the floor, was a beautifully hand-woven carpet which covered a large part of the tiled area.

'This is magnificent!' exclaimed Elise, pointing to the carpet.

'It came from Isilli. My mother's cousin lives and works there, making carpets. She gave that one to Mamma and Babbu for a wedding present. It took her over a year to make it.'

He showed her around the small, single-storey house.

'Claudio and I used to sleep together in this room, but he has it to himself now that I'm away.'

He opened the door next to it quietly. 'And this is where Mamma sleeps.'

The room was dominated by an enormous, carved, wooden bed over which was thrown a geometrically-patterned, hand-woven cover. Above the bed was a large crucifix surrounded by pictures of saints. On a small chest beside the bed lay a Bible, a hymnal and a rosary. A chair stood in the corner with a few clothes on it; apart from that, the room was bare.

'It's like a nun's cell,' remarked Elise without thinking.

'I know. Ever since Babbu died, Mamma has lived like a recluse. She will never change now. The Church completely dominates her life. She is just waiting until she can join him again.'

'Perhaps her faith helps her to face the loneliness.'

'*Boh*. Her life has revolved round this room,' went on Beppe softly. 'Babbu brought her here when they were married. He first made love to her in that bed, and I was born there; so were Claudio and Fran. Babbu died in it, and I expect she will, too.'

He sighed, closed the door behind them and took her back to the living room. There he stopped and kissed her, long and tenderly.

'I love you,' he said, folding her in his arms.

'Is that you Claudio?' called a voice from the doorway.

'No, Mamma. It's me, Beppe.'

A cold shiver ran down Elise's back as the small, black-clad figure advanced and stood looking at them with unmistakable hostility. She felt Beppe stiffen beside her.

'Mamma, this is Elise,' said Beppe, stepping forward to kiss his mother on the cheek. She checked him, saying something sharply to him *in Sardu*. Elise felt his grip tighten on her hand.

Beppe must have inherited his father's eyes, for the widow's were small and mean and flashed venomously as she spoke. Elise couldn't understand a word she said, but her meaning was crystal clear.

Having lashed Beppe with her tongue, she turned on Elise, and, in perfect Italian, hissed, 'How dare you come into my house? You, who are leading my son into mortal sin, for which he has said he will never repent!' She took a step nearer Elise.

'And you needn't think that the fancy crucifix you have given him will save his soul from eternal damnation, because it won't.' Raising her arm, she pointed a finger menacingly at Elise.

'You are married; if you must commit adultery, find someone else. People are talking about my son! Find one of your own kind and leave my son alone, you… whore… you… Jezebel! May you burn in hell!' She spat the words out.

Without a word, Beppe put his arm around Elise and led her out of the house. The widow was still screaming abuse at them in both *Sardu* and Italian when they reached the street.

Beppe closed the doors behind him. Elise buried her face in her hands and burst into tears.

'Don't cry, darling. She can't hurt you now,' Beppe soothed, drawing her close.

'It's not me I'm worried about, Beppe,' she sobbed, 'it's you… and her…'

'I live a long way away from her. She'll get over it, given time.'

'She won't and you know it. Oh, Beppe, please go back and make your peace with her,' pleaded Elise.

'No,' said Beppe firmly. 'She couldn't even observe the rule of hospitality. I'm not going back. Besides, how can I make peace with her? I'm not sorry for what has happened.'

'Oh my God, Beppe – what have I done to you? Please go back!'

'Elise, listen,' he said, raising her chin with his finger to look into her eyes. 'You have given me untold happiness and a purpose for living. You said yourself that if we share the pleasure, we must share the pain. I love you, darling, and no one, but no one, can take that away from us.'

'And I love you, Beppe – so much,' she sniffed.

Taking his handkerchief from his pocket, he carefully dried her eyes and wet cheeks.

'Come on,' he said. 'I think we'd better go back to the villa. I'll just have a word with Claudio and then say goodbye to the others.'

Back in the courtyard, the dancing was once more in full swing.

'Can I have a drink, Beppe, before we go?' she asked, shakily.

'Yes, I could do with one too,' he agreed.

They helped themselves to wine and stood watching the dancing.

It ended to rousing applause, and someone announced the next item.

Beppe bent towards Elise, and translated what had been said.

'One of the women is going to sing a very lovely, but rather plaintive song, the *Desperado Logudorese* called '*Non Potho Reposare* '. It is the record I bought in Cagliari, but it is always better sung by people you know.'

A deep hush descended as the woman began to sing, accompanied by Ignazio, a slow, haunting melody, and although Elise couldn't understand all the words, but they seemed to sum up exactly how she felt. Beppe, glancing at her, slipped an arm around her waist. When it was over, there was a moment's silence before they all cheered their approval.

'Where have you two been?' demanded Claudio, tapping his brother on the shoulder.

'I took Elise to show her our house. Mamma was there, and she went for us like a tigress!'

'Bad move,' said Claudio, grimacing. 'She has taken it badly, Beppe. Everyone reports back to her what has happened.'

'How did she know about Elise's present to me, though? Elise only gave it to me the other night.'

'I'm afraid I told her,' Margherita confessed. 'I noticed you wearing it this morning and guessed that Elise must have given it to you. It's so beautiful. When I saw Claudio, I told him and your mother happened to overhear. I could have bitten my tongue out. I'm so sorry, Beppe, if I've caused trouble.'

'*Boh*. Don't worry about it. It's nothing,' Beppe shrugged.

'The trouble is, Beppe,' Claudio said anxiously, 'Mamma is taking it out on Margherita, because her mother is encouraging you and Elise at the villa!'

'Is this true, Margherita?' asked Beppe, turning to the young girl.

'Well – yes… but don't let it worry you,' the girl added. 'She'll come round in time.'

'She'll have to,' said Beppe grimly. 'I'm a grown man now. Anyway, I think I'll take Elise home. Say goodbye to the others for us, won't you?'

'Must you go?' said Claudio. 'After all, we haven't seen much of you, nor had a chance to get to know Elise.'

'Come down to the villa and see us,' replied Beppe curtly. 'I'm sure Margherita would welcome that.' He kissed Margherita on the cheek. 'Have a good time. We'll see you tomorrow.'

'We will be late. We're all staying up here tonight.'

'Who's doing the work at the villa?' asked Beppe.

'Mamma and Babbu said they could manage; after all, it is Sunday. I don't think they were expecting you back either,' replied Margherita.

'Well, we can give them a hand with the chores. You'd better go and see that Mamma is alright,' said Beppe, looking at his brother.

Back at the villa, Elise joined Beppe in his room for a drink.

'*Fil e Feru*?' he asked.

'Please,' she nodded.

She looked so doleful sitting on his bed that his heart went out to her. He sat down beside her and took her hand in his.

'Darling Elise, there is no going back now,' he said, looking into her hazel eyes. 'I don't care what people say or think about me as my conscience is quite clear. If you loved your husband as you love me, or if he loved you as I do, then no one in Christendom could drive a wedge between you. My Church says that my loving you is a mortal sin, and that I shall be punished in some way or other for breaking that law and wanting you. As God is my maker, it is He, and He alone, who shall decide my punishment!'

That night, while Beppe slept quietly beside her, Elise's thoughts trooped through her head. It was wonderful to slip between the sheets and find herself desirable, and to be able to share her love with a strong, virile lover; so different from the cold rejection she had grown to accept as normal from her husband. True, William was ten years older than her, and he, Beppe, the same age as herself. William had never wanted her unless he was drunk, but with Beppe, there was no humiliation, just honest love.

Elise sighed heavily and looked at him sleeping beside her. She went over what had happened that evening; tossing and turning her mind in turmoil. How would she be able to live among these people if they didn't accept her, and how would Beppe ever manage to earn a living dealing with the farmers if they couldn't accept the fact that he had married a divorced woman? Finally, towards dawn, she got out of bed, dressed quietly and went for a walk along the beach.

CHAPTER TWENTY

Beppe stirred, sighed and put out an arm to encircle Elise. Instead of her soft warmth, however, he encountered a cold, empty space. Instantly awake, he sat up. The bathroom door was ajar, but there was no reply when he called; then he noticed her clothes were gone from the chair where she had laid them last night.

Jumping out of bed, Beppe hurried into the bathroom, put his head under the tap and showered. He groped for a towel, rubbed his hair and face, threw the towel aside and returned to the bedroom. He dressed quickly, dragged a comb through his damp, black curls, and hurried to the villa. On the way there, he glanced at his watch to see it was already nine o'clock; he had overslept.

When he entered the kitchen, Maria was busy making coffee and Efisio was reading yesterday's newspaper.

'Hello, Beppe! What are you doing here?' said Efisio, looking up from his paper. 'We didn't expect you so soon.'

'We came back last night. Have you seen Elise?' replied Beppe.

'Yes. She's upstairs – but don't disturb her. She's gone to get some sleep as it seems that she didn't sleep too well last night,' said Maria.

'She was walking on the beach early this morning, so I went out to see her and brought her in. She'd been crying. She is very worried. Tell me, Beppe, what has happened?' asked Efisio, obviously concerned.

'Have you two quarrelled?' asked Maria anxiously. 'She wouldn't say much to us.'

'No, no,' said Beppe, 'it's nothing like that. It's not between us. I took her home last night and Mamma behaved like a crazy woman. She accused Elise of being an adulteress – and worse – and flung abuse at us both. You know how melodramatic she can be.'

Maria sighed.

'Well, Beppe – you knew what you were doing when you started this whole affair. Your mother has always been a very religious woman, and even more so since your father died,' said Maria as she put a cup of coffee in Beppe's hand. 'Here – drink this.'

'Thanks.' He sat down at the table and took it and sipped the hot liquid absentmindedly. 'I know what I'm doing, but I'm afraid Mamma will take it out on Claudio and Margherita.'

'It seems that Elise is worried about that too, Beppe…' cut in Efisio.

There was a pause, and then Maria said, with some hesitation, 'I know it is none of my business, but… what future does Elise offer you, Beppe? Have you given any thought as to what will happen when she leaves? Beppe, she is married. She's not free to come back to you. It's only another fling; let her go. You have the pick of so many women, why choose a married woman?'

'She is different.' said Beppe.

'They are always different, Beppe,' said Efisio. 'She will go back to England, and you won't hear from her again. Mark my words. Keep sleeping with her and get it out of your system.'

'Thanks, Efisio, I appreciate your concern; but this is something deeper than just a jump in bed.'

Efisio sighed heavily.

'You're going to be badly hurt, young man. Badly hurt.'

'I'm aware of that. But if she divorced her husband, we could, at least, live together.'

'Not in Sardinia you couldn't,' exclaimed Efisio. 'You'd be social outcasts, both of you. And you, Beppe, would be excommunicated. You must know that?'

'Yes, of course I accept all that too. But what I find so difficult is that I have no one to turn to. Mamma is set against anyone who I show any interest in, let alone Elise. Your hands are tied because, naturally, you don't want to spoil Margherita's chances of happiness, and neither do I; believe you me. The only person who would be completely unbiased is Gino, and he's away at medical school in Milan. So – it's something I have to work out for myself.'

He pushed his chair away from the table and stood up.

'Please don't worry, Maria, Efisio. Everything will turn out alright, you'll see,' he said, nodding reassuringly at Maria. He then turned to ask Efisio: 'Is there any work that needs to be done?'

'No, Beppe, there is nothing – for the others will be back later tonight. You and Elise can spend the time together. We can't offer you any help, or advise you in any way, but we can give you time: time to find out what you want to do and whether she really means as much to you as you think she does.'

Beppe patted him on the shoulder.

'Thank you both very much. I do appreciate your kindness, and I won't ever forget it. Efisio, don't you worry either. She is not, as you might think, the first woman I have slept with, but she is the first woman I have fallen in love with.'

Efisio looked up at Beppe with a somewhat surprised expression on his face and added, smiling,

'I knew you had been involved with the occasional female visitor to the villa, but I never thought I'd hear you admit it.'

'Something done on the spur of the moment is completely different from falling in love, Efisio,' Beppe said and he left the kitchen, closing the door quietly behind him.

'His love for Elise was doomed from the moment they first met,' sighed Maria, hurriedly wiping a telltale tear from her eye. 'I know he has raked about a bit, and what man wouldn't when it is thrown at him, but this time he will burn his fingers, Efisio, I know he will. You mark my words.'

'He's certainly going to be badly hurt, one way or another,' said Efisio gruffly. 'So we can only be here to pick up the pieces.'

Upstairs, Beppe let himself quietly into Elise's room. He noticed her clothes were thrown on her chair in a careless fashion. He looked at her lying naked between the sheets, her body golden brown against their sun-bleached whiteness. He sat on the side of the bed, leaned down and kissed her lightly on her cheek. As she stirred, he kissed her again.

Opening her eyes, which were still red from crying, she murmured drowsily,

'Hello darling.'

'What are you doing here?' Beppe asked softly.

'I couldn't sleep last night, so I went for a long walk on the beach.'

'But why didn't you wake me?'

'You were sleeping so peacefully... Anyway, I wanted time to think.'

'Too much of that can be a bad thing,' he said, looking into her eyes. 'My darling, you should not look back on the past, nothing can change it. You should enjoy the present, as we Sards do.' He kissed her again, and she felt the roughness of his unshaven face, making her feel too weak to resist him.

'What about the future?' she asked.

'Oh, we can solve that quite easily,' he said, with a wicked grin. 'There's no future tense *in Sardu*.'

'Now you're teasing me!'

'No, I'm not. We say that the past is finished and there is nothing that can change that. The present is now, and you live it to the full because tomorrow is in the hand of the Gods. You can ask Maria or Efisio, or anyone who speaks both *Sardu* and Italian.'

'That still doesn't eliminate our future,' she said, her smile fading. 'I am worried for you, Beppe. How will you work with these people if they don't speak to you? It's alright now because we are away from everyone here. You don't have to face the rejection of friends and family yet. But if we came together you would have all that to face. Do you understand what I am saying?'

Beppe sat for a few moments in thoughtful silence.

'Elise, will you come away with me for a few days?' he asked. 'We could go down to San Antioco and San Pietro. Nobody will know us there and we can spend some time together, alone, away from all the pressures of the family and the Church. Please say you will.'

'Beppe, have you heard a word I have been saying?'

'Do you love me, Elise?'

'Of course I love you, and it is for that reason that I am trying to look at things as they will be and not as we would wish them to be.'

'Then come away with me for a week so that we can have this time together, away from everything and everyone. Please, Elise?'

'What about Maria and Efisio? Won't they mind?'

'You are on holiday here. If you want to go, there's nothing to stop you.'

'And you?'

'I know they won't mind. Will you come – please?' And this time there was a pleading in his voice.

Elise hesitated.

'Alright, when do we go?'

'Today! This morning! We can find somewhere to stay in San Antioco tonight.' He kissed her again. 'Don't be long,' he said, springing to his feet. 'I'm going to put a change of clothes in a bag. Bring yours down and don't forget your swimming things.'

He ran down the stairs, two at a time, and burst into the kitchen, making Maria jump.

'We're going away for a few days, down to...'

'I don't want to know,' she interrupted, putting her hands over her ears, 'then nobody can wheedle it out of me,' she said, smiling.

'We'll be back by next weekend, Efisio, if that is alright with you?'

'Of course it is. You've earned a holiday – you haven't had one since you came here, and I've always said you drive yourself too hard.'

Elise appeared at the door.

'I thought you were going to get your bag ready!' she scolded lovingly.

'I am, I am, I'm going now! Bye, Maria – Efisio... and thanks.'

He took Elise's large shoulder bag from her and disappeared.

'I'll be with you in a minute,' Elise called after him. Then, turning to Maria, she said, 'I know you can't approve of all this, but there are no words to thank you enough for being so understanding. His mother's reaction has been more of a shock to him than he is willing to admit, but Beppe has been in touch with the outside world, away from Sardinia, and it is difficult for him to accept the kind of life his mother wants for him.'

'Elise,' said Maria, coming towards her and taking her hand, 'whether we approve or not is neither here nor there. All I can say is: *"Let him who is without sin cast the first stone."* None of us are perfect. We are all God's creatures, His children, and He has a way of forgiving even the worst offenders! Just be happy.'

'Beppe is going to need faith like that after I've gone home,' said Elise, her lips quivering. 'And God knows. I shall need all His strength to help me through the time to come.'

A car outside hooted.

'There now – Beppe's getting impatient,' said Maria briskly, her eyes shining with the tears she was fighting to hold back. 'Go, and take care of yourselves. And, Elise, be happy.'

Maria bent forward quickly and kissed the young girl's cheek. The kiss and the squeeze of her hand spoke volumes to Elise.

The car hooted again and Maria waved goodbye to them both as Elise ran out into the courtyard.

CHAPTER TWENTY ONE

'This is one of my favourite roads,' said Beppe, 'the scenery is beautifully wild and the sea down there, somehow adds an air of remoteness.'

They passed Chia and he thought back to that afternoon when they had gone there bathing, before the festival of Saint Efisio. It seemed like such a long time ago and so much had happened since then. The road wound its way through the scenic landscape and turned down towards a huge bay where a small stream meandered along the valley floor. Cattle roamed over the broad, brackish flats, their neck bells clanging with a doleful tone. From there, the road climbed sharply, doubling back on itself until, on reaching the top, it fell away again to the next long stretch in front of them.

Beppe stopped the car and the wind blew in warm gusts through the open window. Below them a spit of land stretched out into the blue sea which, in turn, melted into the hazy sky. Another of the Spanish towers was perched on the end of the point, still watching for possible intruders coming in from the sea.

'Malfatano,' he said. 'Imagine living out there, away from the rest of the world. Just the two of us living in that tower and sharing our life together.'

'Dreamer, you'd never grow peaches out there – it would be too cold,' she teased, and gave him a quick kiss.

They continued along the coastal road until they reached the large bay of Teulada. Here the cliffs were covered in a profusion of vegetation in greens, reds, brown and yellow, that clung tenuously to the windswept rock face. Below, the blue water was white tipped by the constantly breaking sea on the rocks and in the distance the cliff fell away to a long sandy beach.

They took the road towards Teulada itself, which ran through a fertile valley. There were carefully tendered vineyards and almond groves on both sides.

Tall reeds grew thick along the water's edge, choking the

meandering river in places and the wind that came from the sea whispered through them in its familiar, haunting way. Beppe knew this route well, but somehow it took on a new freshness as Elise pointed out the various landmarks or remarked on each scene that unfolded before them.

The road suddenly branched left on its way to Sant Anna and, finally, San Giovanni, where the landscape seemed flat and uninteresting.

'This is the causeway across to the island of San Antioco,' said Beppe. 'It was started by the Carthaginians and carried on by the Romans, and those two stones,' he added, pointing, 'are known as *Su Para et Sa Mongia.*'

'The monk and the nun,' remarked Elise. 'And who were they?'

'They were a monk and a nun in Holy Orders who were on the Island of San Antioco. They fell in love with one another, and they decided to run away to the mainland together, but halfway across the causeway the Divine wrath turned them into stone for their sin. They have stood there ever since, as a reminder to all those who sin.'

'What a lovely legend,' Elise said, but then, seeing the expression on Beppe's face, she said no more.

They stopped for lunch at a small restaurant in a tree-lined street in San Antioco. A friendly young man came forward to welcome them and showed them to a table.

'What would you like?' asked Beppe.

'Linguine with clams, I think,' she replied.

He ordered for both of them and the young man disappeared into the kitchen.

Beppe looked at Elise, took her hand in his, and squeezed it gently. 'Here, away from everyone, and with you wearing my ring, there is a good chance they will think we are man and wife,' he said, smiling.

While they were eating, a large woman came across to greet them and enquired if everything was to their satisfaction.

'Yes, very good indeed thank you,' answered Beppe.

'Are you staying here on the island?' she asked.

'We hope to stay one night here, and then travel on to Carloforte,' he replied. Then he added, 'We want to spend the night in Calasetta and then catch the ferry to San Pietro tomorrow. Do you know of anywhere we can stay?'

The woman beamed as she raised her open hands skyward.

'My sister-in-law lives in Calasetta. She has a small room. Nothing very fancy, you understand, but you could stay there. She will give you a good meal, and the bed will be clean. If you are not in a hurry, I can ask the boatman to arrange it?'

'That would be wonderful, thank you,' replied Beppe. 'We want to go up to the catacombs and we will call back later.'

'That's fine,' said the woman cordially. She smiled and waved as they settled their bill and left, and watched them as they walked, arm in arm, up the street to the Basilica.

The doors of the ancient church stood open and, tying her scarf over her head, Elise followed Beppe into the building.

The inside was dark and dank, lit here and there by the soft light of candles, making the air smell of tallow, incense and dampness. They walked towards the altar where Beppe bowed and crossed himself before escorting Elise to one side of the church. There, towering above them, stood a large statue of a dark-skinned Mauritanian dressed in heavy, purple-velvet robes edged with gold braid. There were flowers in his hair and around the edge of the alcove in which he stood, all delicately carved and painted. He had a beautifully carved bouquet of flowers in one hand, while in the other he carried a copy of the Bible.

'That is Saint Antioco,' said Beppe. 'He originally came from Africa. He was tortured by Adrian for his Christian faith – put into boiling pitch and finally flung into the sea. He was washed ashore at Sulcius, the ancient town here, where the people found and cared for him, nursing him back to health. He, in turn, converted them and became their bishop, and a highly venerated patron saint.'

'Is he buried here?' she asked.

'Yes. So is his mother; in the catacombs of Santa Rosa, which are named after her.'

Beppe led the way to a small doorway beside the statue where on a nearby ledge he found a large number of candles and matches. He lit two candles and handed one to Elise.

'You'll need this,' he said. 'Follow me closely, and watch out for the potholes in the ground.'

He led her through the doorway into a maze of catacombs and ancient burial places. The flickering candlelight caught the roughly cut stonework and emphasised the deep burial recesses.

'Some of these go back to Carthaginian times. There have been many finds here,' he said.

The air was cold and Elise shivered. It was an eerie place with an overlying claustrophobic closeness, so she was glad when they finished their tour and were back in the half-light of the damp church. Beppe blew out the candles and returned them to the ledge where he had found them, then followed Elise out into the bright afternoon sunshine. She slipped off her headscarf and returned it to her bag.

'Do you always carry a scarf in your purse?' he asked, fascinated.

'A trick I learnt in Florence, as you never know when you might come across a small church,' she said, smiling.

She looked around the small square in front of the church and its surrounding houses; on one the plaster had been newly painted, except for one area where the letters 'DDT 1955' were stamped. The greyness of the fading letters contrasted sharply with the glaring new paint.

'What are those for?' she asked, pointing to the markings.

'That shows that the house was sprayed with DDT in 1955. The Rockefeller Foundation sprayed all of the swamp areas. Before then, the island suffered from malaria; the spraying helped to kill the mosquitoes that carry the disease.' He paused and sighed. 'But it didn't save my sister, Francesca.'

'How old were you when she died?' she asked, slipping her arm through his.

'Fourteen, and Claudio was just six. Fran was only ten; I remember her so well. She was really beautiful.'

'Maria told me she believes your mother never really got over losing Fran.'

'She's probably right. But it was when Babbu died, eight years later, that she really changed.'

'In what way?' asked Elise as they sauntered along the road.

'She used to be such a fun-loving person. She was strict, but she enjoyed life to the full; she was always there when we needed her. When Fran died, she turned to the Church for courage and comfort, and then when Babbu died, the church seemed to take over completely; it dominated her life and suppressed her spirit. The local priest has been very good and helps her in many ways, but she has lost her love of life.'

'It must be terrible to lose a child. Even so, she has you boys to lean on for support, surely?'

'I know – but she thinks the Church can offer her more. It gives her the spiritual comfort that she craves so much, and holds the link with the dead. The priest told her to walk in the way of the Church and then she will be spared from further pain.'

'As a prop, yes – but she doesn't really believe she will never be hurt again, Beppe; surely she must know that it's not her fault that people die? It was no fault of hers!'

'She believes it was, and that's what is important. That's why she is so strict with us boys.'

'And you, Beppe? You can't believe that, surely?' she said, turning to look into his face, but his expression betrayed his thoughts.

'My God, Beppe. You do, I can see by your face that you do. You really believe that death is retribution for sin, don't you?' She paused, suddenly realising the full implication of what she had said. 'Then why in heaven's name did you make love to me, or tell me that you loved me?'

He put his arm around her and walked her to the hilltop overlooking the bay.

'I did it, Elise, because I love you. Your love is dearer to me than life itself. My happiness is with you, and that is very precious to me. In the eyes of the Church, it's a sin even to want you – but with you, I could face the Devil himself.' He turned to her and kissed her. 'Anyway, my faith is for me to worry about; it's between me and my Maker.'

Elise drew away and looked out to sea. She felt helpless and lost for words. The wind blew from the sea and lifted her hair from the nape of her neck; she felt his warm breath as Beppe bent forward and kissed her again.

'Darling, please,' he begged, 'don't let's talk about it any more. You must leave me to do the worrying, when and if the time comes.'

She looked up into his dark, limpid eyes.

'You will have to be strong for both of us,' she said, in a low voice, 'for I don't have your faith.'

He held her close, kissing her gently.

'For the next few days at least, we belong to each other. Let's not waste precious time thinking about the future. Now, let's go and find out if we have a bed for the night.'

Siesta was over by the time they returned to the restaurant. A large, weather-beaten man sat outside the door reading a newspaper, and he looked up as Beppe and Elise approached.

'Ah,' he said, putting down the paper, 'are you the two who are going to Calasetta?'

Beppe nodded.

'Come in, come in!' said the man, rising from his chair and beckoning them to follow him. 'My wife is inside,' he added.

He called to his wife and said something in a dialect that Elise didn't recognise. The plump woman came forward, her arms outstretched as if welcoming long-lost friends.

'I've had news from my sister-in-law. She has a room – and I have other good news! She has given a message to the ferryman and he will arrange for you to stay in a small hotel in Carloforte. I hope we did right?'

'That's wonderful! Thank you, signora,' said Beppe, delighted.

'Good, and now here is the address of my sister-in-law. She says to arrive at whatever time you like. I hope you and your wife have a good holiday.'

Elise was at once aware she was blushing, but Beppe accepted their assumed relationship without turning a hair. He took the piece of paper with the address and slipped it into his shirt pocket.

After saying their goodbyes and promises to visit the couple on their way back, they left and started on their way to Calasetta.

The road climbed and descended through land which alternated between vineyards and barren hills. Elise was fascinated by the scene in one field where a blindfolded bullock on a chain walked around and around treading the meagre crop of wheat while the men winnowed the stalks with long, flail-like forks.

Over the next hill, they caught sight of the little seaside village clustered around a domed church. Everything looked so clean, as if it had been newly painted. The streets ran down to the large harbour, and the whole scene appeared to Elise to have more of a North African than a Sardinian aspect.

It didn't take them long to find the terracotta coloured house, in the Via Marconi where they were welcomed like friends rather than total strangers.

That night, as Elise lay back in a large, wooden bed watching Beppe undress, she asked, 'Do they always welcome people like this in Sardinia?'

'People here are very hospitable. I told you that before,' he replied, with a broad smile.

'I know you did, but I didn't realise it applied to complete strangers. Now I know why you are so nice to me,' she added mischievously as he climbed into bed beside her. 'It's only because I'm a stranger.'

She pulled the bedclothes up over her face to hide her laughter.

Beppe pulled at the sheet, but she pulled harder; a tug of war ensued, impeded by fits of laughter – then Beppe gave a final yank and the sheet slipped from Elise's fingers, revealing her smiling face and beautiful, naked body. She put her arms up to him and he fell into them, bestowing her with little kisses.

That night, he made her cry out with the passionate intensity of their love-making. They reached heights of ecstasy they had never known before, and afterwards Elise found it impossible to control the silent tears that rolled down her cheeks. Beppe, kissing her, tasted their wet saltiness.

'Darling,' he murmured, huskily. 'Darling, I didn't mean to hurt you. I wouldn't do that for the world. I've never known such happiness. I'm so sorry I…'

She put her fingers over his lips.

'You didn't hurt me. I promise,' she whispered, holding him close. 'You made me very happy too.'

He looked at her tenderly.

'Tell me, Elise, if you always cry when you're happy, what do you do when you're sad?' he asked, gently teasing.

'I cry too, but that's different!'

She lay in his arms as he slept, and thought of this wonderful man who had changed her life so completely, who had loved her honestly and profoundly. She thought of how she found herself thinking about him all of the time and how much every part of her longed for his touch. In anticipation of the next day and in perfect peace, she finally joined him in a deep sleep.

CHAPTER TWENTY TWO

The clanging bell in the domed church woke Elise early. She slipped out of bed and draped her cotton kikoi round her. She quietly opened the shutters and looked out of the window. The brilliant light poured into the room and she shaded her eyes momentarily against the glare. The street below ran down to the port, where the sea lay blue and reflected the large, cotton-wool clouds that hung in the equally blue sky. Everywhere sparkled and shone in the fresh early-morning sunshine; white-washed buildings and the nearby russet-coloured roof of the church glowed under the incandescent light. Elise watched as a young boy wandered down the street behind his straw-laden donkey whose little feet where the only things visible under his vast load.

Beppe watched her standing at the window, her slim shoulders above the striped kikoi.

'Come back to bed – it's early yet,' he said in a low voice.

Elise turned towards him.

'I thought you were still asleep,' she said. 'It's a beautiful day out there. We should be up and catching the ferry.'

He held out his hand to her.

'Come here,' he murmured with his eyes half closed.

She crossed to the bed, dropped the cotton wrap and slipped in beside him.

'God, I love you!' he moaned. 'You're like a drug. The more I have you, the more I want and need you.'

Elise sighed and surrendered to his lovemaking.

At breakfast, the sister-in-law talked non-stop, declaring how glad she was she could help in putting them up for the night and later she gave them the address of the hotel in Carloforte.

'The ferryman returned with the booking this morning. It's only small, but it's a very quiet hotel,' she added, smiling.

After the meal, they collected their things once more, paid their bill and said their goodbyes. Elise shook hands with the woman and felt a small package being pressed into her hand, together with a bunch of rosemary.

At the port, the ferry was waiting. Beppe drove the car into the boat, and then joined Elise on deck. They watched the port of Calasetta and its red, black, green and white fishing boats bobbing at anchor fade into the distance as the vessel, leaving a foaming path in its churning wake, chugged its way across the narrow channel to Carloforte.

'You've been grinning at me all morning,' she accused, putting her arm through his. 'What's wrong? Have I got a smudge on my nose or something?'

'No. It's just that you have become Signora Giuseppe Zedda.'

'Why is that?'

'You have a bunch of rosemary – right?'

She nodded.

'And I'm willing to bet that the small package in your pocket that she gave you contains rice.'

'Why?'

'Because, in Sardinia, we always give rice to the bride; it's a sign of fertility.'

'You mean… they think we're on honeymoon?' Elise said, her eyes widening.

'Yes, darling tell me, how does it feel?'

'I refuse to answer that on the grounds that it may incriminate me, your honour.'

They hugged each other and laughed, and the breeze ruffled their hair.

It didn't take long for the ferry to churn its way across to the Island of San Pietro. The ferry drawbridge was already clanking into position as they entered the stone-walled harbour of Carloforte. A brown-faced man wearing a beret directed operations from the deck by raising or lowering his arms, and when all was secured they disembarked without fuss.

The wide sea front was strewn with nets drying in the sun. Old fishermen with skins like walnuts sat crossed-legged, mending the tears from the previous night's expedition. Other men in berets, short-sleeved shirts and shorts talked of the night's catch and the day's prices. The rows of neatly white-washed houses were screened by a row of gently waving palms, and with the dhow-shaped fishing vessels resting in the harbour, the place could have been anywhere on the North African coast.

'It's all so clean,' she marvelled.

'It always is. These people came in about seventeen thirty-seven, when Carlo Emmanuel III allowed some Genoese refugees living on an island near Tunis to come and settle here. They are proud of their Genoese descent, and their pride shows in everything they do. They speak a very different sort of language here.'

A young man was walking along the street and Beppe enquired of him the way to the hotel.

'I'm going that way. I'll show you,' he said.

Elise squeezed up to Beppe as the young man climbed in beside her.

He directed Beppe through the maze of narrow streets until they reached a row of buildings overlooking the bay.

'This is the place you're looking for,' he said, leaping from the car before it had halted. His white teeth flashed in a smile as they thanked him, and he was gone.

Beppe collected their bags from the boot of the car. As they approached the open door of the small hotel, a short, smiling-faced man followed by a plump woman came forward to greet them. Her long, dark hair was tied back under a black silk scarf.

'Signore, signora – welcome,' they chorused.

'I'm Signora Sanna. You have come from our friends in Calasetta?'

'Yes,' replied Beppe. 'I am Giuseppe Zedda, and this is Elise.'

'You are not Italian, signora?' said the woman.

'No – I'm English.'

'You speak Italian very well.'

'Thank you, signora.'

'Now please – forgive me for keeping you here. Follow me and I'll show you to your room.'

The little, round figure led them up a narrow staircase and along a short corridor before opening a door and standing back to allow them through. All the windows were open, allowing the gentle sea breeze to flow into the room which overlooked the multi- coloured rooftops and the sweeping blue port.

'It's perfect!' Elise cried delightedly, and drew in a deep breath. 'What a heavenly smell.' She stopped and blushed, realising that the whole bed had been strewn with small pieces of rosemary.

'This is the best room in the hotel,' said Signora Sanna. 'It even has its own small bathroom. We keep it for, well… special guests. I hope you will be very happy.' She smiled and went out, pausing at the door to add, 'If you need anything, please ring the bell beside the bed.'

Beppe swept Elise up into his arms, swung her around, kissed her and set her down again.

'Well, Signora Zedda,' he said, laughing, 'what do you want to do now?'

'Let's go exploring,' she said, giving him a quick kiss.

With a picnic arranged, and the rest of the day ahead of them, they took the road north.

On the outskirts of Carloforte, most of the houses had gardens enclosed with dry-stone walls. Orchards and vineyards were divided off and flowers grew in well-tended plots. Further on, the rolling countryside once more took over. The road was never far from the sea and a welcome breeze tempered the heat of the day.

In a deserted spot near the cliff, Beppe parked the car beneath a solitary clump of trees. The views were magnificent, with gently rising hills behind and the blue sea below. Siesta came easily to both of them after the picnic. They lay in the shade, content in each other's arms, and dreamed away the afternoon.

The following morning, Elise sat in the shade of the trees in the small square at Carloforte and sipped her coffee. Beppe had decided that he wanted a shave and had gone to the local barber for the whole works. From where she was sitting, she could see the barbers who were lathering the men's faces; some had hot damp towels wound around their faces to soften the heavy growth. Others sat having their hair cut.

She became aware of how sensual it was to watch men going about something that was so masculine, and it sent a warm glow through her body. Deep in thought, she saw Beppe get up out of the chair, pay the barber and, with a laugh, leave the shop. He looked around him and saw Elise watching him. He came across, reached down and kissed her on her cheek.

'You smell and feel wonderful,' she sighed.

He took her hand and they spent the morning looking around the shops, before enjoying a superb meal of fish in a small restaurant on the seafront. Elise found herself thinking how wonderful it was to have him to herself without the worry of gossip returning to the family. If only this could go on forever... But she knew that would not be possible.

CHAPTER TWENTY THREE

The days slipped by, each one bringing a new understanding and a greater awareness of their growing dependence the one upon the other. They explored the entire island and found a small cove on the west side, the only access being a steep goat track. They would scramble down it to spend long hours in total solitude. Beppe lay in the sun while Elise sketched him, and he, in turn, having brought, his camera with him, took countless snapshots of her.

On one of these carefree days, Beppe, borrowed a fishing line and some bait from one of Signora Sanna's sons and spent the morning sitting fishing on a rocky outcrop. By lunchtime he had caught two large fish, having put several small ones back.

Elise had spent the time sketching him from every angle.

'You go and find some tinder and wood while I gut the fish,' he called.

When the fire was alight and the fish gutted, he showed her how to spike them on sharp myrtle twigs and then cooked them over the now glowing embers.

'They certainly smell good,' she said, inhaling the rising smoke. 'Do you often cook and eat your food outside?'

'Whenever I can, after all, God gave us the great outdoors with all its bounty, so why not take advantage of it?' He turned the fish again. 'Pass the basket, darling. We shall need the plates.'

She passed it over to him, and he took out the plates and two lemons. Deftly quartering the lemons, he put them on the plates, and then told Elise to cut some bread while he went to fetch the wine. She watched as he bent from the waist, knees straight, to haul out the bottle of wine he had carefully rested in the water to chill. His long, brown legs and lithe body thrilled her as always; the hairs on his legs and arms had turned from dark-brown to a golden colour in the sun. She sighed; she could have watched him forever.

'What are you staring at?' he asked as he came back with the wine.

'The sea, what else is there to look at?' She paused, and laughed. 'You can't be conceited enough to think I'd stare at you when I already know every inch of your beautiful body by heart?'

He put down the bottle and came purposefully towards her.

'No, Beppe, you'll burn the fish! And besides, I'm hungry!' she cried.

'So am I,' he retorted, making a grab at her.

'No, Beppe, please!' she squealed, laughing.

'Oh well,' he said, suddenly kneeling down beside the fire, 'if I can't have you, I suppose fish, bread and wine are the next-best things.'

After the meal, they spread their towels near the rocks and lay with their heads in the shade while the sun tanned their bodies an even deeper brown. Elise was half-asleep, with Beppe lying flat on his back beside her, one arm around her, when he suddenly asked, in his usual blunt manner,

'Tell me, Elise, why haven't you had any children?'

'Because we were told we couldn't have any. Besides, William doesn't want any now,' she replied, a little taken aback.

'You and I would make beautiful children. You know that, don't you, Elise?'

'What makes you think you could give me children, when another man can't?'

'Because ours would be different; they would be conceived out of love. That is important, you know.'

'But not necessary, as many a woman has found to her cost,' she said, smiling.

'I'd like six sons,' he continued. 'Think how proud we would be.'

'What about a daughter?'

'Oh, you can have daughters, too; just as long as I have my six sons. I would take one into the co-operative. One would be a fisherman. One could go into the Church, and still I'd have three!' he said, counting out on his fingers.

'And what about me? When I'm fat from all that child-bearing, and bad-tempered and tired from nursing them when they're ill, would you still love me then?'

'Of course! As a woman gets older and rounder, she enjoys life.

It's only the ones who stay thin who are frigid and loveless.'

'What if we couldn't have children? It is possible, even with all the love in the world!' she said.

'As long as you still loved me, even if I couldn't give you children, I would always love you, just as I love you now.' He turned towards her. 'Do you think your husband will give you your divorce?'

She hushed him with her fingers on his mouth, saying softly, 'We promised – no thinking, remember?'

That night, Elise was restless. Someone was having a party, and the noise made it impossible for her to sleep. She lay thinking about the wonderful times she and Beppe had shared over the past week and suddenly realised that tomorrow must be Sunday. Surely, they would have to start heading back in order to be at the villa by the evening. She felt sick in the pit of her stomach.

Six weeks in Sardinia had flown by, and, at this rate, she would soon be going back to London. She turned to touch Beppe; how good it was to feel his body so close to hers, to hear his slow, even breathing – but most wonderful of all, to know that he loved her. To know that his kisses and caresses were expressions of that love and for Elise, it was ecstasy for her to make love to him, because she wanted and needed him. They had so little to offer each other materially, but what they gave in the way of love was boundless, and given and received with ardent pleasure.

She rolled over onto her stomach and, propped on her elbows, she rested her chin in her hands, watching him sleep. His dark hair curled on the pillow and his long lashes lay on his cheeks. His face was relaxed, and he looked so beautiful. She leant forward and gently ran her tongue up Beppe's outstretched arm, across his shoulder. He stirred sleepily, and she went on bestowing small, quick kisses on him until she reached his neck.

The day's growth of beard felt rough to her lips, but it sent a thrill through her body. She kissed his lips gently and then his eyes; those dark, deep recesses that glowed with love for her.

'I love you,' he said in a low voice.

'I love you too.' she whispered

She ran her tongue over his body, kissing him repeatedly until he could bear it no longer.

'Darling, I'm asleep' he whispered, but she kissed his lips, stopping any protest. With a groan, he pulled her down on him, his arms around her so tightly she could hardly draw breath. She gasped for air and he let her go with a long, low moan.

They lay for a while, in each other's arms, in a contented silence.

'What woke you, darling?' he murmured.

'I haven't been to sleep. There was a party somewhere, and the noise kept me awake.'

She closed her eyes, turning on her side, and snuggled even closer to him. He put his arms around her and pulled her into him.

'Goodnight, my darling,' he whispered.

'I love you,' she replied, sinking into a deep, untroubled sleep.

The church bells pealing across the bay, calling the faithful to early-morning mass, woke them both. For a moment, neither stirred; each afraid of waking the other. Beppe sighed deeply.

'Are you awake, darling?' he asked.

'Mmm,' she murmured.

'Do you realise what day it is?'

'Yes, I do. Where has the week gone, Beppe?'

'I don't know. But I do know that if our life together goes as fast as this, we would grow old very quickly!'

'It has been a wonderful week, Beppe. One I shall never forget as long as I live!'

'It's been perfect!' He paused, and then went on huskily, 'Any regrets?'

She looked at him and smiled.

'Not one. Have you?'

He shook his head and kissed her.

'None!' he said, returning her smile.

Beppe lay on the bed and watched Elise as she combed her hair, wet from her shower. She collected her body lotion from the dressing table and sat with one leg up on the bed. She dropped the cream onto her long legs, and then, starting at her toes, she worked up to her body. Beppe sighed; she was content in herself, relaxed enough with him to carry out her daily routine.

'Would you like me to do that for you?'

She looked up at him and smiled.

'Thank you, darling, but we will never get out today if you do that.'

'This could be us forever, Elise, both of us at peace with one another.'

She rose and kissed him on his lips.

Neither wanted breakfast so they had coffee in their room overlooking the port.

Later Beppe took his case down to see Signora Sanna.

'What time are you thinking of leaving?' asked the signore.

'We want to catch the midday ferry,' said Beppe. 'We shall have lunch in San Antioco and travel on to Pula.'

Upstairs, Elise packed her few belongings and collected their swimming things from the balcony, pausing to take in the beautiful view of the bay below for the last time. Beppe returned from settling the bill and took the bag from her. They both stood for a moment looking out of the window and then at the small room where they had shared so much love together. He pulled her to him and kissed her gently on her forehead.

Downstairs in the hall they were met by Signore and Signora Sanna, who shook hands with them and wished them a safe journey and stood in the doorway of the small hotel until Beppe and Elise disappeared from view down the windey road to the wide sea front. The ferry was rocking gently in the harbour, but the streets were deserted; everyone was in church.

Beppe drove onto the ferry, and then he and Elise climbed to the upper deck to sit and watch the seagulls as they swooped over the sea, snatching fish from the still water. The sun reflected off the water in the harbour like a huge, silver plate; here and there, a wave flashed and glinted in the strong sunlight. Soon, the quay started to fill up and people swarmed the harbour as the churchgoers returned home or prepared to make the short journey across to San Antioco to see friends or relatives. A bell sounded, and the clanking drawbridge lifted. They were on their way back.

At Calasetta the cars were again unloaded and Elise stood on the stone harbour waiting for Beppe. Boats lay at anchor or moored by the wall. Some seemed to be permanent homes; one, Elise noticed with interest, had a large washing line strung from the mast to the cabin, but instead of the usual things one would expect to see flapping in the breeze, there was a row of neatly pegged fish hanging in the sun to dry.

This time as they drove towards San Antioco, the fields were deserted. The restaurant proprietors welcomed them like old friends and enquired eagerly whether they had enjoyed their week at San Pietro.

Beppe told them what happened and how the woman's sister-in-law had arranged everything for them, adding,

'Will you please thank her again for us? Everything was perfect. We really are most grateful for everything everyone has done for us.'

After lunch, having bid their hosts goodbye, they set off for the villa. Beppe took a different road from Teulada to Domus Maria; a winding road, but very beautiful. They said little, each deep in their own thoughts. When they reached the top of a long climb, Beppe stopped the car, as usual, to show Elise the view.

'You have a truly wonderful country,' she said. 'I hope it's never spoilt, like so many other places are in the Mediterranean.'

'I hope so too, but we have a chance here because the Government has bought most of this coastline to help preserve the wildlife and its natural beauty.' He went on: 'Come on, it's downhill now all the way to Pula.'

They passed through the small village, and then the road followed the broad, rocky bed of the river Chia, which was overhung by large Oleander trees with the impressive background of the macchia. The road branched, and they were soon nearing the villa. Dusk was approaching as they drove in through the gates. The great olive tree in the courtyard threw a deep shadow over the villa, giving it a sinister appearance after the clarity of the white-washed houses of Calasetta and Carloforte.

Maria and Efisio were in the kitchen.

'Hello, you two!' Maria greeted them. 'Have you had a good time? Silly question,' she added, laughing, 'I can see you have. Where did you go?'

'We went to San Antioco and then on to San Pietro. That's a beautiful little island. We found a beach all to ourselves, and we were thoroughly spoilt by everyone!' said Elise, bubbling with enthusiasm.

'Are you hungry?' asked Maria.

'No. Not at all,' she replied.

'Well – there is a fire in the sitting room,' said Maria. 'Go in there, and I'll bring you in some wine.'

'I'll get it,' said Beppe, reaching for two glasses and helping himself from the carafe on the table.

He joined Elise in the sitting room, and they sat on the floor, their backs against the fireside chairs, sipping wine and gazing into the embers.

'We've only got two weeks together,' said Beppe softly. 'Do you have to go home? Couldn't you stay a little longer? The villa isn't let; you could stay,' he pleaded.

She nodded.

'I will have a word with Maria in the morning. Then I can help you in the mornings, and we could swim in the afternoons or we could go skiing. I would so love that.'

He put his arm around her and drew her close to him as they sat in contented silence, their happiness as yet unspoiled by the imminent parting that was to come.

CHAPTER TWENTY FOUR

'Elise, are you there? Come quickly – there is a phone call from England,' called Maria as she knocked on the door of the vinery.

Elise jumped out of bed and pulled on the kikoi she had given Beppe.

'Who is it, Maria?' she asked, opening the door.

'I don't know; someone for you, Elise, someone who only speaks English.'

Elise hurried into the villa and picked up the telephone receiver in the sitting room.

'Hello? Elise Raynesford speaking.'

Beppe, having dressed quickly, joined her just as she was replacing the receiver. She sank into a chair, her face as white as a sheet. Beppe knelt beside her.

'Elise, what is it?' he asked, looking into her stricken face. 'For God's sake, tell me what's happened?'

'It's my mother,' Elise said dully. 'She has been taken ill. They are very concerned about her. It seems she has had a heart attack. That was her doctor. He has been trying to get me since Saturday. My mother is asking for me.'

Beppe called Maria, who came into the room, looking anxious.

'Can you bring some coffee?' he said. 'And put some brandy in it. Please.'

She nodded and hurried away.

'I must go,' Elise said and burst into tears. 'But, oh, Beppe… darling… I don't want to leave you! Just when we thought we could have more time together!'

He tried desperately to comfort her as Maria returned carrying a steaming cup of coffee, followed by Efisio.

'Drink that,' said Efisio quietly but firmly, 'then you get dressed and Beppe will take you into Cagliari to get your ticket changed. Do you understand?'

She nodded, drank obediently and then went upstairs to shower and dress, putting on her largest pair of sunglasses to hide her red, swollen eyes.

The Alitalia office was busy with people making reservations or checking flights. Beppe took her ticket, sat her down and went to speak to a young man behind one of the counters.

'It's imperative I change this ticket,' he said. 'The signora received a phone call from England this morning to say her mother is very ill. She must go home at once.'

'The earliest flight is Wednesday morning, I'm afraid. All domestic flights out of Sardinia are fully booked.'

'But this is an emergency; it's her mother! Can't you do something for her?' begged Beppe.

The young man went away, returning with an older man who said, 'It seems that a member of the company is flying tomorrow afternoon. It is the best we can do. We will change the flight over. Will that be alright?'

'Yes, thank you,' said Beppe.

'If you leave the ticket with us for a while, we'll deal with it, signore.'

Beppe told Elise what he had arranged.

'Thank you, Beppe,' she said, obviously still stunned by the morning's events. 'I want to do some shopping anyway.'

'Where do you want to go?'

'To the Via Manno, please. I want to buy Ignazio, Predu and Margherita a button each. They have all been so good to us.' She paused. 'Will it upset things very much if someone outside the family gives them one?'

'No, of course not,' he said, laughing. 'If that's what you want, I'm sure they'll be delighted.'

'What can I buy for Maria and Efisio?'

'They would rather it went to the family. I can promise you that,' he said firmly.

'I'd like to give them something to remember me by...' Elise said, with a helpless shrug. 'I don't know...'

She felt numb, exhausted. Beppe took her back to the shop where she had purchased his gift, and the owner, recognising her, greeted her warmly. Beppe helped her choose the buttons which he thought matched the ones they had already.

'Don't worry if they are not right, I can always change them,' said the man, adding, 'I see you were the lucky recipient of the crucifix, signore. It looks very fine.'

Beppe smiled and winked at Elise.

The man wrapped the buttons in separate red boxes with satin ribbons and then bowed them out of the shop. A little further along the street, Elise saw a large double silver frame which she decided to buy because it would be ideal to contain the sketches she had made of Maria and Efisio.

They collected her ticket from the Alitalia office and returned to the villa, where she sent a telegram to Harvey, William's chauffeur, to let him know her plans. Beppe helped her to pack, leaving the case open on the bed ready for the next day.

'Darling, as your flight leaves in the afternoon, we could go from here early, and I could show you my peach grove,' he said. 'You haven't seen it yet.'

'I should like that very much,' she replied, trying to control the quivering of her lips. She clung to him. 'Oh, Beppe – I'm trying so hard to be brave, really I am.'

He held her tightly, and she could feel his heart beating against his chest.

'My dearest, dearest, love,' he murmured huskily.

The whole family gathered for the evening meal; Maria had arranged for them all to be together on Elise's last night. Word travelled fast and people she had met while staying at the villa sent messages home via Ignazio and Predu saying they hoped to see her again next year, if not sooner, and that they hoped her mother would be better soon. Franco sent a message to say that he was sorry that the bandits hadn't managed to keep her for longer, which made them laugh.

While they were drinking coffee after the meal, Efisio rose and called for quiet.

'We have many people come to stay in this villa,' he said, 'but never before has anyone touched our lives as you have, Elise. You opened your heart to us right from the start, and made us look upon you as family. We shall all miss you very much – and I hope you will not easily forget us. Perhaps you will write and tell us your news, then come back and see us again next year for a holiday or… maybe to stay. And here is health to your mother.'

Everyone clapped and Efisio looked a little embarrassed by his own, somewhat uncharacteristic, rush of sentiment.

'Speech, Elise,' went up the cry.

Elise rose slowly and looked around the table at each attentive, smiling face.

'I hardly know what to say, you have all taken me in like a member of your family. You've shared my laughter and my sorrow. I can only say that, although I've travelled half way around the world, I have never been made to feel as much at home as I have been here.'

She paused for a moment, bit her lip and waited for the threatening tears to pass, and then went on, 'I can't begin to thank you for what you've done for Beppe and me. I ask you not to abandon him, because he, I'm sure, is going to need all his friends. We have bought small gifts, tokens of our thanks, and we hope, when you look at them, you will always remember us as we are now.'

She handed the small red boxes out to each of the children and gave Maria the large one, saying, 'This is for you both. It's to hold the drawings I did of you.'

The young people watched as Maria opened the packet. Holding up the double picture frame, she said tearfully, 'Oh… Elise… it's lovely! Thank you.' And taking a large handkerchief out, she blew her nose.

'Well – aren't you going to open yours?' Beppe asked the others.

They pulled the ribbons and opened their boxes excitedly. Ignazio and Predu sat and stared at their buttons, but Margherita jumped up and threw her arms around Elise's neck.

'Thank you, Elise – oh, thank you! It will always remind me of you and Beppe.' She said turning to kiss Beppe.

The boys stood up and shook hands with Beppe, and threw their arms around him. They kissed Elise on both cheeks and then gave her a hug too. Maria excused herself from the table on the pretence of fetching something from the larder, and Elise followed her.

'I hope you don't mind,' she said, 'but we wanted to buy them something we knew they would like. Beppe said you wouldn't mind. You don't have to tell Claudio or his mother, do you?'

'Elise, it's not that at all. I'm so overwhelmed by such generosity; I don't know what to say.'

'Well – don't say anything. It's not necessary.' Elise took the older woman's arm. 'But there is one thing I want you to do for me, please, Maria. In this envelope is enough money to cover all the expenses that Beppe has had to pay out over the past weeks. I can't give it to him; he would never take it. He would only be offended – but he can't afford to pay for everything as he did.'

'If he married you, he would have to,' said Maria.

'That's different; we wouldn't be spending weeks in a hotel or be going out to meals. Please, Maria. Take the money and give it to him as a bonus or something, but don't tell him it's from me, I beg of you.'

Maria hesitated; then she nodded, took the envelope and slipped it in her pocket.

'There you are, you two!' said Beppe, as they were emerging from the kitchen. 'Are you coming for a walk on the beach, Elise?'

'Yes, do,' urged Maria. 'But before you go, can you tell me what is happening tomorrow?'

'We'll have breakfast, and then I'm taking Elise into Cagliari and up to Santa Cella. I want to show her the peach grove before she goes.'

'Fine. Goodnight, then – and God bless, and thank you both,' said Maria, going back to the kitchen once more.

The air was chilly outside, and the wind, blowing in from the sea, sighed through the trees, shivered on the water and whined in the reeds.

'It usually rustles, like a whisper,' said Elise, shivering, 'but tonight, it's more like a wail. Let's go in.'

They passed the house and crossed under the olive tree to the vinery. A few spots of rain spattered in their faces, and Beppe, attempting lightness, remarked, 'It seems the whole of Sardinia is crying over your leaving tomorrow.'

They undressed each other slowly and climbed into bed.

'I can see everything that you're thinking in your eyes,' Beppe murmured as he stared into her eyes with his own dark gaze.

'Can you? Then you know how much you mean to me,' she breathed.

'Elise, will you call me by my name?' he asked in a whisper.

She smiled and pulled him toward her.

'I love you, Giuseppe Zedda, more than I can say, my dearest, darling Giuseppe.'

He said nothing, but gently kissed her fingertips before moving his lips up her arm to her neck. She felt his warm tears fall onto her shoulder and run down her breast. She ran her fingers through his hair, burying her face against him. Their tears mingled on her body and trickled onto the pillow below.

'No one has ever shed tears over me before,' she said with a break in her voice.

'And I've never had anyone to share them with before.'

'Beppe I want to run my hands once more over your beautiful, beautiful body; feel your breath on my neck and cheek. To feel the weight of your body on mine as you make love to me. Oh, darling, please hold me.'

He made love to her, gently, tenderly, caressing her so that he would remember how she felt in his arms, leaving a picture and an imprint in his memory.

Elise showered him with small kisses, as she too needed to keep the feel of him alive in her mind.

Three times that night, they woke and reached for each other, and at last, at dawn, Beppe opened his eyes with a start, having dreamed she had already gone. When Elise woke, she was conscious of a dull, sick feeling in the pit of her stomach. Beppe was still red-eyed and she knew she must be too from all the tears she had shed.

'Hello,' she said with a wan smile and clung to him.

'Elise, darling, make love to me just once more, please…'

'My dearest, dearest, Giuseppe – I do love you so very much,' she whispered.

He took her left hand and kissed the ring he had given her.

'Don't ever take it off, will you, Elise?'

'No, never – I promise. And no other man shall own my soul. I was sure when I promised you that before, but now I know there will never be anyone to take your place.'

'And I swear, Elise, by this cross and by Our Lady, that there will never be anyone else but you. Swear you will come back to me one day; please swear it.'

'I'll come back, Beppe. I swear it. As God is my witness, I shall come back to you. It may take a little while, but I promise.'

CHAPTER TWENTY FIVE

'What are you travelling home in?' asked Beppe. 'I want to put the case in the car ready to go.'

'I've the white linen dress in the wardrobe. It will be cool... and I'm wearing these sandals. Someone will be at the airport to meet me anyway.'

'Who?'

'William's chauffeur will probably be there. Why?'

'It's another world,' sneered Beppe sarcastically.

'Yes, it's another world,' she snapped. 'One where husbands come home after losing a fortune at the gambling table and beat the hell out of their wives in a drunken rage. Where money is valued more than people; where you judge a man by his club, his car, his house and the number of women he keeps on the side, but most of all, by the size of his bank account. A world where people's feelings are trampled into the dirt and nobody cares!'

'Wow, darling, I'm sorry. I didn't mean to sound bitter. It's just that... that your husband has everything to offer you – money, security, a large house...' Beppe broke in, holding his hands up in defence.

'And I'd trade the whole lot tomorrow for your love and the possibility of having your children,' she sobbed, putting her hands over her face. 'Don't you realise, Beppe, you've shown me more love, more tenderness and probably more understanding in the short time I've known you, than in the years I've been married to William!'

She put her arms around him and reached up to kiss him.

Efisio, entering after a quick knock, gave a small cough.

'This won't do – you will never get to Cagliari!' he said. 'Is your case ready, Elise?'

'Nearly, I just want to change and put these jeans I'm wearing in it.'

She put on her dress and dropped her jeans and put them in the case and closed it.

'Holy Mary!' exclaimed Efisio as he lifted it off the bed. 'What have you packed in here?'

'As many of the shells I've collected as I could pack, and the book Beppe bought me.'

'*Boh*. You'll have to pay excess baggage, you know that?' exclaimed Efisio.

He disappeared down the stairs with the case and Elise said, 'Beppe, please will you keep the wooden dish your cousin gave us? When I come back, we can share it again. I've left lots of shells with it. You said you wanted some for decorating something – and I've left you lots of the watercolours I did at San Pietro and a bottle of my perfume for you, to remind you of me.'

'Thank you, darling, I'll find them,' he said, smiling weakly. 'And I have put the record of *Non Potho Reposare* in your case; you can play it and think of me.'

'Oh thank you Beppe.'

Elise put the final touch to her dress and Beppe watched her every move. She had put on a little weight during her stay, and the dress clung in all the right places, falling softly over her now rounded hips.

Ready at last, the family was outside near the car, and Elise bit her lip as she walked towards them. They were lined up in order of age and Predu came forward first. He kissed her on both cheeks and wished her goodbye. Margherita, already red-eyed, burst into tears and threw her arms around Elise's neck.

'You will come back, won't you?' sobbed the young girl.

'Yes, Margherita, I will. I promise. Besides I want to learn to ski from the beach!' she said, and kissed her.

Ignazio kissed her hand, and then gave her a kiss on each cheek, 'Goodbye, good luck and come back soon!'

Elise turned blindly to Maria, and they embraced, holding each other tightly for a moment.

'Come back, for all our sakes,' whispered Maria, her voice choked with tears.

Efisio stepped forward to kiss Elise formally on both cheeks.

'Have a safe journey,' he said, gruffly. 'May God go with you.'

In a mist of tears, she climbed hurriedly into the waiting car, blew her nose, wiped her eyes and waved a last goodbye as Beppe clambered in beside her and drove away.

They deposited her luggage at the airport, paid the excess that Efisio had predicted, checked her flight – the plane was due to leave at four o'clock, but she had be there an hour earlier – and then they returned to the car.

'Would you like to see the peach grove?' Beppe asked.

'Yes, but what about your mother? Will she be there?'

'It's outside the village. She never goes there,' he said, and swinging the car round onto the main highway, he headed north towards his village.

At Monastir they took a bumpy side road to the right which was flanked on either side by citrus groves and small vineyards. Men and women were working on their pieces of land, scratching what living they could manage from the sun-baked soil. The car turned up a narrow dirt road with groves on either side. It lurched in and out of potholes until Beppe halted with a sudden jerk. Opposite, Elise noticed an arch with a gate leaning against the wall.

'Here we are!' he said.

They got out and went through the makeshift gate into the tree-enclosed groves.

'Gosh, it's hot in here!' she said.

'The trees act as a wind break and keep the groves at a good temperature, which helps to ripen the fruit early. Here,' Beppe added, taking a peach from one of the trees, 'try this. It's one of our new early varieties.'

The skin was warm in her hand and the juice was sweet as she bit into the fruit.

'Mmm – lovely! Its white fleshed; I have never seen that before. Peaches are usually yellow. Tell me, what else do you grow?'

He showed her all the different peach trees, explaining the varieties, and went on, 'There are also medlar, oranges, lemons and some almonds.'

'You and your father did all this?'

'Yes, we worked very hard for this – all of us. Most of the land was virgin soil. It was ploughed and then hand dug over before the trees were planted. We still have to water it all by hand.'

'You must be very proud of it.'

'Yes,' he nodded, 'I am. But I shall give it to my brother.'

'But why Beppe?'

'He will need it when he is married. Besides, as you know, I'm saving up to start a small cooperative, so I can help all of the people in my area. If we combine our crops to sell them, we can get better prices and the haulage charges will be lower. I know it will benefit many people.' He smiled.

They walked on through the grove in silence until they reached the shade of the tall cypress. Then Beppe looked at Elise and suddenly caught her in his arms, crushing her as he held her. They were near the lemon grove and the lemon scent enfolded them, mingled with the scent of the roses and honeysuckle clambering through the prickly pear.

Elise shivered involuntarily and Beppe held her close to him.

'Besides,' he whispered gently, 'I shall need a good business so I can look after you. We could run it together, and then we wouldn't ever have to be separated.'

Tears filled her eyes, and she clung to him.

'Oh, darling Beppe, I love you so much! I don't want to go home.'

'God willing, we shall be together soon; perhaps forever,' he said, tilting her head towards him and kissing her. 'Come – let's go and have a drink. I'm sure we could both do with one.'

He reached up and picked a sprig of orange blossom and gave it to Elise. She smelt it and, smiling, kissed him.

He kept his arm around her as they walked to the car.

'I will come back, Beppe. I promise. And I know I shall always be able to find you here in this peach grove. It may take a few months but I'll be back.'

He collected a number of ripe peaches and took them to the car where he found a newspaper, made a cone and placed the peaches in it.

'Will you take this home with you?' he asked, tentatively.

She smiled and nodded, while new tears flowed down her cheeks, and she put the sprig of blossom in the bag. She would press it in her diary later.

In the neat, white-washed bar the whirling fans helped to keep the room cool. Beppe went to the counter to order the drinks, while Elise chose a table well away from everyone else. Joining her, Beppe reached out, took her hands in his, and looked deep into her eyes. He sighed heavily and bit his lip.

A young girl came over with the drinks, putting a whisky in front of Beppe, before giving Elise her Vernaccia; Elise had become used to the fact that the men were usually served first in Sardinia and, indeed, quite liked the idea.

Beppe let go of Elise's hand and drained his glass and immediately ordered the same again.

'Dutch courage?' asked Elise with a wan smile.

'God, Elise, I need something,' he replied briefly, not smiling back.

She took his hand again and looked at him tenderly.

'Wouldn't it be better to leave me at the airport and go back to the villa, rather than hang around waiting?'

'No. No – I'm alright.'

But when the second glass of whisky arrived and he raised it to drink, she saw that his hand was trembling. They sat talking about everything and nothing, while the hands of the bar's clock crept around to half past two. Beppe wanted this time to go on forever; he dreaded her going. Elise fought back her tears as she watched him trying to compose himself.

The wait at the airport was even more of an ordeal. It was like waiting for a sentence to be carried out, and Elise secretly longed for it to be over. Then, finally, her flight was called. She and Beppe stood and faced each other, awkward, like strangers, until large tears filled their eyes and spilled down their cheeks. Beppe, suddenly seized by fear, pulled her towards him, and with one last, desperate embrace held Elise so tight that she finally had to free herself. Then, to Beppe's despair, she was suddenly gone, swallowed up in the surging mass of fellow passengers.

She hadn't dared look back, frightened that she would not be able to leave. In a merciful daze of numbness, she boarded the plane, sat through the journey to Alghero and on to Milan, where she changed flights for Heathrow. She disembarked, collected her luggage and, still hugging the peaches, she passed through customs and was finally met by Harvey, William's chauffeur, who drove her straight to the hospital.

CHAPTER TWENTY SIX

Her mother looked tired and strained. The nurse who was sitting by the bed rose and quietly left the room.

'Is that really you, Elise?' said a faint voice from the bed.

'Yes, Mother, it is. How are you feeling?'

'A little tired, but I haven't any pain now.'

'Was it very bad?'

'Yes rather. Did you have a good holiday, dearest? You look brown, so well; better than I've seen you look for a long time.'

'Yes. It was wonderful.'

'I'm sorry to call you home. But the doctor insisted. I feel so much better now, but thank you for coming back so soon.'

Elise pressed her mother's hand and saw that she had fallen asleep.

The nurse, coming back at that moment, said softly, 'Don't worry, she sleeps a great deal. She is heavily sedated to stop the pain.'

'What's wrong exactly?' asked Elise.

'It's her heart. She suffered two very bad attacks. The doctor is afraid she may not survive another. But we have discovered she has ovarian cancer so she is a very sick lady.'

Elise spent her days going to the hospital to see her mother, and was pleased to see that there was some slight improvement.

William unexpectedly returned to the London house and insisted that Elise help him entertain some important American business colleagues, and much against her will, she reluctantly agreed; only because she knew them from the last time they had stayed with them in London. The entertaining proved to be the usual round of drinks parties, with William returning home so drunk every night that he didn't even notice that Elise was sleeping in the attic guest room.

At the end of the week, when the Americans finally departed, he stopped coming home again all together. Elise was surprised to find that she was no longer afraid of him, and that hatred had turned to indifference.

William left for Germany and Elise spent time with her mother and seeing her dear friend James about a divorce.

During any spare time she had, Elise wrote long letters to Beppe. The post between England and Sardinia proved to be erratic, and so they took to numbering their letters in order to know how many had gone astray. When she received his letters, she would go to the park and find a bench, away from prying eyes, before reading his news. He would tell her how much he missed her and how his ideas for a co-operative were coming along. He wanted to know when she was coming back and longed for her return. He always ended his letters 'I lovingly kiss you', and to Elise it summed up everything she loved about Beppe.

The summer passed with increasing heat, and Elise took to spending more and more time with her mother. It seemed that the barriers that had divided them for so many years had finally broken down, and they became great friends. They talked about when she was a young girl, and about her father.

Then, in mid-August while visiting her mother, Elise fainted in the corridor. A young doctor, who happened to be present, caught her and insisted on examining her.

'You must go and see your doctor, and in the meantime to try to take things a little easy. You know you are pregnant, don't you?'

Desperately hoping this to be true, Elise took her courage in both hands and went to see her doctor, who confirmed her wildest hopes and the young doctor's diagnosis.

'Yes, Mrs Raynesford, there is no doubt at all that you are pregnant,' said Doctor Shepherd. 'I estimate the date of birth will be around the beginning of March. Congratulations – and don't forget to come for regular check-ups.'

Elise floated home on a cloud of bliss, and sat down to write to Beppe:

My own dearest, darling,

I hope everything is well with you. I am well, more than well; I am amazingly healthy.

Darling, something wonderful has happened. I am pregnant. The 'wedding gift' of rice has worked its magic. I only hope you are as happy as I am.

I have made up my mind that as soon as my mother is well enough (or if something happens), I will come back to you. However difficult it will be on the island for us, it can't be any worse than living apart. I only hope you are as happy as I am with this news.

I miss you and I lovingly kiss you.

My own dearest love,

Your Elise

Not until she had posted the letter, did it occur to her to wonder what his reaction would be. Three long weeks passed before she heard from him, and she opened his letter with trembling hands.

My darling, Elise,

I am sorry I haven't written earlier. I have been away and only just received your wonderful news.

I read your letter and wept. We are to have a son! I say son, as I am sure that is what it will be, having been conceived in such love, and I am so happy.

Please take care of yourself and as soon as you can, please come back to me. We can work things out on the island, I am sure.

I am so excited because suddenly my life has meaning. I have you and our child; hopefully the first of many. Six boys, I think it was! I will work night and day to see you all have everything you want.

I love you, Elise, and I ache for you. My thoughts are always with you.

If you don't hear from me for a week or so, don't worry as I am going up north to try to secure some contracts for supplying the hotels there and the south of the island.

The idea of a co-operative is going slowly, and I am looking into plant importation, as more and more people are using the small tractors now. So in the meantime, I am working on supplying the hotels and restaurants that need fresh vegetables, now that tourism is taking hold on the island.

I will be in touch soon. I love you, Elise, take care of your self and our son. I lovingly kiss you.

Your Beppe xxx

She read, and then re-read its contents, slipping it in her handbag before going to see her mother.

CHAPTER TWENTY SEVEN

'Is that husband of yours ever at home?' enquired Elise's mother.

'Not often.' said Elise as she sat beside her mother's bed.

Her mother frowned. She was having one of her good days and didn't seem to be in too much pain.

'It's not right, Elise. Perhaps you should go with him on these trips.'

'I did to begin with – you know that, Mummy. But they're only excuses for cocktail parties and drinking orgies. I'm just not interested.'

'You're looking well, though, Elise,' she commented, eyeing her up and down, 'and I think you've put on a little weight. It suits you.'

'Yes, I have,' Elise paused and took her mother's hand. 'Mummy, I'm going to have a baby in March.'

Her mother's eyes lit up.

'Are you? Oh, Elise, that's wonderful news! I am to be a grandmother at last. You must be thrilled. What a pity your father is not alive he would have been so proud. When did you say it was due? And what does William think? Perhaps this is just the thing to make him settle down,' she said, running all her words together in her excitement.

Elise smiled at her mother.

'It's due at the beginning of March – William doesn't know yet.'

'Well, you'll be able to tell him when he comes back from Germany. When will that be?'

'Next week sometime, I think.'

'My dearest girl – so I'm to be a grandmother, at last,' she repeated, gleefully. 'I was beginning to wonder if it would ever happen.'

Elise leaned across and put a hand on her arm.

'I'm so glad you are pleased,' she said, deciding not to tell her mother just yet about Beppe.

In the early hours of the morning came the phone call Elise had been dreading. She was told her mother had slipped into a coma and she had better come as soon as possible.

Elise never had the chance to speak to her mother again. She was glad she hadn't told her about Beppe, she was sure that she would not have understood; besides, she had died happy in the knowledge that she was to have a grandchild.

Elise now had to arrange the funeral, which was to be in the country. Her mother would be laid to rest with her father in the small parish churchyard. James, her friend and solicitor, helped organise everything. William was noticeable by his absence, but she knew it wouldn't be long before she heard from him. She didn't have long to wait, because two days later William phoned her at her parents home to say he was back and wanted to see her urgently.

It was late evening when she arrived in London. Elise let herself in at the front door of their large house. The place was in darkness, except for the strip of light under the study door. She was about to cross the hall and climb the stairs when the study door opened. Her husband stood there, a drunken, stooped figure silhouetted against the light of the study. Elise could smell the drink on his breath from where she was standing.

'Goin' somewhere?' he slurred, propping himself against the door frame.

'Yes, I'm going to bed. I'll see you in the morning when you're sober.'

'Jus' you come here, my fine lady,' William snarled, lurching forward. He barred her way, holding on to the newel post for support, leering at her.

'I've been celebrating,' he said, mockingly. 'I think you've shhome thin' to tell me, don't you?'

'What do you mean?' she retorted, turning cold.

'Doc Shepherd rang this afternoon to say he wanted another check-up. I was quite surprised when he congratulated me on the fact that I was soon to become a daddy!'

He reeled towards her, thrusting his face in hers; his eyes narrowed.

'Who is the father, eh? Some greasy little wop you met on the beach? You bitch. You little whore!'

'I'm not prepared to discuss it with you while you're in this state,' said Elise, forcing herself to speak calmly. 'I have seen James already about a divorce. In the meantime, if you are staying here, I shall move to a hotel.'

'There'll be no divorce. I shall see to that!' said William.

'Why? You don't love me. All you care about is your women, the bottle and your gambling.'

'You're damn right I don't love you! I never have – but you had a good-sized bank account at twenty-one, and it was credit to me in the gaming houses. If you go, my credit goes too; and there will be nothing left after all the creditors have been paid, I can assure you!'

Elise stood there, speechless. William, aware of the position he was in, immediately turned on the charm.

'After all, Elise,' he wheedled, 'you don't really think you could be happy, do you, living in some squalid little village surrounded by a hoard of snivelling kids?'

'How could you possibly, in a thousand years, know what makes me happy? You've never once considered me since the day we were married!'

'And I suppose that jumped up little wop has!' he shouted.

'He's a thousand times the man you are. At least, he's proved himself, which is more than you've been able to do. You're not a man; you're just a... a drunken soak!'

With a curse, William rushed at her and struck her on the side of the head, sending her reeling against the wall. Then he stood in front of her, his mouth contorted in a triumphant sneer.

'I found all your letters in your father's desk, and I thought you'd like to know that I've burnt them.'

Elise looked dumbfounded, and tears welled up and spilled down her cheeks as she saw where her father's desk had been forced open. The remains of Beppe's letters lay in ashes in the grate.

'You bastard,' she said weeping and began thumping him on his chest. He pushed her away from him sending her reeling on the floor.

'Maybe, but before you pack your things, you'd better read this!' He said leaning over her and hurled a letter at her, which hit her in the face. 'Seems the lover boy is dead, been killed in a car crash, leaving his poor bastard child to you!'

Elise climbed slowly to her feet, ice cold with shock, her fingers so numb she could hardly hold the letter. It was short and to the point:

Signora Raynesford
Giuseppe Zedda was involved in a car accident outside Cagliari with a friend and the funeral took place yesterday. The family has asked me to return your crucifix, and has stated that they wish no further communication with you, whatsoever, regarding this matter.
Signed: Father Guido

'This was with it. I believe it's yours!' William dangled the coral crucifix in front of her, laughing. Elise reached up and snatched it from him. 'Well,' he went on, 'I don't want the bastard child!'

'You won't have it. I'll see you in hell first!' she cried.

With a roar, he sprang at her and began beating her unmercifully around the face. She defended herself as best she could. She lashed out at him and caught him off balance, sending him sprawling across the floor. Before he could get up, she ran to the door, wrenched it open and fled, weeping, into the street. She ran as fast as she could, her aim to get as far away as possible. A cruising taxi approached and she frantically waved it down.

'You alright, Miss?' asked the cabby, peering at her bruised and bleeding face. 'Ope the other bloke is worse!'

'Yes, yes, I'm alright now.' She managed a smile. Thank heaven for the London cabbie. 'Please take me to Cheyenne walk.'

She slumped back in the taxi, still panting and gasping for breath. It was then she realised she was still clutching the crucifix and the letter in her trembling hands. In that brief moment, she saw Beppe's face.

He was smiling and saying, 'You will only have it back when I die.'

The taxi stopped. She stumbled out, asked him to wait and fell against the doorbell.

The door was opened and Elise collapsed into James's arms.

When she regained consciousness, Elise found herself in bed. James and a stranger were standing over her. James took her hand and said, gently:

'Thank God you've come round. This is Doctor Peters. I called him in; you were in a terrible state. What in heaven's name happened to you?'

Elise looked from one concerned face to the other.

'Is… is my baby alright?' she asked quietly.

'Yes – don't upset yourself. You have nothing to worry about on that score. I've checked the heartbeat, and everything seems to be in order,' said the doctor, who then turned to James.

'I'll go now. She'll be alright. I have given her a very mild sedative and I'll call in to see her again in the morning. You stay with her – I'll see myself out.'

James sat down on the edge of the bed.

'What has happened, Elise?' he asked again. 'Did William do this to you?'

'It… it was, yes,' she whispered, struggling to control her tears.

'I see,' said James grimly. 'Well, try to sleep now, my dear. You're quite safe here, I promise.'

He stood up to go.

'James… he's dead. Beppe is dead. What am I going to do without him?'

'What do you mean he's dead? How do you know that?'

'I had a letter that William opened. Beppe was killed in a car accident. Where is the crucifix?'

'Over there, on the table. Don't worry now, just you get some sleep.'

'James, life was bad enough being apart from Beppe, but at least I knew he was thinking of me and that he was alive and well. What am I going to do now he has gone, and I will never see him again; and he will never see his child?' she wept. 'And William found all his letters and burnt them. I only have the last one he wrote.'

'Hush, Elise, my dear I am so sorry but you must sleep now and we will talk later.'

She did sleep, surprisingly well. When she woke it was a moment before the realisation hit her. Beppe was dead; she would never see him again, never feel his touch or know his kisses. Tears fell silently, she felt totally devastated and her head was pounding.

James' housekeeper, Mrs Simons, came in and tentatively asked whether there was anything she could do to help.

'I've a terrible headache. Have you something for it?' Elise asked her tears flowing freely as she struggled with all her emotions.

Mrs Simons disappeared and Elise, dressed in James' pyjamas, slowly climbed out of bed to brush her hair. She was unprepared for what she saw in the mirror. Her face was black and blue and grazed where William's knuckles had struck her. Her eyes were swollen from crying. She sat staring at herself, gently pressing the bruised marks.

'You shouldn't be out of bed,' said Mrs Simons, returning with the pills. She helped Elise back into bed and was tucking her in when James knocked at the door.

'Can I come in?' he asked.

'Yes, do,' replied Elise.

He was carrying a tray with fresh coffee, toast, butter and marmalade, which he put on the table next to the bed.

Elise turned her head away, saying in a muffled voice, 'Please don't look at me. My face is a terrible mess.'

'Don't you worry about that,' he replied gently. 'Come – sit up, I'll pour you some coffee. Thank you, Mrs Simons,' he added to his housekeeper, 'I'll look after her now.'

When she had gone, James placed the tray in front of Elise. He sat down in a chair beside the bed and looked at her tenderly.

'Now – I know about Beppe, but don't you think it's time to tell me the whole story.'

'I… I hardly know where to start,' stammered Elise, fighting her tears.

James took her hand and squeezed it gently.

'Try starting at the beginning – from the moment you stepped off the plane in Sardinia.'

CHAPTER TWENTY EIGHT

It was late September when James and Elise were chauffeured down to Suffolk. It was one of those golden days when summer seems to linger, giving a warm, mellow feeling to the countryside.

'It's on days like this, I would like to throw everything up in London and practise in the country,' mused James as he watched the countryside slip by.

'Don't be silly; you couldn't exist down here without your clubs, theatres and general social life. You know that.'

'Maybe, but I know you will be happy here.'

James looked across at Elise. She looked wonderful, radiant; pregnancy had given her a healthy glow. He smiled at her, and she squeezed his hand.

'I don't know what I would have done without you over these past few weeks, James. Thank you for all your help and for letting me stay with you. I couldn't have stayed at the house alone.'

'It's been a pleasure, Elise. Tell me, are you nervous?'

'No, not at all, I love my grandfather dearly, and it will be wonderful for the baby to grow up on the farm.'

James took Elise's hand and gently squeezed it.

'I heard from William's solicitors yesterday. The London house has been put in the hands of the agents and it will sell very quickly. It seems that William has insisted on organising everything, so I have let him and his solicitors sort out the sale of the lease, et cetera. I know you don't want anything from the house, other that your father's desk. Do you want me to forward any mail to you?'

'No, I have no one I want to hear from, and there will only be bills and letters for William. There will be nothing for me. I want a complete break, please, and I certainly don't want William turning up at the farm.'

'You have no worries on that, my dear. He has a restraining order on him. If he so much as contacts you, let me know at once and he will be in court. Besides, he is off to the States with a new, very rich American widow next month.'

'She will need to be rich with his tastes in gambling. I can't believe how much money he went through. But then thanks to you, I have a large amount of it back. However did you manage that?'

'It was quite simple really,' said James with a broad smile. 'I told him that if he didn't allow you to divorce him and reimburse you with the money, I would make sure that the photos I took of you after he had beaten you up would be sent to his new, rich widow.'

'God, James, whatever did he say?'

'He called me a blackmailing queer and paid up. He was frightened that she would leave him.'

Elise smiled at her old friend, squeezed his hand again, and added, 'Thank you.'

'Elise, there is one other thing. I wrote to Father Guido in Santa Cella about Beppe, but I am afraid I have had the same reply: they do not want any contact with you. I am so very sorry, my dear.'

Elise turned away and fought the oncoming tears that stung the back of her eyes. It was over, Beppe was dead and nobody wanted to know her any more. She was on her own. She sighed.

'Thank you for that. I miss him so much James. I wake in the night feeling him near me. I think I hear him call my name and he is not there. If only we could have said goodbye.' She turned to James. 'I have written to the villa to Maria and Efisio, but have heard nothing from them either. It seems no one wants to know me now. I feel so guilty. I feel responsible for his death in someway; if I had gone back to him earlier or not left him, perhaps he might not have been doing whatever it was he was doing and still be alive,' said Elise.

'You mustn't think like that, Elise. Promise me; try to put those thoughts out of your mind. It is time to make a new life, with the baby and being here at the farm. At least you have something wonderful of his.'

Elise looked at James and fighting back her tears nodded at him.

They turned into the long drive up to the farm, and Elise put on a smile as she saw her grandfather come out to greet them. Francis, his housekeeper, was with him and they all hugged one another in greeting.

Lunch was served out on the terrace under the shade of a large

Judas tree. The garden was still in full flower. Her grandfather loved his garden, and it showed. Francis had laid on a magnificent spread of cold salmon and fillet of beef with salad, followed by homemade ice cream. Port with cheese and biscuits rounded off a great meal. James sat back in his chair and complimented Elise's grandfather George Farthing on his splendid hospitality.

Finally, the time came to say their goodbyes as James made ready to leave for London again. He turned to Elise,

'I'll let you know when the money comes through. In the meantime, take things easy and keep in touch. We can decide what you want to do with your parent's house in the months to come.'

He shook hands with George Farthing, thanked Francis again for a wonderful meal and her hospitality towards his chauffeur, kissed Elise and with a wave of the hand was gone.

Elise settled well into the farm life, and insisted on helping whenever she could. It became her job to collect the eggs from the large hen houses, just as she had as a child. She sorted them into sizes, washed them and carefully packed them into boxes of six or twelve to be sold at the farm gate.

One day, in early October, when she had finished all her chores, she wandered across to the greenhouse where her grandfather was working. There had been a frost that night and the leaves from the trees in the orchard had fallen in pools around the trunks; it looked magical. She had the peach stones with her that she had so lovingly kept with the few things she had of Beppe's.

'He gave me these peaches when I was in his peach garden. It was the last time we were together,' she said handing them to her grandfather, silent tears running down her cheeks.

He took them from her, and smiled. 'We will see if we can grow them. It will make an interesting challenge.'

The two of them tended them carefully over the following months. During this time together, she would tell him about Beppe and all the things they had done together on the island. He listened and asked her many questions about the island and its people. She found it easy to talk about those times and was grateful to her grandfather for all his interest.

Elise was physically well, but had terrible days of depression when she found it difficult to stop crying. On better days she would sit and sketch the places and people of the island from memory. She wanted a record for the baby, so she could tell him about his island and his father and all the wonderful things and happy times they had spent together. She was still sure it was going to be a boy.

Christmas loomed, and her grandfather arranged for James to come down for the holiday week. This time, he drove himself down to the farm, arriving with a hamper from Fortnum and Mason, a crate of champagne and presents for everyone. It was a good time; the weather was cold but the farmhouse was warm and smelt of cooking from morning until night.

Christmas day came with turkey and all the trimmings, followed by Francis's homemade pudding and mince pies.

James and George Farthing retired to the study to smoke cigars and enjoy another brandy while Elise went to bed for a rest before the evening festivities and fell into a deep and dreamless sleep and awoke refreshed for the first time in ages.

In the following days James and Elise wrapped up warmly and spent time together going for long walks in the countryside, returning to sit in front of a roaring fire in the sitting room, for tea and toast. Everyone helped with the domestic chores and the cooking. When the festivities were over, James returned to London, taking a large rib of beef which George had given him, knowing how partial he was to a good roast.

After Christmas, George asked Francis's daughter, Sarah, to help and to be a companion for Elise. She had finished her nursing course and was looking for a job. Being the housekeeper's daughter the two girls had grown up together and shared the same interests. Sarah had always helped Elise if she had found a wounded animal or if a lamb on the farm needed fostering. Sarah loved children and she regularly walked all the dogs, which allowed George time to put his feet up.

Elise and Sarah soon picked up the threads of their friendship and became close, just as they had been in childhood; this was a great comfort to Elise. Sarah never tired of Elise's stories of the island, and asked her time and again to retell the story of her meeting Beppe and the things they had done together.

In early March, the weather turned warm and the spring sun made the last days of her pregnancy enjoyable as she walked in her grandfather's garden. Elise had decided that she wanted the birth to be at home, and the local midwife now visited her every day.

She was woken in the early hours of a Friday morning with back pain and the realisation that she was going into labour.

Although George Farthing was a longstanding stockman, well used to the traumas of birth, he surprisingly went into a state of panic, summoning assistance from every conceivable source. He rang the midwife, begging her to come quickly. He then rang James for moral support. James dropped everything and went on an immediate spending spree before heading down to Suffolk.

The labour proved to be long and difficult for Elise, but finally, early in the evening, she gave birth to a beautiful baby boy whom she named Joe. Elise held her son in her arms and cried tears of joy. The midwife allowed all the family in briefly. George looked at his great-grandson and the big man fought back his tears of joy. James couldn't have looked prouder if he had been the father, and Sarah was completely overawed by the whole thing.

Elise turned to James and her grandfather, 'Will you two be godparents to Joe?' she asked. And then, turning to Sarah, she said, 'And will you be godmother, please?'

Sarah nodded and burst into tears. Her grandfather bit his lip and smiled tenderly at his granddaughter and James, who looked as if all his Christmases had come at once, bent and kissed Elise on her forehead. At that point the midwife finally ushered them all out of the room so Elise could get some rest.

While Elise slept upstairs, the godparents and Francis all celebrated the arrival of the baby with a good meal and copious amounts of champagne, thoughtfully provided by James in way of a present to them all. They retired late, and in the early hours of the morning Elise woke to the sound of Joe wanting his feed. She picked him up and suckled her beautiful son. Her tears fell onto his tiny face, and she wiped them away. She thought of Beppe and sighed heavily. If only he had lived to see his son; life could be so cruel.

She smiled through her tears; he had said it would be a boy and he would have been so proud of his son, who was just like him with his pale, olive skin and dark hair. She felt a flood of joy and pride spread through her as she looked at her son nestling in her arms. She had called him Joseph James. Joseph after his father and James after her dearest friend, but he would be known as Joe. At that moment, she promised herself that they would be friends, not just mother and son, and that she would tell him all about his wonderful father and his beautiful homeland.

So Joe was nurtured in a house of love and harmony. He would learn to love the land from his grandfather, respect for others from James, literature and Italian from his mother, and friendship from Sarah. All this would lead to him growing into a young man of whom any father would be proud.

PART TWO

CHAPTER TWENTY NINE

England

April 1991

Joe settled himself in the seat of the plane. The flight to Milan would only take a couple of hours. He closed his eyes and thought over the last month. He had flown in from Milan to spend his twenty-first birthday with Elise at the farm. She had joined him at the table for breakfast, kissed him and handed him a small package.

'Happy twenty-first birthday, my darling boy,' she had said, dropping a kiss on his head.

He opened the present, and read the letter inside.

My dearest, Joe,
Where do I start, and how do I thank you for being such a wonderful son and giving me such an insight into your father.
I would like you to have this as it is all I have to give you that belonged to Beppe.
I love you, Joe.
Elise

Joe swallowed hard and had taken the coral crucifix from the box in which she always kept it. He knew it had originally come in a green velvet box when she gave it to Beppe, but only the crucifix had been returned. The chain felt heavy in his hand.

'Here,' Elise said, 'let me help you,' as she came round the table to place the chain around his neck.

'Are you sure about this, Mamma? It is yours, and you have nothing else of his,' he said, rising and kissing her on her cheek.

'I have you. And I still have his ring,' she said, smiling, at the same time turning the ring on her wedding finger.

Joe knew the cross was her most beloved possession; Elise had given it to Beppe when they were together in Sardinia. He had been overwhelmed by the gift. Also, tucked in an envelope was the letter from the priest telling her of Beppe's death.

'Can I get you something to drink, sir?' said the young flight attendant, bringing him back to the present.

'A coke, please.'

He took the drink, thanked the young girl and sipping it slowly, went back to his thoughts.

Sarah had also wished him a happy birthday and given him a present.

'You only have one twenty-first, and I hope it brings you everything you could wish for.'

Joe had looked at the neat little gift.

'Well, open it. It won't bite,' she said in her usual no-nonsense way.

He opened it to reveal a pair of gold, fox-mask cufflinks.

'Wow, Sarah, these are lovely; you shouldn't have, but thank you.'

'Well, it's not every day my godson turns twenty-one. I'm so glad you like them.'

He rose and kissed Sarah on both cheeks, and she had hurried out of the room, trying to hide her blush.

James and Elise had arranged a small dinner party at James's club in London, he was well known as the service had been excellent. It was a celebration for Joe's birthday, and it turned out to be a very special day. The chauffeur was sent to collect them from the farm, and they arrived at James's house just after two o'clock. James and Joe went out to do some shopping and Elise went to have her hair done.

Later, they all met up in the elegant sitting room at James's beautiful home in Chelsea.

Elise entered the room wearing a new, navy silk dress. She looked stunning.

'My, you two men look very smart in your dinner jackets,' Elise said as she kissed Joe on his cheek. 'Happy birthday darling.' She drew back and stared at him. 'Are you wearing a new cologne?'

'Yes, do you like it? James took me out to choose a new one.'

'It's *Eau Savage*. Did you choose it?' said his mother.

'Yes. Why, Elise, don't you like it, and how do you know that?'

'It was your father's favourite cologne. He always wore it. His dear friend Matteo introduced him to it and he said it was his one luxury. You smell as fresh as a bag of lemons.'

He felt a thrill of excitement run through him at the mention of his father. How strange he should choose the same cologne as him.

'Are you alright with it? Do you want me to change it?' he asked.

'Of course not, Joe; but you are so like your father, so like him. He would have been so proud of you.'

'It must be difficult for you, watching me and seeing him all the time?'

'It's not like that, darling boy. You are you, and I love you; but you also remind me of Beppe, and that is wonderful too.'

He put his arms around her, and noticed that she was forcing her tears down as she fought her memories. He also became aware that she had lost weight; she felt so much smaller in his arms.

'Are you alright, Mamma?' he asked, somewhat concerned.

'Yes, of course, silly.'

James broke the tension by calling for a toast.

'To Joe, twenty-one; my duties as a godparent are officially over. However, Joe, you know – as I hope you do too, Elise – that I am always here to help, should you need me.'

They toasted him, and James gave him his present. Joe had opened it to find a stainless steel and gold Rolex watch, and was momentarily taken aback by the generosity of the gift.

'James, thank you. I don't know what to say.'

'Wear it and think of me, and perhaps one day you will be able to hand it down to your son.'

The words had poignancy about them because James would never have children of his own. Joe had put his arms around the neck of his life-long friend and godfather, and hugged him.

'Steady on. All that Italian touchy feely is a bit much.'

And they all laughed.

The meal went well. James and Elise spent time remembering the past.

'Do you remember the first time we met?' asked Elise.

'I do. It was in an art gallery in London.' James turned to Joe. 'It was the time of hot pants and beehive hairdos, and your mother walked into the gallery where I was trying to help out a client of ours. She looked amazing. Her hair was cut in a long bob, much as she wears it now. She had a Chanel-style suit and low, patent-leather shoes. She looked so elegant compared to the other girls.'

'I didn't know you worked in an art gallery,' said Joe.

'It was an office must-do job. Help the client; help your career. The owner was a personal friend of my boss in chambers. He liked racing and had taken my boss with him, so someone had to run the gallery. Anyway, that day there were a pair of Italians in the place trying to make me understand, and Elise dropped in to get out of the rain. She took over, sorted everything out and put a red sticker on the painting they had bought; so I took her out that evening on my commission!'

They had all laughed. It had certainly been a great start to a life-long friendship.

Joe was now returning to Milan in order to finish his course, with four weeks left to study and revise for his horticultural finals.

Elise had been insistent that he did his studies in Italy.

'I want you to have the same background as your father, and then you can come back and expand the farm and start your nursery in England.'

He had been reluctant at first, but now, after two years in Italy, he was grateful to his mother for her persistence.

He fingered the coral cross around his neck. The heavy chain lay on his chest. He had loved it from the first time he had seen it when, coming into Elise's study, he had found her holding it and crying. She had told him that it belonged to his father, Beppe, and how it had been returned to her after his death.

Joe sighed heavily.

He had been due to go straight back to Milan, after the birthday celebrations, but Elise had taken him into her study, sat him down and told him that she had ovarian cancer; she only had a very short time to live. She'd had no idea how ill she was until after a very mild heart attack they had discovered that the cancer had gone too far. Joe had been devastated and begged her to go into hospital, but she had been adamant she wanted to stay at home with Sarah to look after her.

'James knows, but I begged him not to tell you until after the celebrations.'

Joe had been devastated.

James visited regularly and they all spent the precious remaining time together. The doctor came in daily, and as the pain became worse, he sedated Elise. Joe spent as much time as he could with Elise, talking to her and telling her he loved her.

Two weeks after the celebrations, Elise had suffered a second heart attack. The doctor had come and heavily sedated her. It had been a beautiful morning and the sun had filled Elise's bedroom as Joe sat beside her. Elise had taken his hand and looked at him.

'I've come back, my darling,' she said, looking at Joe. He had held her hand to comfort her as she slipped into a coma from which she never awoke.

Joe had been inconsolable and had shut himself in Elise's study for two days while Sarah tried to tempt him into eating something. James had made all the necessary arrangements for the funeral while they all struggled to cope with Elise's early death. At forty-nine, she should still have had a full life ahead of her.

When the day of the funeral arrived, Joe watched the rain of the spring storm beat against the window. The rivulets of water ran down the panes, joining others, growing larger and larger.

The little church had been cold and draughty, and the black-clad vicar was only too glad to draw the proceedings to an early close. When they went outside, the rain had eased and the sun had begun to show, intermittently, from behind the scurrying, slate-grey clouds. Everything had looked vivid in the storm light; so green and fresh, making drops of water that hung on the branches sparkle in the sunlight.

The grave had been waterlogged, and a trickle of water had flowed over the canvas edge, splashing into the well of darkness below. Even the canvas straps were soaked, which made the lowering of the coffin difficult. It had caught against the damp patches, causing it to descend into the gaping hole with a jerking movement as if reluctant to leave the light of the day for the eternal darkness waiting below.

Joe shuddered. Elise had hated the dark and the rain; now she was a victim of both, with only the coffins of her parents beside her for cold comfort. But she was with Beppe now, and he hoped that she had found peace at last.

He looked around at the number of people who had come to Elise's funeral and was both proud and surprised to see so many had come to say their farewells.

After the funeral, Joe had been staring out of the farmhouse sitting room window.

'Here, take this,' James had said.

Joe turned and smiled at James; he took the proffered glass of wine. His godfather was a strong, good-looking man who was gently turning grey at the temples. The years had been kind to him though, and he still carried himself well. James Bennett, always there in his life for as long as he could remember and always there whenever Elise needed him too. Never too busy to take him out as a young boy and do the things boys usually do with fathers or uncles. James was a busy and much respected family lawyer who worked tirelessly to help others. No doubt if he hadn't been gay, Elise might well have married him, he thought.

'She died thinking I was Beppe,' Joe said.

'She loved you both so much,' replied James, and then looking at his Godson he continued 'She asked me to give you this.'

James pulled a package out of his brief case and handed it to Joe.

'What is it?' asked Joe.

'It contains Elise's diary when she was in Sardinia, the last letter from Beppe and a small silver plaque.'

Joe opened the package and took out the contents. He picked up the plaque. It was oval, about four inches by three inches, and solid silver. It had been hand engraved in Italian: *In loving memory of my beloved Beppe. Always with me in the Spirit of Sardegna. Elise*

So, here he was on the flight to Milan and then on to Sardinia to carry out Elise's last wishes and take the plaque to Santa Cella.

The flight attendant came past and reminded him to put on his seat-belt for landing. The plane touched down at Milan airport; Joe collected his luggage and went to find the flight desk for Cagliari. There was a flight in two hours. He bought a ticket and waited to be called. A couple of days and then he would be back in Milan.

He needed to see his father's village, to see where he had grown up, and he wanted to visit his father's grave. It had been a surprise to receive his mother's diary and the plaque with the request to take it down to Santa Cella. She had never been back to the island. She was afraid she would be rejected by Beppe's friends and that the memories would be too painful. But with all the talk of the past at his birthday party and having read parts of her diary, Joe found he was curious about his parentage.

Finally, his flight was called and he headed down to Sardinia. The flight was good and he looked down at the island with its mountains and patchwork fields and sighed.

Joe stepped off the plane at the new Elmas Airport in Cagliari. He collected his case and found a taxi.

'A hotel in the centre of Cagliari, please,' he said in perfect Italian.

A discussion ensued with the driver as to which type of hotel, and after much deliberation Joe chose the Jolly. Having signed in to the hotel, he went out to explore Cagliari.

He wandered through Casteddu, the old part of the city, taking in the sights and sounds. It was just as Elise had described it from all those years ago. She had sketched many of the places she had visited and the people she had met. They had spent long hours in the winter together when she told him about her time on the island.

He found himself at the Piazza di Yennes; her stories and pictures came to mind of the festa that Elise had watched opposite the municipal building at the bottom of this street with Maria and the family. It was all so familiar. There was the broad street of Largo Carlo Felice, where she had watched the candle light procession. On the opposite side of the road was *Libreria Cocco*, where Beppe had bought her the beautiful book on Sardinia; they all matched her vivid description in the diary and her sketches.

He walked on in the late-afternoon sun. He felt at peace, and as if he belonged here. He loved Milan, but this felt like home.

Joe crossed the road to the book shop where he bought a map of the area, and then, thanking the tall assistant, he retraced his steps to the hotel.

'I'd like to hire a car for tomorrow morning. Please can you arrange that for me?'

'Certainly signore for how many days will you want the car?'

'Two days will be enough. Thank you.'

'I will see to that for you, sir. Is there anything else I can help you with?'

Joe produced the map of the area and laid it on the desk. 'I want to go to Santa Cella.'

'No problem signore.' Coming round the counter, he pointed the way on the map. 'Straight up the Sassari road to Monastir and then you turn off to the right; it's easy. It is about half to three quarters of an hour from Cagliari.'

'Thank you,' said Joe. Folding the map, and wished the man a good evening.

Joe decided to eat away from the hotel and walked down to the Via Roma. The wide arcade overlooked the port of Cagliari, but despite only being mid-April, the air was warm.

He found a small restaurant and sat outside, watching the evening world of Cagliari pass him by.

'Would you like something to drink?'

A young Sardinian girl stood beside him, pen and pad in her hand. Her dark eyes sparkled at him.

'Yes a Sardinian beer please.'

She nodded and disappeared, returning moments later with a glass and a bottle of beer.

'Thank you,' he said and watched as she poured the golden liquid into the glass.

'Would you like something to eat, signore?' Her pad was once again poised in her hand.

'What do you have?'

She disappeared to find a menu and returned giving Joe a broad smile.

He looked through the comprehensive list of offerings; he wasn't that hungry.

'*Malloreddus*, please,' he said, watching the young girl as she wrote with concentration. It had been Elise's favourite.

'And for anti-pasta?'

'No. Nothing, thank you.'

'And second?' Her hand still poised over the pad.

'No, nothing, thank you. But I will have a glass of your local wine to go with the *Malloreddus*.'

She hurried away with her small order, and Joe settled down to listen to the sound of motorbikes and cars roaring past as people returned home from work. Gradually, the traffic noise gave way to the chattering of the promenaders on the Via Roma.

His pasta came, together with a glass of dark wine.

'*Cannanou*,' said the young girl, '*va bene?*'

Joe nodded his approval, and she went off to look after another customer.

He took the wine and gently swirled it in the glass. The liquid hung on the side of the glass, indicating its strength. He smiled. Elise had always said that the Sard wines were strong. He raised his glass in silent salute to Elise, and to his father, Beppe. Elise had been afraid of rejection, but for him, though, it was different. No one knew who he was or where he came from. He was tall enough to pass as an Italian from the north, and his accent from Milan would not cause any problems. So when James had given him the contents of the package, he had been more than happy to carry out Elise's wishes.

He was so deep in thought he had not touched his meal.

'Is everything alright?' asked the young girl, looking concerned, bringing Joe back from his thoughts again.

'Oh, yes, thank you.'

He began eating. The *malloreddus* was excellent, and he tucked in heartily, suddenly realising how hungry he really was.

Later, back in his hotel room, he took out the letter from the priest in Santa Cella from all those years ago, and the last one she had received from Beppe. It was the only letter she had of his as William had found and burnt all his others. Joe opened the letter from the priest carefully. It was dated August 1969 and was written in shaky handwriting. No preamble, just straight to the point.

Signora Raynesford

Giuseppe Zedda was involved in a car accident outside Cagliari with a friend and the funeral took place yesterday. The family has asked me to return your crucifix and have stated that they wish no further communication with you, what so ever, regarding this matter.

Signed: Father Guido

He read the letter again. He looked at the envelope, which was addressed to Mr and Mrs Raynesford. How odd he thought; why would the priest write to them both rather than just Elise.

Joe looked at the other letter; opened it and began to read.

My darling, Elise,

I am sorry I haven't written earlier. I have been away and only just received your wonderful news.

I read your letter and wept. We are to have a son! I say son, as I am sure that is what it will be, having been conceived in such love, and I am so happy.

Joe caught his breath.

Tomorrow, he would see Beppe's village. He would go to find the priest and see if he knew more about the accident. The idea filled him with an unexpected excitement, tinged with both fear and regret.

CHAPTER THIRTY

Joe turned off the main road at the sign pointing to Santa Cella. Clouds of dust rose up in the air behind him as he drove along the road. He passed small fields of barley, vineyards and neat rows of peach, orange and lemon trees. The village proved easy to find, just as the man at the hotel in Cagliari said it would be. He could see the square outline of the church and made his way towards it, knowing that it would be in the centre of the village.

Suddenly, he found himself in a large garden area which was the middle of the square, full of flowering trees and shrubs, the scents of which he recognised as being the same as those in his mother's garden at home.

A young man on a bicycle came towards him, whistling an unfamiliar tune. Joe parked under the shade of a large fig tree and crossed to the church. Inside, it was cool and quiet. A number of people were praying, but there was no sign of a priest. He was turning to leave when a hand touched his arm.

'You look lost, signore,' said an old man, looking him squarely in the eye and speaking Italian with a strong Sard accent. He was bent and leant heavily on a stick. His face was like a walnut, but there was a twinkle in his eyes.

'I'm looking for the priest here,' Joe replied in Italian. 'Father Guido, I think his name is.'

'Then, alas, you look in vain,' said the old man. 'Father Guido died a number of years ago. Father Domenico is the parish priest now, but he's not here either at the moment. He is administering the last rites to an old woman in the village.'

'When will he be back?'

'That I don't know, signore. But if your business is important, I suggest you see the doctor. He usually helps the Father when he can.'

'Where does he live, please?' asked Joe.

'In that house over there, the one with the high wall,' said the old man, leaning on the door and pointing with his stick. 'His name is Doctor Garcia.'

'Thank you. You've been very kind.'

'My pleasure, signore,' replied the old man with natural courtesy. He stood watching the young man as he left the church and crossed to the other side of the square.

The large iron gates creaked slightly as Joe pushed against them, and then slammed shut behind him. The garden was full of almond, lemon and pomegranate trees, and the smell was hypnotic. He climbed the stone steps and knocked on the door. Eventually, it was opened by a rather shy-looking young girl.

'Can I help you?' she asked.

'I hope so. Is this the doctor's house, and is he at home?'

'It is the doctor's house, but I'm afraid he's not in at the moment. Who wants him, please?'

'My name is Joe Warwick. I've come from England. There is something I have to do in the village. I've been to the church, but the priest isn't there either. An old gentleman told me to see the doctor.'

'Please come in,' said the girl. 'The doctor should not be very long.'

She opened the door wide to let Joe enter a hall with a marble floor and dim lighting. It was cool inside after the brilliant sunshine outside. The girl showed him into a large room with closed shutters, which was very pleasant after the morning heat. She offered him a glass of lemonade, which he gratefully accepted, and presently she returned carrying a tray with a large jug and a tumbler. As she poured the lemonade, Joe studied her. She was a pretty girl of about eighteen, with long, black hair and striking eyes.

'Have you travelled far?' she asked, handing him the glass.

'From England,' he said, taking the glass from her. 'I'm staying here for a few days as I have some business in Sardinia.'

'You speak excellent Italian.'

'Thank you. I studied in Milan for two years.'

'Where do you come from in England?' she asked. But before Joe could reply, the front door slammed.

'Ah – that will be Babbu,' she said, excusing herself and hurrying out into the hall. Joe heard brief words exchanged in su Sardu,

216

which he did not understand, and the girl came back accompanied by a tall, dark-haired man. The doctor stepped forward, stretching out his hand in greeting.

'How do you do, signore? I'm Doctor Gino Garcia. I understand I might be able to help you?'

'My name is Joe Warwick,' said Joe, taking the outstretched hand and shaking it firmly.

He smiled but felt somewhat uncomfortable, for the doctor's eyes were fixed intently on his face. Aware that he was staring, the doctor suddenly blinked and made an apologetic gesture.

'I'm sorry to stare at you like that, but the likeness is quite remarkable. You remind me so much of a friend of mine when he was about your age. Still... they say everyone has a double, somewhere.'

'Your friend... would he be a man from this village by the name of Beppe Zedda?'

'Why... yes,' replied the doctor, clearly taken aback. 'But...'

'It's him that I've come to see you about, or at least indirectly.'

'What can I do?' asked the doctor, still visibly shaken.

'I have come to see his village and find his grave. I have been to the church, but the priest wasn't there, and I was advised to come to see you. My mother wanted a plaque put in the church for him.'

'Of course!' The doctor's eyes suddenly widened. 'Holy Mary! You're not... You're Elise's son?'

'Yes, I am. But however do you know?'

'But... her name wasn't Warwick. It began with an R. Ric... Ray...'

'Raynesford,' said Joe.

'That's right!' said the doctor, amazed, and still clearly taken aback.

'She changed it back to her maiden name when she divorced William Raynesford.'

'Divorced him? When was that?' asked the doctor, now looking concerned.

'The same year I was born, in nineteen seventy.'

Doctor Garcia drew in a deep breath and released it, blowing out his cheeks as he did so.

'I need a drink,' he said, 'and I think you will, too. Please sit down.' He opened a large cupboard, from which he took a bottle and two glasses, and as he poured the wine he said, 'Rosie, go and tell your Mamma there'll be another for lunch.'

'Ah, please – don't put yourself out for me,' Joe began, but the girl had already gone. He held up the glass, admiring the wine's rich straw colour. 'It's very kind of you to ask me to stay. Thank you, did you know Beppe? He added.

'Yes. *Salute*,' said the doctor, raising his glass to the young man. '*Salude*.'

'Vernaccia,' went on his host. 'It is a great wine; one peculiar to this island. We Sards are very proud of it.'

Joe sampled the wine. It had the quality of unfortified sherry, with a hint of port.

'Excellent,' said Joe. 'You have every right to be proud of it – it's a beautiful wine.'

'But, now, you didn't come here to discuss the merits of our wine,' replied the doctor. He gazed intently at Joe. 'Tell me, how much do you know about Beppe?' he said, signalling for Joe to sit down.

Joe settled himself into a large, well-worn leather chair beside the doctor's desk, and rested his drink on a nearby table.

'I know my mother came to Sardinia for a holiday. I know she fell deeply in love with a man called Beppe Zedda from this village, and I know that when he died, a part of her died, too. I also know that Beppe Zedda was my father.'

'Died?' Gino Garcia frowned. 'Did Elise tell you all this?'

'Yes. I always knew he was dead. He died before I was born. He had a car accident and was killed. Elise never said anything much about it. She talked about my father all the time, so much so that I feel I know him. She told me how wonderful he was, and how much I was like him. But she hardly ever spoke of his death. She said it was too painful.'

'You certainly look like him; but who told her Beppe was dead?'

'She received this letter from Father Guido, of this village, telling her that Beppe was dead, killed in a car crash outside Cagliari, and that the family didn't want to hear from her any more. They returned this crucifix of Beppe's at the same time.' Joe said, taking the priest's letter from his pocket and pulling the crucifix out from under his shirt.

The doctor took the letter and thought for a moment, then asked, 'Do you know why she divorced her husband?'

'Things hadn't been right between them for a long time before she came to Sardinia; but she and William were both due to come down and stay while he did work at Saras. But William was suddenly sent to America, and Elise decided to come down here on her own. The villa was paid for, so her friend, James, persuaded her to come, but when she returned to England, things were even worse.

'One night, when William returned from Germay, she returned to the house to collect her mail to find him there. He had discovered she was pregnant and he had opened Elise's letter from the priest. He beat her in a drunken rage, found and burnt all Beppe's letters and she left him. She went to live with James, who is the family solicitor and my godfather, for a few weeks. He also contacted the priest, but the result was the same: they wanted nothing to do with her.' Joe paused trying to catch his breath and fight the dryness in his throat and continued.

'It was after this that she went to live with her grandfather in the country. My mother changed her name back to Warwick to stop further gossip, and to protect me as I grew up. William, was involved with the rich widow of an American ambassador, went to live in America with her.'

'And Elise is she still alive?'

'No she is dead.' replied Joe.

'It's a very sad story,' said Gino slowly. 'Sadder than I ever imagined.'

'Why do you say that?'

'Joe...' The doctor began, and then he hesitated and sighed heavily. 'Joe, there is no easy way to say this, but... Beppe Zedda isn't dead. He's alive and still living in the village. In fact, I only treated him about ten days ago. He said he saw Elise, and that she had come back to him.'

Joe looked at the doctor, not understanding what he was saying.

'But he can't be,' he stammered. 'It must be a different Beppe

Zedda. Is it a common name here?' asked Joe, unable to take in what the doctor was saying.

The room was beginning to spin and he felt as if his world was about to tip upside down. The doctor came forward and put Joe's head between his knees. The ringing and hissing in his ears stopped, and the world became still again.

After a moment Joe looked up at the doctor.

'I'm sorry, this is a shock. Is it a common name?' Joe repeated.

'No, not very – and I can promise you, it is the same man. But it's incredible!' the doctor added.

'What is?' asked Joe, with a mounting concern. He was having trouble taking all this in. Words still kept spinning in his head.

'Are you alright?' asked the doctor, looking concerned.

'Yes. I'm sorry; this is rather a lot to take in. What were you saying?'

'It is the same Beppe I can assure you.' continued the doctor. 'Beppe has always suffered from periods of deep depression at about this time of year. At first, when Elise went back to England, they were very bad, and then as time passed they became less marked. The other week, he became terribly depressed and drank himself insensible. The following day, he declared he'd seen Elise in the peach grove. She promised she would come back, and he thought she had.'

'What day was that?' asked Joe, aware of a cold shiver running down his spine. 'Would it have been last Monday week, around midday?' he asked, feeling his throat close and his mouth go dry as he took a sip of the wine.

The doctor thought for a moment.

'Why, yes. However, do you know?' asked the doctor. Then, seeing the expression on the young Englishman's face, he added, 'Your mother died then, didn't she?'

The doctor rose, fetched the wine bottle and replenished their glasses.

'Yes,' replied Joe.

The colour had gone from his face and he felt drained. 'But why didn't Beppe write to her? That's what I want to know. If he wasn't dead, why did he let her go on believing that he was? Didn't he want her anymore; didn't he love her anymore?'

'Of course he did. They wrote constantly to one another, and then suddenly the letters stopped after she told Beppe that she was expecting you. He wrote several times, but the letters came back unopened. One had even been torn into small pieces and put in a new envelope. I wrote, and my letters came back marked 'not known at this address, gone to the USA'.'

Questions were going round in Joe's head; nothing made sense. His mother was dead and his father alive. It had always been the other way around. He turned to the doctor.

'You wrote too? But why?'

'When I came back from Milan, I took over the practice in the village, so Beppe, obviously, became one of my patients. We were always friends. We were two of the few who had left Sardinia and gone to the continent. We had a wider understanding of the world. We both liked music and books, and so we spent time together. He was working hard in the groves with his brother, at the same time starting the new co-operative.'

The doctor took a sip from his drink and slowly replaced it on his desk.

'As I said, he had bouts of depression and used to drink heavily at such times. I heard rumours and gossip, but I wanted to hear the truth from him. One day, he broke down and told me the whole story. Elise had written telling him she was to have his child. She had said she would come back to him if her mother recovered or if she died. He was delighted – ecstatic. He knew she would leave her husband now and come to him, and he wrote to tell her so, saying he would do all in his power to make her and the child happy. However, he never heard from her again.'

The doctor paused again and sighed.

'He wrote again and again to her, but as I said, all his letters came back unopened. He was determined to see her, so he organised a flight to England to try to find her. There was an accident, and Luigi was killed and Beppe injured. After the accident, he said he was going to the north of the island, but flew to England. He went to her house, but it was all shut up. At that point, Beppe came home a broken man, believing that Elise had abandoned him completely.'

Joe reached for a drink and swallowed it in one, still trying to take in everything the doctor was saying. The doctor rose and refilled Joe's glass.

'Thank you,' said Joe, 'please go on.'

'Beppe told me that life without Elise was going to be hell on earth, and that he wasn't sure that he wanted to live if she wasn't there in his world. Needless to say, we watched him day and night until his fighting spirit returned.'

The doctor's words went round in Joe's head. His father was alive; he had been alive all that time and Elise had not realised. How cruel was that? Tears stung the back of his eyes as he tried to keep his emotions under control.

'I can hardly believe it,' said Joe with a break in his voice. 'But it must have been because she moved to the country after receiving the letter telling her that Beppe was dead. She wouldn't have expected to hear from him after that, naturally. It must have been William who returned the letters, out of sheer spite. I know she left William to sort out everything in London, and he put it in the hands of the selling agent; she went to live with her grandfather. She was frightened that William would cause her trouble. He owed so much money in gambling debts, so she would have covered her tracks fairly well.'

The doctor stood up and put a comforting hand on Joe's shoulder.

Joe looked at the doctor and said. 'Why did fate deal them such a blow? Why did they suffer so? They only loved one another, what was the crime in that? My God, they could have been together all this time, and now my mother is dead.'

Joe felt the tears run down his cheeks. Turning away from the doctor, he took out his handkerchief and wiped his face.

The doctor bit his lip and said,

'Beppe saw it as retribution for what he called his mortal sin; and his mother and the old village priest nagged him continually, reminding him of his duty as the eldest son. Duty and responsibility have always lain heavily on Beppe's shoulders.'

'Surely he couldn't believe in retribution like that? How can loving someone be so bad?'

'It went against all the teachings of the Church, and he was brought up by his mother to be a strict Roman Catholic.' The doctor sighed. 'Let me tell you something, Joe, to try to help you understand. When I was at medical school in Milan, there was a very bright student from Africa. He was top in everything, but when he was diagnosed as having cancer himself, he packed his bags and went back to the witch doctor in his village. Lessons learnt at our parents' and grandparents' knees are hard to shake off.'

A silence hung between them.

'He must have felt very bitter towards my mother,' said Joe sadly. 'He must have felt she had abandoned him.'

'I don't think so,' replied the doctor. 'You see, he still loves her and believes she will, one day, come back to him. I know the old priest insisted that Beppe confess his sin, but as Beppe told me later, he couldn't do that. He would have to be penitent in order to receive absolution, but he wasn't. He loved her and still wanted her, even though she hadn't returned. The priest then threatened him with excommunication, but thankfully he died before the application was made to the authorities. When the new and younger priest came, with fewer rigid ideas, the whole thing was dropped.'

'Beppe's mother must have hated Elise,' said Joe as quiet tears still pricked his eyes and he fought to keep them at bay.

The doctor put a comforting hand on Joe's knee. 'Perhaps, she was certainly a very jealous, possessive woman with a deep, morbid religious conviction. While I can't condone what she did, I have to admire her for doing what she thought was right for her son. Nevertheless, it was a wicked and senseless thing to do.'

'Poor Beppe. How is he going to react when he hears about Elise's death?'

'Badly, I think. So I need to see him and tell him first.'

Rosie knocked at the study door, and came in to say that lunch was ready.

'Thank you, my dear. We're just coming,' said her father, and then, turning to Joe, he asked, 'Have you any other letters with you by any chance?'

'I have one letter that Beppe wrote to her; it was his last one; as I said William had found and burnt all his letters to her. I do have her diary, but you should also take this,' he said as he undid the cross from around his neck. 'Elise gave it to me for my twenty-first birthday. She gave it to Beppe all those years ago. It was returned with the priest's letter.'

'May I take them with me this afternoon?'

'Of course, but there is one thing: the letters Beppe wrote to Elise were addressed to her, but this final letter, from the priest, was addressed to Mr and Mrs Raynesford; as if they wanted her husband to read it too.'

The doctor took the letters and the crucifix and examined them and then, without commenting, slipped them in his pocket. He rose slowly and signalled for Joe to follow him to the dining room.

'I think you should call me Gino.' said the doctor putting his hand on Joe's shoulder.

'Thank you Gino. Also.' said Joe. 'Elise wrote to the villa, to Maria and Efisio, who lived there, but she never heard from them either.'

The doctor shook his head and sighed.

'Let me show you to the cloakroom. I'm sure you would like to freshen up before lunch. By the way, that is a fine ring you're wearing on your little finger,' said the doctor. 'Did you buy it here, in Sardinia?'

'No, it belonged to Elise. She wore it on her wedding finger. I don't ever remember seeing her without it. Beppe gave it to her.'

'It's an antique Sardinian wedding ring. It must have belonged to his family.'

In the dining room Joe was introduced to his host's family: the doctor's wife, Lucia, and then his two other daughters, Daniella and Graziella, together with Rosie. He was made to feel most welcome, and they all enjoyed the delicious meal together.

As they ate, Gino Garcia said to Joe, 'I hope there is no need for you to return to Cagliari tonight. I think it would be a good idea for you to stay here for a few days and to meet Beppe as soon as possible. I would like to break the news to him myself, before anyone else has a chance to tell him.'

'That's very kind of you,' said Joe, 'but I don't want to be any trouble – besides, what if he doesn't want to see me?'

The doctor laughed.

'Do you really think he has worked so hard all his life just to throw you out of the door? I don't think so. You need have no worry on that score. You are more than welcome to stay here as long as you like. As for Beppe – well, after the initial shock he will be delighted, I can assure you of that. There are some things he will have to know, which will be painful to hear, but it will be alright, I promise you. Now, while I'm gone the girls will give you coffee and my wife will prepare your room. I promise you, Joe, everything will be alright.'

After lunch, the doctor took Joe back to his study, gave him a *grapa* and said he would return later.

Joe fell into the leather chair and, putting his head in his hands, he wept for his mother.

CHAPTER THIRTY ONE

Doctor Gino Garcia drove slowly to Beppe's house, turning over in his mind all the events that had come to light that morning. Beppe and Elise had paid dearly for their love; there was little doubt of that. God, fate and some evil conspiracy had dealt them a bitter blow.

Maria opened the door to his knock and greeted him warmly.

'Beppe isn't here,' she said, looking anxious, 'but I expect him back at any moment; he's gone to the co-operative.'

'While he's not here, perhaps you would answer a few questions for me?'

'If I can Doctor.'

He led Maria to a chair and sat beside her.

'You knew Elise Raynesford, didn't you?'

'I did.' Maria's lips became compressed in a grim line. 'And if you ask me, she's the cause of most of Beppe's problems.'

'Why, do you say that?'

'Well… you know how it was with Beppe and Elise: they were lovers; he adored her and worshiped the ground she walked on, and she, for her part, said she loved him. She took us all in,' replied Maria with a sneer.

'Did you know she had a child by him?'

'I knew she was expecting one. Beppe told me. I remember how happy he was.' said Maria her face lighting up. 'He had been away up north on business so it was quite sometime after Elise had written before he had the news. She had said she had decided to return to him when something happened to her mother. He wrote at once, asking her to come to him, and then waited anxiously every day for her reply, but none came. He wrote again and again, but his letters all came back unanswered. I watched him die a little every day after that. He saw her in the market, in the peach grove, down at the villa everywhere they had been together, and he always heard her laughter.'

Maria's lips became compressed again as she continued.

'When the owners of the villa sold it that winter, we were without a home. He found us all somewhere to live, and the following year Claudio and Margherita announced their engagement. Beppe became withdrawn and started working even harder in the co-operative. He drove himself and everyone else to the limit, and then more. He was so determined to make something of himself; for Elise and their child.'

'Tell me, Maria – when Beppe was so thrilled about the child, did his mother know?'

'Oh yes, she knew alright. As you can imagine, she was furious and vowed she would stop it at any cost.'

'Did she ever talk to you about it? After all, you had been close friends. Did she ever say how she would stop them?'

'We were not that close and then, after Fran died, we grew apart. You see, I had Margherita. But she did say she would never let Beppe marry Elise, and that she would see to it that she never came back to Sardinia.'

'What did she mean by that exactly, do you think?' asked the doctor.

'I don't know. She and Father Guido spent a lot of time trying to wear Beppe down. Jesu, his own mother!' she said, throwing her hands heavenward. 'The priest said Elise only wanted his child because her husband couldn't give her one. They were very hard on him.'

'If that was the case, why did Elise bother to write and tell Beppe about the baby in the first place? She didn't have to tell him anything.'

'Perhaps she changed her mind, or she wanted to rub salt in the wound. I don't know,' said Maria bitterly.

'Did you know he went to London to try to find her?'

'He went with Luigi that day the young lad was killed, but Beppe didn't get to London. He was in the hospital.'

'He went to London after that to see if he could find her, with no luck. You didn't know that?'

'No. He went up to the north of the island not long after the accident, but he said it was business.'

The doctor fumbled in his pocket. 'Have you ever seen this

before?' he asked, holding up the coral crucifix.

The old woman peered at it and frowned. 'Why, yes, that was Beppe's. Elise gave it to him. Wherever did you get it from? It has been lost for ages.'

'Elise's son has brought it back. He's at my house.'

Maria turned pale and sank back into the chair.

'Wh... what are you saying?' she breathed. 'Elise's son? Where did he get it from? And what is he doing here?'

'It was sent to Elise with a letter from Father Guido saying that it was Beppe who had been killed in the car crash, and that the family didn't want to hear from her any more.'

'But... It was years ago when he had that accident – and as I said, it was Luigi who died!'

'Apparently, Elise wrote to you at the villa but had no reply. Did you not receive her letter?'

'No, we never heard from her. I never received a letter or anything,' said Maria, 'but we did move out that year.'obviously concerned.

The doctor put a finger to his lips as he heard footsteps on the outside stairs. Beppe opened the door and Maria, excusing herself, scurried into the kitchen.

'Hello, Gino. What brings you here? Checking on me again? And what have you been saying to Maria to send her scuttling off like some scared rabbit?'

'She... err... she needed to attend to something in the kitchen,' stammered Gino, trying to gather his wits.

'Well – what do you want? Have you come to give me another lecture, or perhaps see if I am now ready for the funny farm with all my weird hallucinations?'

'Not exactly,' said Gino, looking embarrassed.

'You look as if you've got something on your mind, Gino. Want a drink?' Beppe took a bottle of wine from the sideboard, poured out two glasses and handed one to his friend. 'Here – relax and tell me what's bothering you,' he went on, falling into the nearby chair just vacated by Maria. 'Well, what is it? Apart from the fact that I'm working too hard and, perhaps drinking too much.'

Gino hesitated. Then he slowly produced the coral crucifix.

'Beppe, I believe this is yours,' he said quietly.

The colour drained from Beppe's face. He put his drink on the table and took the cross with trembling hands, staring at it. When he spoke, his voice was hoarse and dry.

'My God, Gino, where in hell did you find this?'

'Before I answer, will you tell me when you last saw it?'

'I was wearing it when we had the car accident. I always wore it.' said Beppe, looking visibly shaken.

'Where were you and Luigi going that day exactly?' asked his friend.

'I was on my way to catch a plane to England, to find Elise and bring her back. Luigi knew all about Elise, and that she was having our child. He said he wanted to help. He was driving. He swerved to avoid a loose horse on the road. Then swerved again to avoid a young child standing on the other side of the road with his mother; he missed them all. The next thing I remember was waking up in hospital. Mamma was there; they were all wearing black and wailing. Then I was told that Luigi was dead. She and his family blamed me. Mamma had found the ticket to London and believed I was being punished for my sin. The cross was missing then; they said it was stolen from the wreckage and that I would pay for my sin.'

'It was stolen, but not by the person who has returned it. Of that I can assure you.'

'And who has returned it?' said Beppe, looking at the doctor curiously, a slight touch of anger in his voice.

'A young man from England called Joe Warwick. His mother received the cross from Father Guido with a letter telling her that you were dead and that your family wanted nothing more to do with her. He was given it by his mother, his mother's name…'

'Is Elise Raynesford; it couldn't be anyone else.' cut in Beppe.

Gino looked at his friend, whose face showed all the agony of his lost love.

'Joe Warwick, your son, is at my house,' continued the doctor, 'and he wants to meet his father. He has always known about you, and now he wants to see you; but he thought, as Elise did, that you were dead.'

'And Elise, is she still alive?' whispered Beppe.

'She died last Monday week. The day you saw her in the peach garden, she came back, Beppe.'

Beppe gasped and turned away as the enormity of what Gino had said hit him like a canon shot. He fell back in the chair, dropped his head in his hands and wept.

'Oh God, Gino, I did see her. Oh God, Gino. But why is his name Warwick? Did Elise marry again?'

'No. She divorced her husband and took back her maiden name. There was some scandal and she didn't want the boy to be affected. Elise still loved you, Beppe.'

Beppe stood up and started to pace the room.

'Why didn't she write? Why didn't she come back to me if she was free? Wasn't I good enough? When did she get divorced?' cried Beppe in anguish.

'She believed you were dead, Beppe. The family had said they wanted nothing to do with her; so she went back to live with her grandfather. All the letters you and I wrote were returned – you know that. Her ex-husband saw to that, and when he sold the house, nobody knew where she had gone. She was divorced in nineteen seventy.'

Beppe put his hand on his forehead and ran it back through his dark hair, desperately trying to fight the emotion he could feel building up inside him.

'Oh my God, Gino, what terrible twist of fate has done this to us? All those lost years. Why couldn't we have come together like other lovers?' His voice trembled with emotion.

'Because you weren't like other lovers; Elise was married. You could never have married her even when she obtained her freedom. You certainly couldn't have lived on the island together, not then. And you would never have survived in England, you know that. What life would it have been for you both and the child, shunned by everyone? Things are a little different today. You might, slowly, have been accepted now, but not then.'

'And what kind of life has it been without her?' demanded Beppe. 'Oh Gino, all this time I was convinced she didn't love me; all the uncertainty,' he sighed.

'She did love you, Beppe.'

Beppe frowned. 'How do you know that?'

'Your son told me so.'

There was a poignant silence; then the doctor went on softly:

'Your mother thought she was doing the best for you. She took the crucifix and gave it to the priest, and he, no doubt, wrote to Elise with her approval. Your mother was a very strong-willed woman; there is no need for me to tell you that. Indeed, even I thought that, perhaps, after four years, when I came back from Milan, the whole thing had faded from your memory. The depressions weren't as marked as they used to be. It wasn't until last week that I realised you have never really forgotten her and that all your problems stem from that love you still hold for her.'

'How could I forget her, Gino? She was everything in the world to me. I thought she had gone back and that perhaps her husband had accepted the child as his own. I wanted to see Elise, but Mamma said that she probably hadn't told her husband anything about me and that it would disrupt her life. She also said that he could give the child far more than 1 ever could. I thought I was doing the right thing. How could I know she still thought of me – still loved me...' His voice trailed away as he tried desperately to master his emotions.

Suddenly, with a muttered curse, he hurled his glass into the fireplace.

'I went to London to find her. There was nothing there. I tried to find her, but she had disappeared. Gone to America with her husband and I had lost her. To hell with the Church, with all its hypercritical teachings! Damnation to its comfort and strength! All it's brought me is heartache – and a terrible feeling of guilt!'

Gino rose and put out a restraining hand to his friend.

'Beppe, don't be too hard on yourself. You were both victims of circumstances. It may be little consolation now, but you and Elise were blessed with a love not known to many. You only know and remember the good things about each other. You have never faced the realisation that your love has died; never known the enmity that can grow between two people, once madly in love – the dividing line between love and hate is small, and when that love turns to hate, there is little to be done – or maybe indifference, and then no feeling at all. You have known none of these things.'

Beppe put his head in his hands, listening to his friend, and then raised a ravaged face.

'I know,' he sighed. 'All that's true, But I would have put up with that just to be able to have the good times, for they would have outweighed all else. Such love, such pain, and to think I thought my mother was trying to help me. All the time she was making sure that I never saw Elise again. I can't believe it. And Elise, she was going through the same; and she was free.' Beppe wept.

'Beppe, your union with Elise was blessed with a son. He is the image of you as a young man, I recognised him immediately, except that his eyes are hazel. You must make the boy welcome; don't let him sense any bitterness, any regret. You and Elise gave him the gift of life and he wants to know all about you. Don't you think he might need you as much as you need him?'

'There is no bitterness, no regrets towards him.'

There was a long silence, and then Gino stood up and made for the door.

'What did you say his name was?' asked Beppe.

'Joe short for Joseph. Giuseppe in Italian,' said Gino with a smile.

Beppe sighed.

'Elise named our son after me. How wonderful is that? Will you take him to the villa tomorrow? I would rather meet him there. Take him there tomorrow morning, please, Gino. I need time tonight to sort myself out. And, Gino, thanks, I know it couldn't have been easy for you, and I'm going to need all your help.'

'You will have all the help you need. Just keep off the drink, Beppe, for God's sake.'

Beppe found sleep an elusive partner that night. He sat up, wide awake. The early morning air was cool and outside the window the large fig tree stood stark against the blue-black light. In the distance, past the tops of the uneven roofs of the sleeping village, he could just make out the outline of the cypress and juniper trees that surrounded the peach grove.

The grove... once more the events of the previous week came flooding back. The sight of Elise as a young woman, looking happy and so young; she had come back. Tears sprang to his eyes again.

He clambered out of bed carefully; his head still felt a little light. He put the music player on and played the *Bruch violin concerto* that Elise had given him all those years ago. He fumbled for the trunk under the bed and dragged it out. He took a key from a small box on his chest of drawers and opened the trunk. Numerous things lay in there. Old photograph albums from his time in the army. Souvenirs of places once visited, and people all forgotten now. But the one thing he searched for seemed to evaded his eager fingers.

He lifted out the green velvet lined box in which his crucifix had been given to him by Elise and felt the cross on his chest and sighed heavily.

He searched again in his trunk, his searching became frenzied as he turned the boxes out from their dark hideout, until, at last, right at the bottom, his fingers found the once-familiar shape of the shell-covered box. He grasped it with shaking hands, and drew it toward him. A layer of fine dust which permeated everything covered the box decorated with shells. He gave it a quick blow, sending a cloud of particles into the air and revealing an intricate pattern with the initial 'E' worked in smaller shells. He sat with his back against the pillows and stared at the box. He had made it so many years ago. He remembered collecting the shells on the beaches at Pula and San Pietro. The pictures were crystal clear in his mind, as if it was yesterday, but a lifetime had passed since those carefree days. With trembling hands, he opened the lid.

Inside laid a collection of faded letters, cards and photographs – much handled and obviously cherished – along with shells and an empty perfume bottle. He reached out and turned on the side light. He felt compelled to open and re-read this chapter of his life, although he had been forced to obliterate every part of it. He had tried, God knew he had tried, to push it out to the remotest part of his mind, but he hadn't succeeded. Indeed, his efforts had resulted in him becoming the dour, relentless and somewhat embittered character he knew himself to be.

He took out the photographs. They were a little faded, but there, smiling back at him, was the same fair-haired, brown-skinned girl that he had seen approaching him in the peach grove. Claudio had seen nothing, but she had come back to him.

He fumbled through the letters, each one in its envelope, the paper so stiff and dry it crackled at his touch. He picked one up and smelt it; did it still carry her perfume, or did he always imagine it?

He opened one at random and read:

My darling, you are forever in my thoughts like a beautiful melody that plays in the background of my mind. You have my soul, and I live with a part of you in my heart, and it feels and keeps every touch or kiss you ever gave me. Know that I will always love you.

Beppe felt a terrible wave of emotion wash over him as tears stung his eyes and fell down his cheeks. An intolerable lump swelled up and ached in his throat. Clenching the letter in his hands, he wept unashamedly for his long-lost love, and those precious days spent together. He had carried the burden of his sin all these years, and was paying for it still. Elise had never married again in all those years, and they had a son. He had seen her that morning, so clearly. She was there; he had not imagined it like so many times before when she had first left. She was dead, but she had loved him and had come to him. His mind was in turmoil. Deep sobs racked his body until; finally, he fell back into a dreamless sleep.

He woke with a start on hearing Maria in the kitchen. The sunlight was pouring through the open window. He still held the letter in his hand and all the others, plus the photos, were scattered over his bed. He sat up quickly and replaced them in the box; all save one snapshot, which he slipped into his wallet. Then he put the box on the chair beside his bed. Joe would want to see it, he thought.

The sun was reflecting from the roofs of the houses; it would be another hot day. He felt restless and knew he couldn't stay in bed. He wanted to be out, to wander around the village, to be away from everyone. He showered, dressed quickly and then quietly let himself out of the house.

The smell of freshly baked bread hung over the streets. Women carried bundles of washing down to the river; some used washing machines, but many preferred the old ways. Young children darted about and played in the alleyways and courtyards. School would begin soon; donning their smocks, they would disappear into the small building and silence would again settle on the streets.

Beppe wandered on down through the old part of the village. The beaten dirt roads were dry and dusty from the lack of rain, and when he idly kicked one of the loose stones a cloud of dust rolled up behind it.

Most of the large wooden entrance doors were shut against prying eyes, but occasionally, where one was left ajar, the beautiful courtyards could be seen with their masses of bougainvillea, passion flowers and oleander; some had grape vines that twisted and knotted their way over the old houses, while others were ablaze with clambering varieties of geranium.

He carried on through the village until the houses gave way to the start of the neat groves and gardens. Men, women and young children were all labouring there with the watering, weeding and general care that occupied the whole of their lives. Ahead lay the river, where the women laughed and chattered as they beat their linen on flat stones and small children played hide and seek among the bushes, just as he had as a child.

The wind whispered through the reeds, making them rustle. He remembered standing here with Elise, some twenty-odd years earlier. Very little had changed during the years, women still came every day to do their laundry, laying the clothes out on the sweet-smelling myrtle bushes to dry and, then carried them home in large baskets. Nowadays, the baskets were plastic. When he was young they were made from asphodel, woven by the women themselves during the long winter evenings. They still carried them on their heads, balancing them elegantly, and in doing so acquiring their distinctive upright carriage.

Turning to go, his eye caught the square outline of the church tower. The skyline hadn't altered much. One or two new houses had been built. He had helped to build one for Claudio and Margherita. When the villa was sold at Pula, he had moved back to the village to be near the family. Then, when his mother died and as the business grew, he had built his own house, and Maria, after the death of her husband, Efisio, had moved in to look after him. Time stood still on the island and in the small villages. Only people grew old; changing and dying – the thought depressed him.

With a long sigh, Beppe shook himself out of his gloom. He looked at his watch and smiled, remembering that Gino was taking his son to the villa this morning. He would collect Maria and they would leave to open the place up ready for Joe and Gino.

CHAPTER THIRTY TWO

Gino drove Joe down to the villa at Pula, having returned the hire car to Cagliari and travelled on in the doctor's car.

'I didn't know Beppe owned the villa. I understood from Elise that he only worked there.'

'He didn't, not when they were together. But when she returned to England, he was sure that she would come back to him, and so he worked hard building the co-operative and starting the plant-importing business. He was like a man possessed, wanting to have something to offer you both.' Gino paused and looked at Joe, who was watching him intently. 'He was determined and drove himself, and everyone, to achieve his goal. Then, when the villa came up for sale again, he bought it and had it put back exactly as it was when they were together. It is his sanctuary.'

'What are we going to do if he doesn't like me?' Joe could feel the anxiety mounting and, not for the first time, he wondered if this had been a good idea and that Elise had been right not to come back.

'As I said, you have no worry on that score,' replied the doctor, smiling.

They came to Pula and passed through the clean and obviously prosperous little community. Just outside the village they turned left down a newly tarred road. There was a farmhouse on the left and a small chapel on the right, shaded by an old olive tree. The road ended at a large, plastered wall, and they turned in through a gate into a courtyard dominated by a huge olive tree under which Gino parked the car.

Beppe had been pacing his study like a caged animal, continually glancing at the clock. At half past ten exactly he heard the car come down the lane and stop in the yard. He heard footsteps echo across the yard and up to the room in the vinery. The door opened and Gino came in, followed by a tall, dark, curly-haired young man.

'I know this room,' gasped Joe.

Beppe stared at them both. Gino's voice, when he spoke, came from far away.

'Joe, this is your father, Beppe Zedda.'

Joe stared at his father. It is hard to imagine the difficulty of meeting a man you know is your father but is a total stranger. You carry his genes, have his mannerisms, the same features, but he is unknown to you. He has never scolded you, never passed judgement, never praised you, and never told you that he loved you. No contact, nothing. However, you know he is your father. You will come to love him, but it will be a different love from that of parents. It is love for a man who cares for you but has never physically cared for you. It is a remote but familiar love. Joe felt all of these emotions race through his mind as he stared at the man; his father whom he resembled in every way, except his eyes. Beppe's eyes were black, but with a fleck of green, and the long black lashes gave them a deep-eyed appearance. Joe smiled and went toward his father, finding himself immediately drawn to this man.

Beppe read his son's thoughts, and as father and son gazed at one another for a long time without saying anything, Beppe felt his heart racing as if to burst. True, the boy did look like him, but his eyes, they were Elise's eyes looking at him, fearless but questioning. Beppe went forward, threw his arms around the young man and kissed him on both cheeks. Then he drew away and held Joe at arm's length to look at him. Smiling, he asked him:

'Why did you say that you know this room?'

'Because at home Elise's study is exactly the same with all the books on Sardinia along the walls, together with lots of Italian and French poetry books. The records and the record player; the record you gave her. I was always teasing her and telling her she should have a modern player. The desk where she used to work and the lamp, just like this one. Where you have the sketch of her, she had a sketch of you on one side and a pressed orange blossom on the other. You gave it to her the day she left.'

Beppe caught his breath.

'Where you have your beautiful rug she had a Persian rug.' Joe continued, giving Beppe time to compose himself.

'She used to spend a lot of her time in there. Where you have your bed, she used to have a single day-bed against the wall. When I was young, and if I was ill, I would be allowed to sleep in the bed while Elise worked. There were times when I would go into the study and find her asleep across her desk because she was so tired, and times when I would find her crying.'

The two men looked at one another, an understanding passing between them. Elise would have felt close to Beppe in her study, remembering the times they spent together in the vinery.

'Did she think of me?'

'Every day she said I was a constant reminder of you. When she spoke of you, she always lit up.'

Beppe smiled. There was no awkwardness between them; it was if they had known each other all their lives.

'Are you alright?' asked Beppe.

'Yes. You know when she was very ill, they sedated her. She woke one time when I was there, and she must have thought I was you, because she held my arm and said, 'I've come back.''

Beppe felt the hairs on the back of his neck rise.

'I saw her in the peach garden, and she touched my arm and told me she had come back.'

A silence fell between the two men.

Beppe turned to Gino and said quietly,

'I told you I had seen her.'

Gino nodded.

'Did she never want to come back?' asked Beppe.

'No, she was frightened of her memories. I wanted to come, but she was adamant.'

Beppe turned away and bit his lip; all the wasted years when they could have been together. He turned to Joe, smiled and put his arm around his son's shoulder.

'I think a drink is called for, and we will see if Maria has everything ready for lunch.'

'Not for me,' said Gino. 'Forgive me, but I must get back to Santa Cella. I have patients to see to.'

Joe put his hand out and touched Beppe on the arm.

'I just know she always loved you; there has never been anybody else. And it seems it has been the same with you.'

Beppe sighed. 'I have your crucifix, which I understand from Gino that Elise gave you for your twenty-first birthday.'

'It's yours, please keep it. It rightfully belongs to you.'

Beppe smiled as he fingered the crucifix.

'We have so much to talk about,' he said huskily.

'I'll say goodbye, Beppe. Keep in touch. I'll see you soon,' said Gino.

He shook Beppe's hand, then, turning to Joe, he took his hand.

'I told you it would be alright.'

Joe smiled at his father, who touched him on his shoulder.

'I would like to phone my godfather, if that's possible,' said Joe.

'There is a phone in the main house. Gino will show you where you can find it on his way out…'

As they left the room, Joe was aware that Beppe was weeping.

Joe rang James and it proved to be a long and emotional conversation.

Maria prepared lunch, and the three of them sat together around the table and talked of the time when Elise was at the villa.

'Are you the Maria who lived here at the villa when Elise was here?' asked Joe.

'Yes.' replied Maria rather coldly as she rose to clear the plates.

'When the villa was sold that winter,' said Beppe, after Maria had gone into the kitchen.

'Maria and Efisio, her husband, went back to the village to live. Then the following year, Claudio and Margherita became engaged and married, but when the grandchildren started coming along, the house was too small. The co-operative was doing well,' continued Beppe, 'and the new business of plant importation was doing better than I could have ever imagined; so I built a house for my brother and Margherita. Then Mamma died, and soon after, Efisio died too, so Maria moved in, in order to look after me when I rebuilt my house.'

'And Maria has lived with you ever since?' asked Joe.

'That's right. About four or five years ago, the villa came on the market again. I bought it and Ignazio, Maria's eldest son, and his wife, Madelena, moved into the cottage with their two children after I had extended it.' He smiled. 'Children! Tomaso is eighteen and engaged to Daniella, Gino's eldest daughter, and Rosa is seventeen now!'

Joe looked at Beppe and said quietly,

'And all this happened and Elise knew nothing about it. She fell in love with Sardinia. I know she felt the island was her natural spiritual home. She taught me to love it too.'

'I'm glad you like it, but then you should – you are a Sard, it's your island too,' Beppe said, laughing.

'And you never married then?' ventured Joe.

No. No one could have taken Elise's place, and I was sure she would come back to me someday. Maria was the only one who could put up with my moods.'

'By the way,' said Beppe changing the subject. 'I have asked Maria to organise a party for the weekend,' he added, beaming. 'We haven't had a celebration for years, and I feel like celebrating. After all, it isn't everyday a man finds his son. Besides all the family is complaining that I'm keeping you to myself, and they all want to meet you.'

Joe smiled. He had already grown fond of this gentle and sensitive man, and could understand why Elise had fallen so deeply in love with him.

'We shall have roasted suckling pig and all the trimmings,' said Beppe gleefully. 'It was Elise's favourite.'

That evening, Beppe took Joe down to the co-operative. There were two large buildings, one where the locally – grown grapes were pressed, and the other where the olives were processed. And it was obvious to Joe that Beppe took a great pride in everything he had achieved.

'All the people in the area bring their grapes here. We pay them for their crop, make the various wines, and then sell them on.' said Beppe.

'Did you start all this yourself?'

'I did,' said Beppe, with obvious pride. 'But with Elise's help.'

'That's wonderful, but how did she help?

'When she left she gave Maria all the money back I had spent when we went to the hotel and more. She made Maria promise not to tell me, but to give it to me as a bonus. Well Maria isn't a very good liar so I soon got it out of her. That money bought my first big order for the cooperative and I have never looked back. So I always say she started by business. It took time and quite a bit of persuasion, but it has paid off now. We do the same thing with all the fruit and vegetables; enabling the small growers to specialise and not have to grow meagre amounts of everything.'

'And you obviously enjoy it?'

'I do now. It gave me something to do at first, to keep my mind off things. I still help Claudio in the peach grove when I have some free time. Physical work can be quite relaxing after mental stress, besides, I needed something for you and Elise when you both came back.'

Father and son sat into the late hours, talking of Elise and their separate lives; each getting to know the other and finding out that they had much in common.

The following day Beppe took Joe up to the peach garden, and Joe experienced the heat and heavy scent of the area. The trees were laden with the unripe fruit, and they hung like small baubles on the branches. The ground was stony and reflected back every drop of the heat.

'Is this where you saw her?' asked Joe.

'Yes. She was so real, but so young,' Beppe sighed.

'You gave Elise some peaches from this garden the day she left.'

Beppe stopped in his tracks.

'How do you know? I had forgotten. I was so distraught that day, but yes, I did.'

'She gave the stones to her grandfather and they managed to raise two young trees. They now grow in the walled garden at our farm and produce small white peaches. Elise always said they were Beppe's peaches.'

Beppe fell silent. He was again struggling with his emotions.

His son put an arm around his shoulder. 'You must have loved each other very much.'

'We did,' said Beppe, sighing deeply. 'I have loved her with a deep intensity which has sustained me throughout the years we have been apart. She gave me an understanding of love that I never thought possible and she gave me you – and for these things I will be eternally grateful. She gave meaning to my life.' Beppe turned to Joe and, smiling through his tears, he continued, 'And to know she loved me too, all this time, is wonderful. Now she has gone, and the thought of not seeing her again fills my soul with sorrow. If only I could have said goodbye.'

'I can see why Elise fell in love with you. We were both blessed by having her love, and I am so proud of you and love you both. You were everything she needed with your love of the land, poetry and music. Your island, it really is beautiful and surprisingly unspoiled and she loved that too,' said Joe.

Beppe turned away and bit his lip.

That evening in Beppe's room they continued their stories about Elise.

Joe told him how Elise had insisted on sending him to learn Italian and to appreciate the arts, as her father had done for her. Then on to Milan to study for his degree.

'She always said that I should know my father's language, and that every man should have some knowledge of the arts.'

Beppe smiled contentedly at his son; pride coursed through him. Elise had done such a wonderful job, all on her own.

'Tell me, did you always call her Elise rather than Mamma?' asked Beppe.

'Yes, we were very close, more like friends than mother and son. Obviously, when I was at school she was my mother; but when we were alone together, she was always Elise,' said Joe.

Beppe looked at Joe.

'I missed her so much. She had become part of my life. I had all her letters. Without them, I would have had nothing to remember her by; they were proof that I hadn't imagined the whole affair.'

'I understand from Doctor Garcia that you went to look for Elise in England.'

'I did. I must say, Elise was right; I would have found it impossible to live there.'

'Tell me about it.'

Beppe rose collected two glasses from the cupboard and poured them both another drink, drew in a deep breath and began to tell his story.

He had arrived on the Alitalia flight into Heathrow. It was late

September, and the weather was warm for England. He found his train from the airport to London. He sat and watched the countryside flash by. England, in late summer, looked a bit like Sardinia with its harvested fields and cropped grass. But the unfamiliar chatter of English made him feel alienated. He took his notebook out of his pocket and read the address for the hundredth time. Why hadn't Elise contacted him? He had been so sure she would come back to him. Her letters had stopped, and his had been returned stamped NOT AT THIS ADDRESS. He felt his stomach tighten at the thought of her, and he wondered if she was alright.

He reached the station and followed the crowd in the hope of finding a taxi. He watched a queue of people as they stood waiting. Families with young children, businessmen with briefcases, old people fussing with one another and making sure they had everything. Soon, it was his turn. He handed the address to the cab driver, who had said something he couldn't understand, and Beppe climbed into the back of the taxi with his overnight bag.

He had looked out of the taxi window and watched the afternoon traffic fight its way through the streets.

'Here you are, mate,' said the cabbie, indicating the house on the address.

Beppe saw the amount of thirteen pounds registered on the fare. He took out a twenty-pound note and told the cabbie: '*Va bene così.*'

The cabbie removed his cap and thanked him, and Beppe knew he had tipped him too much.

Beppe stood on the pavement outside the house. It had a large sign outside that read For Sale. The house was obviously empty. He turned back to see that the cabbie was still watching him.

'No good, mate?' He gestured to Beppe to get back in the taxi and drove to the address on the board. It was a large estate agent's in Sloane Square. He parked his cab and beckoned to Beppe to follow him. They entered the large offices, and the cabbie stood talking to a young man in a suit. Beppe, somewhat bemused by the whole thing, watched on.

The cabbie was making demands to the man, who left and returned with a smart young girl with dark hair and darker eyes.

'I understand you need some help?' said the young girl in perfect Italian.

Beppe smiled, and turned to the cabbie and shook his hand.

The cabbie spoke to the young girl, who then translated.

'It seems your cabbie's father was in Italy during the war, and was helped when he fell behind the lines. They fed him and helped him escape into the mountains until the Americans came. This is his way of saying thank you.' She smiled.

Beppe thanked him profusely.

'Now, can I help you?' the young girl asked.

He gave her the address and asked about the fact it was up for sale. He wondered if all the English were this kind, like Elise, or had he just been very lucky?

The young girl returned with a file.

'I'm sorry,' she said. 'It seems that the house is for sale and that the owners have left. We have had no contact with them for two months. I understand they have gone to America. There is a forwarding address if you would like it?'

Beppe's heart jumped.

'Yes, please.'

Had Elise gone with William after all? Had she really decided that a life with William would be better? He felt sick.

The cabbie asked a question to the young girl, which she put to Beppe. 'Your friend wants to know if you are alright, and is it some woman?'

Beppe had explained that he was looking for a dear friend, but she had obviously gone.

'Women, they will be the death of you,' replied the cabbie after he had understood the problem.

The cabbie was talking again.

'I am to tell you his name is Fred, and that he knows a place near the station which is clean and reasonable,' said the young girl, at the same time handing Beppe the cabbie's visiting card.

'Fred,' she said, indicating the cabbie.

'Beppe,' he replied, and they shook hands again.

'He will take you to the place and make sure you are alright.'

Beppe thanked them all profusely and took the address in America from the young girl. Then he followed Fred out to his cab.

The cab was parked in an area which was especially for taxis, and there was a small hut nearby where men came and went with cups of tea or coffee. Fred signalled and asked if he wanted something to drink. Beppe declined; he felt drained and overwhelmed by this man's kindness. He climbed into the taxi.

After a while, they arrived outside a neat-looking house, and Fred beckoned him out. It was in a leafy street with rows of identical houses all painted in different colours. At the knock of the door a large, portly woman welcomed Fred with a huge smile. Fred was obviously explaining what had happened, and the woman turned to Beppe and welcomed him inside. Before entering, Beppe went back to the cab to check the fare on the meter and turned to Fred.

'Quanto?' he said, putting up his fingers and counting them.

'No, mate, this one is for my dad. Mio padre,' he said, smiling.

Beppe put forward his hand to shake Fred's hand, and was totally unprepared for the big bear hug he received.

'Good luck, mate,' said Fred; and with a wave of his hand, he was gone.

Beppe spent the night in a small, cosy room and shared the bathroom at the end of the corridor. Breakfast consisted of cereal, toast and marmalade, and probably the worst cup of coffee he had ever tasted. Finally, he had thanked the lady as best he could, paid his bill and hailed a taxi to the station. At Heathrow, he found the Alitalia desk and checked in on his open ticket to Milan at twelve o'clock, and then there was the connecting flight to Cagliari at six.

He sat back in his seat on the Milan flight and fought back the tears that threatened to overwhelm him. Elise had gone to America. She hadn't contacted him, and she hadn't even left him a note. He ordered a whisky to try to numb his senses. By the time he reached Milan, he had drunk at least four more, and he hazily found his way to the *Alisard* desk for Cagliari. While waiting to be called, he managed to down another two double whiskeys. A young girl from the desk came to tell him that his flight was about to close, and led him unsteadily to the gate. Beppe felt himself stumble up the steps to the plane where he finally sank into oblivion on the flight, first to Alghero and then Cagliari.

The attendants helped him out of the plane and led him to an office in the corner of the lounge. They searched his belongings, found his address, called a taxi and sent him home.

Beppe awoke in his bed in the early hours of the morning. Claudio was there and was looking most concerned.

'God, Beppe, where the hell have you been?'

Beppe stumbled out of bed and rolled down to the bathroom, where he threw up noisily.

Life without Elise was going to be hell on earth, and he wasn't so sure he wanted to live if she wasn't there. The world spun and then he had passed out.

'I was at my lowest ebb at that time, I didn't want to live without Elise, but I knew she was carrying our child and it was that thought that kept me going and finally got me back on my feet. But I missed her so much.'

At this point Joe looked at Beppe, and put his hand on his knee. 'And all the time she was in Suffolk, how very, very sad.'

CHAPTER THIRTY THREE

Beppe and Joe crossed the yard to meet the family. The sound of voices and laughter echoed around the villa. When they opened the hall door silence fell, and Joe found himself feeling a little bit shy. The long table had been laid in the huge room that served as both sitting room and dining room, and it looked resplendent with all the cutlery and glass twinkling under the lights.

Maria came forward and took Joe's hand. She looked uneasy as she stared into his eyes. 'Please forgive me, Joe. I have been thinking about Elise, and I got it all wrong. I thought Elise had gone away with the baby...'

Joe put his finger to his mouth.

'That is all forgotten now.'

Maria nodded and smiled.

'Thank you. Joe.'

All the family came forward, one by one. Ignazio stepped forward and introduced his wife, Madelena, and his two children, Tomaso and Rosa, to Joe. Claudio and Margherita introduced their children: Efisio, Margherita and Claudio. Finally, Predu stepped forward with his wife, Maria, and their two young sons, Predu and Franco.

Beppe watched as Joe was kissed and hugged and welcomed by all the family, and finally moved forward to sit next to him at the head of the table. Then all the others took their places at the table, and Beppe noticed that Rosa made sure she sat on the other side of Joe. Ignazio said grace, and Joe realised that he had taken over the role from Efisio, as Elise had said he always said grace when he was at the villa.

Maria arrived with plates of anti-pasta, salciaccia, olives, meats and freshly baked bread. Carafes of homemade wine were placed on the table and the family settled down to chatter among themselves.

Malloreddus followed and finally the roast suckling pigs which had been cooked by the open fire, and were served by the girls.

Beppe sat beside Joe and introduced him to all those who arrived to join the party.

News had travelled fast in the small village, and later friends arrived to congratulate Beppe and to meet Joe, who found their hospitality overwhelming. Joe was amazed at how many people he had never seen before paused to ask him how he was, and that they knew he was Beppe's son. For if they hadn't been told, it was easy to see the likeness as it was so marked. He was touched, too, by the warm way in which they received him and included him in their invitations to their homes.

Those of them who had known Elise were only too eager to tell Joe about her.

Franco came and introduced himself. 'I am Franco and I am the one who told Elise about the *banditti.*' He said. 'Unfortunately they did not kidnap her and keep her, otherwise she might still be here.'

Franco filled Joe's glass 'I remember how lovely she was: I am sorry to hear she is no longer with us. You must miss her.'

They were standing at the wine cask, when Margherita came up to join them.

'Hello,' she said, 'Sorry Franco but I haven't had a chance to welcome Joe yet. Beppe has kept you to himself! You look just like Beppe.'

Franco nodded and went to find his wife.

'Hello,' said Joe, taking her offered hand and smiling.

Margherita went on earnestly:

'I remember Elise very well. I was terribly fond of her. When she didn't come back, many people thought the worst; they said she no longer cared. But I knew she would never forget Beppe, and I always said so. I knew, by the way she looked at him, that she felt about him the same way as I do about his brother.'

A young man came up to them, saying,

'Excuse me, Mamma, but Babbu wants you to help.'

Margherita smiled at the youngster.

'This is Efisio, our eldest,' she said proudly. 'Efisio, this is your cousin from England, Zio Beppe's son.'

The youth smiled, shook hands with Joe and then was gone.

'So how many children do you have?' Joe asked.

'Three. Efisio, Margherita and little Claudio,' she replied laughing. 'It must be difficult for you to take it all in at one go.'

Joe smiled at her.

'Yes, but you certainly have your hands full then!'

She laughed too and nodded in agreement.

'Excuse me, I must go and help,' she said, looking around her. She beckoned to her niece, who was standing nearby.

'Rosa, will you look after Joe for me? See that he has everything he needs.'

Rosa looked up at Joe. The eyes that met his gaze were the deepest and most bewitching that he had ever encountered, and the heart-shaped face, with its olive skin crowned with jet-black hair, was strikingly beautiful. He had seen a lot of her recently during his stay at the villa, and she had made sure that she sat next to him at the first supper, but tonight she looked particularly appealing, dressed as she was in traditional dress. Joe spent the rest of the evening talking and dancing with Rosa, watched over by a beaming Beppe and Ignazio.

Beppe was in great form, happy in a carefree manner. Joe had seen him change over the past week from a withdrawn, remote being to a man with a positive joy in living.

'You certainly have done him the world of good,' said Gino smiling at Joe. 'I hope you will be able to come back to the island often, for it will be wonderful for him to have his son around. You have done more good than all the medicines in the world.'

'And I hope he will come to England to see the farm Elise loved so much,' replied Joe.

The evening passed with each family telling their stories to bring everyone up to date. They listened intently as Joe told them of his life in England, and the moment when he learned that Beppe was still alive. Beppe lightened the event by retelling his story of when he went to England to try to find Elise.

Beppe and Joe finally said goodnight to all the company and Rosa came forward and wished Joe '*buonanotte.*'

Father and son walked slowly back to the vinery.

'Vernaccia, Joe?' he asked.

Joe looked at him and smiled. 'Please.'

They sat in his study, sipping their drink and listening to the music. No words were needed between them as they sat in complete harmony with one another. Beppe rose and filled their glasses, and Joe walked across to the bookshelves. He ran his fingers lightly along the spines of the books, taking in their colours and designs.

'I still have that wonderful book you bought Elise. She used to tell me about all the things you did together.'

Beppe watched him intently.

'Elise used to run her hands along the books just like that. She loved them.'

'She has many of these at home in her study.'

Beppe sighed, and Joe, finishing his drink, said goodnight and went to his room.

He lay in his bed thinking about all that had happened during the past week and Rosa. Time had flown by. Here he was, staying in the villa where Beppe and Elise had first met and fallen so deeply in love with one another. He had come to Sardinia to find a grave, but had found, instead, his father and his family alive and well. If only his mother could have been here. Life could be so cruel!

Over the days that followed, Beppe and Joe spent their evenings together reading Elise's diary, and in the daytime Beppe took Joe to all the places that Elise had written about. Joe saw for himself the wonderful colours of the island in late spring, with its riot of wild flowers. They travelled up to Barumini and Beppe pointed out the ancient ruins. Joe remarked on Las Plassas, with its smooth sides and small castle on the top, and the little church nestled at the base. Joe was as eager to learn about the island as Elise had been, and Beppe's life filled with joy as father and son shared the same things as his mother had done all those years ago.

They went to Cagliari, and Beppe took Joe to the little shop where Elise had bought him his crucifix and found Joe a beautiful, plain, antique coral cross.

'Thank you, Beppe. It is lovely,' said Joe.

'It is the least I can do, seeing as you let me have mine back. It is my twenty-first birthday present to you,' said Beppe with a grin.

Beppe had a spring in his feet as he introduced everyone to his son; life took on a new meaning.

'Next week, I'll take you down to San Antioco and on to San Pietro; they are the two small islands off the mainland. Elise and I stayed there, and I believe you were conceived there too,' said Beppe, a wide smile on his face.

That night, after returning from the day in Cagliari, Joe was woken by the wind which had sprung up and banged the shutter against the window. Getting out of bed to close the shutter, he noticed on the sea the small lights of fishing boats trawling for the night's catch. The wind blew again, making the reeds below his window whine along the river's edge. He shivered, and for some reason thought of Elise. He closed the shutters and the window, and went back to bed, where he soon fell asleep.

Later, he was again woken suddenly by a confusion of sound: running footsteps, voices calling and the slamming of doors. The wind was howling around the villa and moaning in the nearby trees. Dressing hastily, he ran downstairs and into the kitchen. Rosa was there, making coffee.

'What's happening?' he asked, seeing her anxious face.

'A sudden storm came up. There are some fishermen out there. Babbu and Beppe have gone to help.'

Joe raced out of the villa and down to the beach. The waves were crashing on the churning sand and the wind cut through his clothes like a knife. Madelena was busy with Tomaso, wrapping a wet, unconscious young fisherman in a blanket.

'I'll carry him to the house,' said Joe, lifting him up into his arms.

Madelena looked up gratefully.

'Thank you. Rosa is in the kitchen making coffee. Tell her to put some brandy in it,' she said.

The young Sard had regained consciousness by the time Joe had carried him to the villa so, leaving him to Rosa's ministrations; he hurried back to the beach.

The wind howled off the sea, beating the waves into a mounting fury. Thunder boomed in the distance, and sheet-lightning flashed on the sea with a silver light and then forked across the horizon. To Joe it was more like the east coast of England than the Mediterranean, but he knew sudden and violent storms were commonplace in this otherwise blue and peaceful sea.

Everyone was standing in a huddle around another figure lying on the beach. It was an old man, his hands cut and bleeding. He looked half dead.

Joe looked around the group.

'Go and ring the doctor,' called Claudio, his words snatched by the wind.

'Where's Beppe?'

'He's out in the boat. Get someone to get a doctor.'

Joe ran back to the villa and caught Maria.

'Can you ring for a doctor? We are going to need help here. Please,' he begged.

Then he ran out again into the teeth of the howling gale.

'Where's Beppe?' he asked again, tugging on Claudio's arm.

'He's on the fishing boat. He's still out there. There is one more boat, and Ignazio is with him,' cried someone.

Beppe could be seen struggling on the little boat. Suddenly, a huge wave picked up the fishing boat and slammed into the side of Beppe's motor boat. Joe watched, transfixed, as he saw the little boat rise and Ignazio was flung into the churning sea. Peering out to sea, Joe saw a small light flashing as it dipped and rose with the rolling waves.

Without hesitation, he stripped off and dived into the churning water. He was a strong swimmer, but the boat suddenly felt miles away; by the time he reached it, he could barely summon the strength to climb aboard. There was no sign of Ignazio in the water, but Beppe was in the bottom of the boat; he was conscious, but blood was pouring from a cut somewhere on his body.

The trawling net, Joe noticed, had been torn away by the sea. Frantically starting the engine, he steered the boat towards the lights on shore. A huge wave caught the little vessel and carried it at breakneck speed onto the beach. The noise was deafening as the waves broke over the boat and drove it ashore, pouring tons of water on top of Joe as he fell on his father in the hope of holding onto him. He was vaguely aware of being dragged out, coughing and spluttering; then, nothing.

The storm had blown itself out by the dawn. The brilliant sunshine pouring in at his window gave little evidence of the previous night's bitter weather. Joe stirred in his bed and tried to sit up. He groaned and lay back. He was sore and ached all over and there was a pounding in his head.

'Careful. You must take things easy,' said a voice. It was Claudio, who was standing over him, looking pale and drawn.

'Is Ignazio alright?' asked Joe, suddenly seized by apprehension. 'He wasn't in the boat. Beppe was lying in the bottom of the boat.'

'Yes… Joe… Ignazio is fine; he swam to the beach.'

'And Beppe? He was alright when I got to him, but he was bleeding.'

'He was conscious when you brought him to shore by holding on to him, but I'm afraid Beppe's dead.' replied Claudio. 'We thought he was alright. He called for Elise and then lost consciousness. The doctor tried desperately to resuscitate him, but he lost the battle. I'm really sorry, Joe.'

Joe felt the world come in on him; first, his beloved mother, and now his wonderful father. Beppe had seen Elise when he was in the peach grove the morning she had died and he had obviously seen her this morning as he had called her name.

He wept, and Claudio comforted him as best he could.

Later, he handed Joe a large coffee laced with brandy.

'Here, drink this. You have lost a father and I have lost a brother,' he said looking distressed.

An hour later, Joe washed and dressed. A little recovered from the initial shock of grief but still visibly shaken went to the vinery. He gently pushed open the door of his father's neatly furnished and familiar room. He walked slowly over to the bed where Beppe had been laid out, a linen sheet covering his body. He pulled the sheet away from Beppe's face. The agony on the face of the crucified Christ hanging over the bed made a startling contrast to Beppe's peaceful expression. His dark hair lay in a tousled mass on the pillow, and the coral crucifix still hung round his neck, which was badly marked where the heavy chain had pulled on his skin. A large gash ran down his chest where he had obviously caught it on something. His body was badly bruised and marked.

Joe caught his breath.

'It's all over. You're together at last,' murmured Joe as he bent to kiss his father's pale, cold cheek. 'It's all turned full circle.' His voice broke and he fell to his knees, weeping bitterly for the loss of both his beloved mother and father.

Outside a gentle breeze shivered in the great olive tree, quivered through the vineyard and whined in the nearby reeds as it tried to whisper words of comfort and consolation to a grieving son of the island.

Rosa entered and came to stand beside Joe, who was still kneeling by his father. She bent over and gently removed the crucifix from Beppe's neck and gave it to Joe. He rose and, taking off the cross that Beppe had given him, gave it to Rosa, who put it round her neck. She smiled at him and taking Beppe's crucifx from Joe, she reached up to put it round his neck. Then, without saying a word, she took Joe's hand and gently led him toward the door of the vinery.

Once outside, she led him to the river. The sun shone and the water trembled as the wind gently passed over it and on through the reeds. Nora stood out in the early morning light in the distance. Rosa put her arm through his and pulled him close to her. Joe turned to her and smiled as he looked into her dark, beautiful eyes.

'Look,' she said, pointing along the river's edge towards the sea. 'That's where they are. Somewhere out there, Beppe and Elise will be chasing through the reeds and running along the sand; their two souls will reach out to one another, and they will spend eternity as one. You will always be able to hear them together, throughout the island, in the whispering wind.'

EPILOGUE

After Beppe's death, Joe experienced the same bouts of depression that his father had suffered all his life.

James had flown down to be with Joe to console him and help in any way he could.

They buried Beppe under the shade of the olive tree in the small churchyard near the villa. Joe had been taken aback by the hundreds of people who came to the funeral of an obviously well known and loved man, all too eager to tell him about his father and what he had done for them. It seemed he had helped so many people either to start their own businesses or had pulled them into the cooperative making selling their produce so much easier.

After the funeral, Joe decided to go back to Milan to complete his degree which he did with honours. Then, returning to England he tried to settle back into farming. James was always there when Joe needed him, and Sarah made sure he was well looked after. Elise's study became his refuge, because he knew it was the same as Beppe's at the villa.

But Sardinia seemed to call to him so in the spring of the following year; Joe decided to return to the island where he learned that Beppe had left everything to to him. Beppe's business was on the decline because it now lacked proper management, and Joe became involved in putting it back on its feet.

He reluctantly returned to England in the late summer to find that Sarah, who had had an on off relationship with Phillip, the younger son of the neighbouring farmer, had announced that she was finally going to marry him. Joe delighted at the news asked Phillip to manage his farm in his absence; his great grandfather Farthing having died a number of years earlier.

Phillip proved to be more than a capable man, and Joe decided he would live in Sardinia for three months at a time so that he could oversee both businesses.

Joe took over all of Beppe's business, and it wasn't long before he fell under Rosa's charms, and Joe found himself wanting to be in Sardinia all the time.

Two years after Beppe's death, Joe and Rosa were married in the little church at the villa. They went on to have four wonderful children, two boys, Beppe and Luca and two girls, Margherita and Maria, all the apple of grandfather Ignazio's eye.

With Phillip running the farm in England, Joe spent more and more time in Sardinia. So when it came to the time to put the children in school, he and Rosa settled in Sardinia, much to the delight of all the families.

During this time with the money Elise had left him, Joe bought a large vineyard outside Santa Cella, and with Claudio, Ignazio and Predu's help they produced some fine wines.

Maria retired, and Joe converted one of the buildings at the other end of the vinery into a small flat from where she could still organise any help at the villa and enjoy her grandchildren.

Joe and Rosa travelled across the island whenever they had time in their busy lives.

In spring they would take the children and go to the mountains to see all the wonderful flowers and in the winter, they would all go beach combing for the odd coins or small treasures that were washed up by the storms. In the summer they spent long days on the beach at the villa. Joe would sit with Rosa watching the children and continually found himself counting his blessings.

Joe and Rosa use the big bedroom in summer, as Rosa likes to see the beach and Nora in the distance, where she can watch the stream below as the wind whispers in the quivering reeds and where she is sure she hears Beppe and Elise's laughter on the wind. They move into Beppe's room in the vinery during the winter, which is cosy, and makes Joe feel close to both his parents and he knows that he is home.

THE END

Dear Reader

Thank you for reading *The Whispering Wind*, I hope that Beppe and Elise's story touched your heart as it did mine.

If you enjoyed the book, it would be wonderful if you could find the time to write a review either with Troubador or Amazon.

I love receiving feedback from my readers, as it is incredibly rewarding, whether good or bad, and I have made some wonderful friends among my readers.

I look forward to hearing from you.

For news of my latest book *Children of the Mists*, please visit me at my website:

www.lexadudleywriter.co.uk
www.facebook.com/lexa.dudley
www.twitter.com/LexaDudley